Nickname:	Pelican State
Date Entered Union:	April 30, 1812 (the 18th state)
Motto:	Union, justice, confidence
Famous Louisiana Men:	Louis Armstrong, *musician* Geoffrey Beene, *fashion designer* Truman Capote, *writer* Van Cliburn, *concert pianist* Bryant Gumbel, *TV newscaster*
Bird:	Eastern brown pelican
State Name's Origin:	Named in honor of France's King Louis XIV
Fun Fact:	Louisiana has the tallest state capitol building in the United States; the building is 450 feet tall, with 34 floors.

"No kiss?"

Lisette whirled around. Nate was in bed, propped on one elbow, the quilts pulled midway to his chest. "I beg your pardon," she said.

"When you tuck in Monika and Franz, you give them a kiss."

Horrified by his audacity, Lisette gathered her dignity around her and gave him a cold smile. "One doesn't ask forgiveness only to deliberately go back into the same sort of sin, Mr. Rambler. Good night."

She escaped into the hallway and closed the door behind her. For a moment she just stood there, trembling, her icy hands pressed to her fiery cheeks.

She could no longer deny that she was drawn to Nate Rambler or that he was drawn to her, and she knew that if Nate thought she were anyone but Sister Dominique, he would have already tried to get her into his bed....

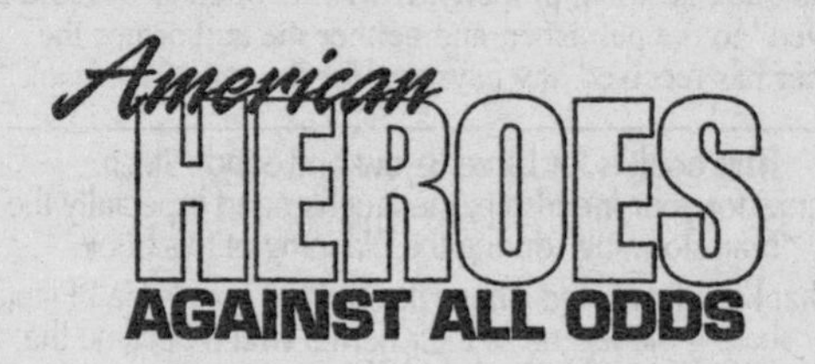

PENNY RICHARDS

Originally published under the name Bay Matthews

Rambler's Rest

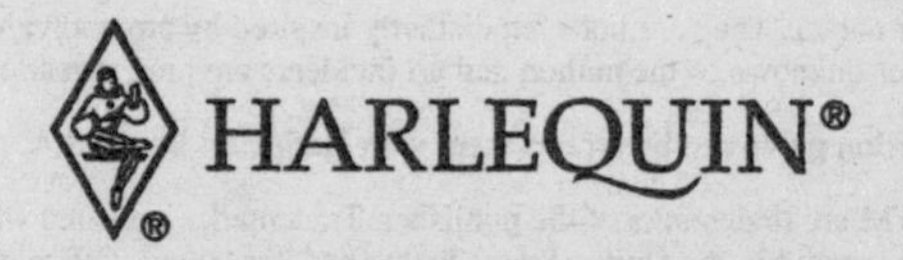

TORONTO • NEW YORK • LONDON
AMSTERDAM • PARIS • SYDNEY • HAMBURG
STOCKHOLM • ATHENS • TOKYO • MILAN • MADRID
PRAGUE • WARSAW • BUDAPEST • AUCKLAND

This book is for Laree Bryant and Sandy Steen.
Thanks for your friendship, the laughter and especially the "brainstorming" during the planning of this book.

Special thanks to Frank and Anne Fitzgerald of Loyd's Hall Plantation, for sharing the legend of their home, which became the springboard for this story.

Thanks to Diane Wicker Davis for listening and sharing her knowledge of Louisiana, and to my nieghbor, Bill J. R. Wilson, Haughton's resident cockfighter.

HARLEQUIN BOOKS
225 Duncan Mill Road, Don Mills,
Ontario, Canada M3B 3K9

ISBN 0-373-82216-2

RAMBLER'S REST
Originally published under the name Bay Matthews

This edition published by arrangement with Harlequin Books S.A.

Visit us at www.eHarlequin.com

Printed in U.S.A.

About the Author

Penny Richards also has written under the pseudonym **Bay Matthews**. Claiming *everything* interests her, she collects dolls, books and antiques. She's been a cosmetologist, an award-winning artist, and worked briefly as an interior decorator. She also worked as a short-order cook in her daughter-in-law's café. She loves movies, reading, cooking, catalogs, research, redoing old houses, learning how to do anything new, Jeff Bridges, music by Yanni, poetry by Rod McKuen, flea markets, gardening (she's a Master Gardener), finding a bargain and baseball. She has three children, nine grandchildren and lives in Arkansas with her husband of thirty-six years in a soon-to-be-one-hundred-year-old Queen Anne house recently added to the National Register. She supports and works with her local garden club, arts league, literacy council and Friends of the Library. Always behind, she dreams of simplifying her life. Unfortunately, there is paper to be hung and baseboards to be refinished....

Books by Penny Richards

Silhouette Special Edition

The Greatest Gift of All #921
Where Dreams Have Been #949
Sisters #1015
**The Ranger and the Schoolmarm* #1136
**Wildcatter's Kid* #1155
Their Child #1213
The No-Nonsense Nanny #1279

*Switched at Birth

Previously published under the pseudonym Bay Matthews

Silhouette Special Edition

Bittersweet Sacrifice #298
Roses and Regrets #347
Some Warm Hunger #391
Lessons in Loving #420
Amarillo by Morning #464
Summer's Promise #505
Laughter on the Wind #613
Sweet Lies, Satin Sighs #648
Worth Waiting For #825
Hardhearted #859

Silhouette Books

Silhouette Christmas Stories 1989
"A Christmas for Carole"

Harlequin Historicals

Rambler's Rest #9

Dear Reader,

The germ of the idea for *Ramber's Rest* came after touring Loyd's Hall plantation in Louisiana. As the story goes, one Lloyd son caused his parents so much grief he was given some money, instructed to go to America and change his name. Lloyd became Loyd, and despite everything, the ne'er-do-well became a success. *Rambler's Rest* is the prequel to *Laughter on the Wind.* Some of you may remember Silvie, the ghost. With a historical, I could go back in time and show how/why she died. Also, I'd always loved the movie *Two Mules for Sister Sarah,* with Shirley MacLaine masquerading as a nun. Hmm. A self-centered outcast, a phony nun and a ghost—what fun elements to weave together! I hope you enjoy the results.

All best wishes,

Penny Richards

Prologue

London, 1850

Tongues of blue flame licked at the massive logs crackling in the huge grate. The candelabra had not yet been lighted, and the fire chased the gathering evening shadows into the corners of the salon. The chill of winter had burrowed into the very core of the rock walls and seemed loathe to depart, though All Fools' Day was but a memory.

Firelight cast dancing shadows over the lavishly appointed room, which was occupied by three people—and the rage and despair engendered by one man's lifetime of rebellion.

Lord Phillip, Baron Ramble, who had inherited the formal title of baron from his father, stalked the width of the room and back. His gray-flecked hair stood on end, the result of well-manicured fingers furrowing through it like a plowshare through the fertile lands of the farm at Devonshire. The baroness sat near the fire, attacking her embroidery with the vengeance of the kitchen tabby loosed on an unwelcome mouse.

The flames were reflected in the sheen of the impeccably

polished black Hessians that covered the narrow feet of the Honorable Jonathan Garrett Ramble—youngest of the baron's four sons—who sat with one long leg draped over the arm of the chair, waiting for his father to speak. Jon might be a gambler and a womanizer and the bane of his parents' lives, but he was not disrespectful.

"You've gone too far, this time," Lord Ramble said at last, stopping before his son's chair and pinning him with a wintry gaze. "The Duchess of Langsford, for God's sake!"

"I don't suppose you'd like to hear my side of the story?" Jon asked with a quirk of a heavy black eyebrow.

Lady Ramble glanced up from her sewing, a look of expectance on her pale face.

"No, I would not!" The resonance of his lordship's voice bounced off the tapestry-covered walls and sent the lady's eyes back to her busywork. "Whatever story you might concoct is no reason to cuckold a duke."

"Not even if the *lady* made all the advances?"

"It matters little who instigated the affair when the woman in question is wife to the Queen's favorite!"

Jon scowled and unhooked his knee from the arm of the chair. "The Queen's favorite! Why the duke is a pompous old fool who—"

"Whose wife you took and whom you wounded in a duel," the baron interrupted. "Perhaps fatally." Lord Ramble shook his head. "For the life of me, I cannot understand why you are so determined to bring this family to ruin."

"That, sir, is not my purpose."

"Then what is your purpose?" the baron pressed. "To gamble and whore yourself to an early grave?"

"What else is there?" the younger Ramble asked with a shrug. "Phillip gets the title—not that I'd want to be a slave to a parcel of land and all the responsibility it entails."

"What you object to then, is a hard day's work," the baron said with exaggerated sarcasm.

Jon leaped to his feet and faced his father. "I object to someone telling me how to live my life, which is why I continually refuse your pleas to join the military or the church—which seem nothing to me but other forms of enslavement."

His lordship's nostrils flared. "In the name of God, what is important to you?"

The fury in his father's voice reminded Jon of the futility of this conversation, a repeat of several over the past two years. The question filled him with the growing and familiar unrest. "I do not know, sir," he said truthfully. "I am still trying to find it."

"And you expect to find it at the gaming tables and the brothels?"

"I expect, sir, not to find it at all." Jon turned to leave the room.

"Where do you think you're going?" the baron thundered.

Jonathan faced his father. "Away from here."

"If you leave this room before we come to some agreement, you leave forever."

Lady Ramble took a wrong stitch and pressed her lips together.

"First my allowance, and now threats. What next, Father?"

Lord Ramble's face reddened. "This is no threat. Your mother and I are disgusted by the life you persist in leading, and we grow weary of hearing your name whispered about."

"And who would be so crass as to mention my peccadilloes to you?" Jon asked in a perfect mimicry of the baron's earlier sarcasm.

"The Queen."

Jon blinked but refused to let his father see his surprise. While it was no wonder to learn that Queen Victoria's prudish sensibilities were shocked by his behavior, he couldn't imagine why she should worry herself with his actions. "Since when does the Queen concern herself with the affairs of a lowly baron's son?"

"Since that son wounded a valued friend. And since he is, according to her majesty, the only thing standing in the way of my chance of obtaining a dukedom."

Jon let his father's words sink in. "I see," he said with a slow nod. "Because I am an object of speculation among the so-called people who matter, I am a stumbling block in your quest for a higher title."

"Yes," the baron replied, his eyes steady and fierce.

"And this is very important to you."

"Very." Lord Ramble sighed. "I had hoped it wouldn't come to this, but repeated pleas have gotten us nowhere. You refuse to mend your ways, and I cannot bear it any longer. No, I *refuse* to bear it any longer."

He went to the secretary and drew out a leather pouch, which he tossed across the room. Jon made the catch automatically. The sound of coins clinking together brought a sudden chill to his bones that had nothing to do with the inclement spring weather.

"There is enough money there for passage to America."

Lady Ramble's needle sank into her finger. Her gasp drowned out Jon's sudden, indrawn breath.

"If you don't gamble it away, there should be enough to last until you can find some means of income."

"You are disowning me?"

The baron refused to meet his son's gaze. "I will not go so far as to do so publicly, if you will promise never to set foot on England's soil again. A story about your succumbing to the lure of the Americas should go down easily, I think."

Jon struggled to hide the pain welling inside him; his gambler's insouciance stood him in good stead. He tossed the pouch in his hand, and a bitter half smile lifted a corner of his upper lip. "A fair trade, do you think? The loss of a son, for the gaining of a title?"

Lord Ramble straightened his wide shoulders. "You will not shame me into changing my mind. I've suffered shame enough."

They stared into each other's eyes for long moments. One set of blue eyes held sorrow; the other held the strength of conviction. Without a word, Jon pivoted on his heel and started for the door.

"Jonathan!"

He turned.

"When you get to America, I'd like you to do one thing more."

"And what is that, sir?"

"I ask that you change your name, so that your mother and I will not have to suffer any more embarrassment."

"Do you think the gossip mongers will follow me to the States, then?"

"I think the gossip will follow you wherever you may go."

Jon swallowed the lump forming in his throat. "Consider it done."

The baron nodded, and Jonathan Garrett Ramble left the room, closing the door behind him without a sound.

When he was gone, his mother set her sewing aside and broke into a storm of fierce, heartrending sobs that were ignored by her mate.

Lord Phillip Ramble, Baron of Wiltshire, went to the window. He peered out, his shoulders drooping as if burdened by a terrible weight. Through the gloaming, he saw his son climb into a carriage drawn by a pair of high-stepping bays. He watched as they pulled from the door-step, watched until they rounded a corner and disappeared from his sight…and his life.

Chapter One

South of Thibodaux, Louisiana
July 1852

"She's as wild as the wind, *Maman.* She talks back, and she won't listen to me at all. I've tried to explain that people will gossip, but she's so headstrong, so sure she knows everything, that she refuses to heed anything I say!"

Lisette Antilly blinked back the tears stinging her eyelids and clutched the pointed finials of the wrought-iron fence that surrounded the small cemetery. Her mother, the beloved Elizabeth Antilly Duschene, had passed away in February. Gastric fever had left her dizzy and weak and had finally sent her into a coma that lasted until her heart gave out.

She missed her mother's chatter and her quick smile, both so much like her wayward sister's. Silvia—or Silvie as she was called—was more like Elizabeth than Lisette would ever be, but Lisette had been close to their mother, nonetheless.

Since her fragile control over her younger sister was slipping, Lisette's visits to the place where her parents were buried had become increasingly frequent. It was as if she felt that sharing her fears with her mother could help. Logically she knew the only help she was apt to get were memories of the advice Elizabeth had given while she was alive, but something about the visits to the cemetery gave Lisette strength.

Taken with fancy, romantic visions and incorrigible inquisitiveness, Silvie was of a mind that life was made for fun and that nothing would dare spoil it for her. Lisette worried about her sister, but if the truth were known, she was a little jealous of Silvie's devil-be-damned attitude.

There were times Lisette envied her sister's cocksureness, but this time she knew Silvie's actions were trouble with a capital *T,* the same trouble that had plagued their lives ever since Henri Duschene had carried their mother over the threshold.

Etienne Antilly had died of yellow jack when Lisette was twelve. It seemed they had hardly seen the last clod of soil thrown onto the casket when her mother had met and married Henri, the handsome cousin of a friend who lived north of Thibodaux, near Donaldsonville.

Lisette had been horrified and furious that her mother could cast aside Etienne's memory in the space of a few months, especially since Henri knew nothing about plantations or planting...or anything else that Lisette could see—except, perhaps gambling.

Yet while Lisette begrudged her mother's happiness, eight-year-old Silvie hadn't minded the new addition to their family. Indeed, she adored the charming, handsome Henri, who enticed her into his lap and good graces with peppermint sticks and licorice. The problem was, Henri was still enticing Silvie.

Just because Lisette had reached the age of one and twenty without taking a husband, she was not blind to what was happening beneath her very nose. Nor did the fact that she had not succumbed to the advances of the young men who came to call when she began showing herself make her ignorant of the things that went on between men and women. She had spent enough time with Elizabeth at the quarters to know that the kind of looks Henri was giving her sister, the kind he had given their mother, led to one place—a moss-filled mattress.

It was a look Lisette had grown familiar with through the years. Many was the time she had seen that look extinguish the light of battle in Elizabeth's eyes. And when combined with a kiss, the look had transformed her mother's irritation to sighs and smiles.

Lisette had seen Elizabeth change for the worse before her very eyes. She had gone from a no-nonsense person who stood for what she believed to a woman who was dependent on her younger husband's touches and caresses. She'd coveted Henri's infrequent smile and begged for his kisses. That she had loved him went without saying; that he had used that love to manipulate her was equally obvious…at least to Lisette.

And now, it was happening all over again with Silvie.

At fifteen, when Silvie had put away her dolls and taken down her schoolgirl's plait, she had made her debut by sitting on the bank of the plantation's park and "showing herself." Neighbors traveling the bayou spread the word of her eligibility, and young men began to call. Though Silvie was as pretty as the spring wildflowers and had a plethora of suitors, she had so far refused to make a choice.

Silvie, who had just celebrated her seventeenth summer, hardly spoke of the beaux who came courting; she scarcely paid any heed to them at all. Instead, she trailed after Henri as he rode around the plantation, or shut herself up with him in the study so that he could teach her to play chess. Through the weeks, Lisette listened with growing concern and anger while Silvie regaled her with talk of Henri's grand plans, which changed from day to day.

Henri planned to do this. Henri was going to do that. Monsieur Bordeaux, the former owner of the plantation next to them, had lost both his plantation and a fortune in sugar, and—wasn't it wonderful?—Henri's newest plan was to buy the land and expand Belle Maison's sugar fields. Why, he might even put in a sugar mill—better than the one at Laurel Valley!

Henri, Henri, Henri... Lisette was sick of the name and the man, but there was nothing to do but endure. Etienne had willed Belle Maison to his wife and two daughters but, as a woman, Elizabeth had had no say in its affairs. Under the law, only a man—a brother, an uncle, or someone appointed by the courts—could take on the responsibility of running the plantation.

The same held true for Lisette and Silvie. Though the plantation had passed into their hands when Elizabeth died, Henri held the reins. As for her stepfather's plans to expand their sugar operation, Lisette would far rather see him take proper care of what he had. She would like to see him do something within the realm of his expertise—like replace the shingles on the dovecote or repair the loose railing of the back of the *galerie* that circled the two-story house. Considering the way he squandered money, Lisette hoped they could hold on to their home.

The situation between her sister and Henri was never far from her mind. Silvie pooh-poohed her fear, and thus far, Lisette had been unable to gather sufficient courage to confront her stepfather.

"I don't know what to do with her, *Maman,*" she said to the white stone angel guarding Elizabeth's grave. "I'm at my wit's end."

Giving a sigh, Lisette picked up her skirts and turned toward Belle Maison. Dodie would have lunch ready soon, and it was doubtful that Silvie, who had gone off somewhere with Henri, would be there to help.

Not a breath of air stirred as Lisette picked her way through the woods toward the house, a scant quarter mile away. Beyond the house and the grass of the park, which grew over the levee to the water's edge, the bayou glittered like a ribbon of green silk shot with silver.

Humidity hung like a miasma in the air, and the bodice of her dress clung damply. With another sigh, Lisette stepped out of the shelter of the trees into the radiance of the July sun. The heat settled its weight upon her narrow shoulders, like the worry that beset her at every waking moment.

Her talk with her mother had yielded no help, and Lisette knew that if Elizabeth was there, she would tell her that there was no use fretting over what she couldn't change. No doubt it was good advice, but as her mother had also said, advice was meant to be given, not taken.

Chapter Two

Silvie and Henri entered the wide hallway arm in arm, their faces flushed, their hair mussed and their clothes awry, as if they had been loosened because of heat—or perhaps, Lisette thought with pounding heart, donned in haste.

"Where have you been?" She was glad Dodie was out back in the kitchen, unable to witness her sister's dishabille.

Silvie's smile vanished. Instead of answering, she took an automatic step toward Henri, who flicked his riding crop against the soft leather of his knee-high boots and pinned Lisette with a challenging look.

"We've been riding. Is something amiss?"

Lisette raised her round chin to a haughty degree. "I believe you know what's wrong. A man as worldly as yourself must be aware of the harm your—" she paused, searching for the right word "—liaison with Silvie will do to her reputation."

Henri's mocking laughter filled the hall. "I'm the child's father, her guardian, for God's sake. No one will think a thing out of the ordinary."

"I beg your pardon, but you are not her father, and she is certainly no child, as the bevy of young men who parade through this house can attest to."

Silvie took off the small hat that matched her riding outfit and jabbed the hat pin into the ruched trim. "Will both of you please stop talking about me as though I weren't here?"

Placing the hat on a marble-topped table, she planted her small hands on her hips and stamped her foot. "I'm tired of you running my life, Lisette, and I want you to stop!"

"I'm only trying to take care of you the way *Maman* would," Lisette said, though she knew she might as well be talking to Charlie, the Catahoula cur dog that insisted on destroying her herb garden. "You know how she felt about keeping up appearance."

"Well, you aren't *Maman,* and she isn't here, so it's of no consequence. If I want to spend time with Henri instead of those gawking, immature *clods* who hang on my every word, I shall!"

She picked up her skirts and flounced up the stairs, leaving Lisette with their stepfather. Feeling the sting of futile tears, she turned to leave.

"Lisette," Henri said.

Clenching her hands at her sides, she blinked the moisture from her eyes before facing him. "Yes?"

"Why do you hate me so?" he asked. He stepped nearer, a quizzical expression in his night-black eyes. "Why have you always hated me?" He brushed the knuckle of his index finger down the curve of her heat-flushed cheek.

Lisette's startled breath caught in her throat. The bluntness of the question took her by surprise, and the intimacy of his touch filled her with a raging anger.

"I would like very much to be good to you...to give you things the way I always have with your sister. I want to make you happy."

The look of desire in his eyes sent a wave of panic to war with the fury sweeping through her. Lisette wanted to take Dodie's razor-sharp fillet knife and sink it deep into

Henri's hard stomach. She forced herself to meet his glittering gaze. Showing him any sign of weakness would never do.

"I don't hate you, Henri," she said, promising herself she would do penance for the tiny lie and her sinful feelings. "But I have everything I need, thank you."

The look in his eyes underwent a swift transformation from desire to gemstone hardness. "Then perhaps you should leave your sister's future to me and concern yourself with the running of the house."

"If you can convince me that your concern with her future and her happiness is genuine, I would be happy to do so," Lisette replied. "If you will excuse me, now, I should help Dodie with lunch."

Not a whisper of air stirred. Lisette lay with her arm flung over her face, listening to the silence and praying for sleep, even though she knew her prayers were in vain. No whippoorwills called; no mockingbirds filled the night with stolen songs; no owls wondered "who-who cooks for you all?" Even the bullfrogs' infrequent bass *rrribbits* sounded lethargic. She dragged the hem of her batiste gown to a position an inch shy of scandalous and flopped to her side. It wasn't just the heat that kept her from rest. It was the dilemma of what to do about Silvie.

Memories of their earlier confrontation paraded through Lisette's mind as relentlessly as the heat stalked the night. She had to find a way to make Silvie understand. Lifting the mosquito *barre,* Lisette eased her bare foot to the padded stool sitting beside the high bed. Moonshine slipped through the leaves of the magnolia tree outside her room, dappling the floor and lighting her way as she tiptoed across the smooth, heart pine floors.

So as not to disturb Henri, whose room was across the wide hall, Lisette tapped lightly on the door that connected her room with her sister's. Through the closed door, she heard the bed creak and the shuffling of covers. Without waiting for an answer, she eased open the door. "Silvie, are you awake?"

The soft closing of another door was muffled by her sister's voice. "What is it, Lisette?"

The sharpness of Silvie's voice stung. "I...thought we should talk."

Silvie was propped against the carved headboard, the neck of her gown unbuttoned and her throat bared to the heat of the night. "Talk? Lecture, you mean."

"I'm sorry if it appears that way to you, but you must know I'm so stubborn about this because I care about you."

Silvie tossed her dark hair away from her face. "You care about what people think."

"Yes," Lisette said fervently, "but only because I don't want them thinking badly of you."

"Why should they?"

The obviousness of the answer should have been clear, but the fact that it had escaped Silvie's will-o'-the-wisp mind was just another indication of her immaturity and her refusal to recognize the seriousness of life. The unconcern in her voice triggered the feeling of despair that dogged Lisette's days. Again she was left with the nagging notion that things between Silvie and Henri were rushing out of control, like the bayou in spring. Swollen with rains, the bayou was wont to seek out any unmended crevasses in the levee, bursting through and flooding the fields for miles, leaving devastation in its wake.

"You are barely seventeen," Lisette said in her sternest voice. "Henri is too old for you. You must stop spending so much time with him."

"He is not too old for me. There are only eighteen years difference between our ages. Why, look at Melinda Carlisle! She's *Maman's* age, and Charles is sixty if he's a day." The moonlight illuminated the thoughtful look on Silvie's face. "I'm not sure I could stand for him to kiss me, though."

"Charles?"

Trying to keep up with Silvie's quicksilver thoughts was like trying to gather the elusive ingredients of Tante Mabel's *Poudre de Perlainpainpain*, a powder of supposedly mystical qualities prepared by young ladies to snare the unsuspecting hearts of the gentlemen who filled their thoughts.

"Not Charles, goose," Silvie said loftily. "Henri."

"You have allowed Henri to *kiss* you?" Lisette couldn't disguise her shock.

Silvie sighed. "I couldn't help myself. He's so strong, and when he touches me—"

"Silvie..."

"I get all quivery inside, just like Dodie's grape jelly."

"Silvie!" Lisette whispered harshly. "This is madness!"

"Stop being so sanctimonious!" Silvie snapped. "Henri is a man. Everyone who's come to call is so boring, a fact of which I'm sure you are well aware." She tilted her chin in defiance. "I have no intention of becoming a *talon jaune* like you, so you may as well get used to the idea of me and Henri."

Lisette wasn't sure her gasp of surprise was because Silvie had called her by the derogatory name given to a young woman who had passed her eighteenth birthday without marrying, or because her sister had all but said she had no intention of putting an end to the dangerous game she played with their stepfather.

"I plan to marry him, and become the mistress of Belle Maison."

"Marry him?" Lisette echoed. "He's proposed?"

"Not in so many words," Silvie said with a shake of her

head. "But he cares for me." There was smugness in her voice. "Does that surprise you?"

Lisette knew that just as she was determined to live her life without any romantic entanglements, Silvie needed that element in her life as surely as she needed the humid bayou air to breathe. "I know you want to be loved. We all do. What surprises me is that you believe Henri is sincere."

"Why wouldn't he be? You're just jealous, sister dear. You're pea green because you don't have someone as handsome as Henri who cares for you."

The accusation stung. Lisette had no intention of tying herself to a man and being subject to his whims for the rest of her life, but the thought of having some strong arms to carry the everyday problems of the sugar plantation was one that plagued her more and more of late.

"Handsome is as handsome does," she said, pushing aside her disquiet.

"And what does that mean?"

"It means that you can judge a person by their fruit. *Maman* was miserable married to Henri. You know what a flirt he is. How can you be so sure he's as serious about you as you are him?"

Silvie's small, perfect teeth gleamed in the moonlight. "Oh," she said with a soft, silvery trill of laughter, "I know."

Chapter Three

New Orleans, September 1852

The command was given to pit, and Nate Rambler, formerly Jon Ramble, watched as the Negro trainers faced the gamecocks off on two lines drawn exactly eighteen inches apart.

The thrill of victory raced through his veins. Normally he didn't bet on cockfights, but Beau Navarre was fighting his new Claiborne cock, a courageous breed introduced by a man of the same name and fast becoming popular with the young men of the gentry. Beau was certain his rooster would win and, taking into consideration the trainers and the breeding of the two roosters, there was little doubt in Nate's mind which cock would be the victor. He had three hundred dollars riding on the outcome, and if there was anything he'd learned the past two years, it was to consider every possible angle before laying down his money.

The first thing the whoring, rakehell son of Baron Ramble had done when he left London was lose the biggest part of the money the baron had given him. The ripples left by the ship's anchor had hardly faded into the placid waters of Boston Harbor when Nathan Rambler, as Jon had decided to call himself, was introduced to the game of poker, which appeared to be a version of *poque,* a similar game of cards played in France. Down to his last few pounds, he made his way to New Orleans.

New Orleans. Paris of the Americas. The city with the longest social season, the most gaiety and culture and the most widespread gambling. What better place for a young gambler who spoke French like a native and lived for a throw of the dice? Nate was able to experience every game of chance that tickled his fancy—from whether or not the rains would flood the city by overflowing the sewage-filled gutters to which poor fool would be killed beneath the Dueling Oaks. And that was exactly what he had done the first few months after his arrival.

The baron's hope that his son would grow up were in vain. Nothing but Nate's name and his social status, which fluctuated with his luck and the coin in his pockets, changed. One day he was sitting quite prettily in luxury's lap—better known as the St. Louis Hotel—dressed as befitted his station, and the next he counted himself lucky to have two coins to rub together and the dubious good fortune of a doxy's bedroom to shelter him from the noxious night air. It was true that he won almost as often as he lost, but he didn't like losing...which always seemed to happen at the most inopportune times.

He had been a year in New Orleans when, deep into a game of poker that had stretched from twilight into the dawn of a new day, he began to wonder just what someone of his background might do to earn the "honest" living so important to his father...and, perhaps, he admitted with some reluctance, important to his own well-being.

No longer the recipient of an endless supply of funds and unused to anything remotely resembling poverty, Nathan

Garrett Rambler had finally come to the reluctant conclusion that trusting his existence to the turn of a card was foolhardy, something Jonathan Garrett Ramble had never been able to see.

Several days later, the answer had become crystal clear when a hot-blooded, hotheaded crony asked for Nate's help in honing his skill with a sword. Nate knew in a heartbeat what his new calling would be. Since swordplay was an art he knew well, one he had used many times to end the frequent disputes that occurred when young ladies or cards were involved, he decided to open up an academy for sword and rapier training.

Renting a place on the corner of Exchange Alley and Conti Streets, Nate set up his own *salle d'armes*. Highly skilled—as was evident by the near-fatal wound he'd inflicted on the Duke of Langsford—students flocked to his studio.

Next to Bastile Croquere, the mulatto who was considered to be not only the most skilled swordsman but the most handsome man in New Orleans, Nate was the best fencing master in the city. There was even a strong core of supporters who believed he might actually be the best, since Croquere's mixed blood limited him to teaching the finer points of swordplay and prohibited him from actual participation in a duel.

Nate's new position had just one drawback. It didn't take him long to see himself in the petulant faces of the young men who played the part of fool to some woman's whims—or those who were hell-bent on being parted with the money so readily available from their doting families.

Realizing that the young men he tutored were replicas of himself was a hard dose of medicine to swallow, one he vowed to change. Though his income was steady, he was far from becoming rich. Gambling was the only way to make it big, and there was a far bigger future in owning a gambling den than in contributing coin to someone else's coffers.

The problem was financing. It would take no small sum to build a place such as he pictured in his mind. No sleazy rat hole for the son of a newly appointed duke. No fly-spotted mirrors and soiled doves for Rambler's. Yes, he thought. He would call the place simply...Rambler's. It had a ring to it, reminiscent of White's or Almack's, both the quintessence of success.

Rambler's would have gold velvet draperies and damask-covered settees. Only the finest liquors would be served, and complimentary Havana cigars would be given out as long as a customer put his money on the tables. There would be a dining room appointed with Spode china, imported paintings and crystal chandeliers, where one might partake of a feast fit for the prudish Queen Vicky herself...prepared, of course by the finest chefs he could locate....

Reality had pulled Nate's dreams up short when the president of the Louisiana State Bank informed him that his chances of getting a loan without collateral were as slim as the straight legs of his tailored trousers.

With a sigh, he had given in to the inevitable. There was nothing for it but to finance his venture the only way he knew how: gambling. But not just willy-nilly gambling. He would choose the time and the place and the players. He would gamble not for the thrill, but for the money.

He became a student of faro, roulette, *vingt-et-un*—and people. He came to realize that how you played your hand was as important as the cards you drew. He honed his nonchalance and practiced his poker face. And he learned to count cards. Within weeks it began to pay off and, as any respectable baron's son would, he had put the money into the bank and saved it until the day his burgeoning account could support his dream....

* * *

There was a roar of voices and a whir of wings as the cocks met in midair, trying to inflict as much damage as they could with the sharp metal gaffs that replaced their natural spurs. Curses and cries of jubilation melded with frantic voices urging the cocks to do it, to get the other. Minute by tense minute passed and, despite Beau's predictions, it began to look as if the cocks were well matched.

Nate pulled out his gold pocket watch. Damn! Maria would be furious. He was supposed to have been at her hotel an hour ago. Not all his pastimes had changed since he had boarded the clipper ship that brought him to the shores of America.

Though he had conquered his impulsive gambling, Nate was far from ready to settle down. He flitted from one beautiful woman to another and was a frequent visitor of the quadroon balls. His current *affaire de coeur* was with Maria Donatti, a flame-haired opera singer touring the country. Her soaring soprano, which spurred the most jaded hearts, had made her the darling of the city. Her plump petiteness had made her Nate's darling.

"That Claiborne breed is dead game, hey, Nate?"

The comment brought Nate's stray thoughts back to the match. Both roosters looked pretty well spent, but the cock opposing Beau's seemed unable to rise. Nate shifted his gaze from the expiring chicken to the young man standing next to him. Taking a sip of his *tafia,* he nodded.

"Old Beau's cock may very well win this one," he said in a voice whose British accent had already begun to meld and merge into the speech patterns of the multilingual city.

"I believe so."

They watched as the losing cock gamely gathered himself. Finally he stood on his own and the two started flogging each other again.

"Nate."

The voice belonged to Raoul Desmoulins, a student at

his academy and one of the few people in his new homeland Nate could claim as a friend. He slapped the newcomer on the back. "Raoul. What are you doing here? I didn't think cockfighting was your cup of tea."

"Nor yours," Raoul countered.

Nate shrugged. "There was money to be made."

"That's why I'm here. Scottie sent me to tell you that some bigwigs are getting together for a few friendly hands at the Fleur d'Orleans. He thought you might be interested."

"What kind of bigwigs?"

Raoul lifted one shoulder in a Gallic shrug. "A banker from Boston who is here visiting friends. A sugar planter from somewhere near Raceland. The governor's cousin by marriage." He grinned. "The usual easy pickings."

"I've heard of the governor's cousin," Nate said thoughtfully. "Rumor has it that he plays quite well."

"But not as well as you, hmm, *mon ami?*" Raoul said with a challenging smile.

Nate grinned back. "When I finish here, we'll have to look them up and find out."

He glanced into the pit and saw that both cocks were down. Cheers of encouragement melded with groans of dismay. As he watched, Beau's rooster rallied enough to make a final, halfhearted peck at its opponent. The crowd cheered. The cock to make the final move was declared the winner. Pleased, Nate smiled. His winnings would come in handy for the poker game. Maria would be furious that he'd deserted her, but she would just have to understand.

Chapter Four

Conrad Krueger was in trouble. He had come to New Orleans with every cent he possessed in his pockets and the idea in his mind of winning enough money to get him out of his present financial bind. He had let everything go since his Helga had died giving birth to their daughter four years before. Fair-haired, blue-eyed Helga had been the light of his life, and every day without her was a little harder for him to bear.

He had promised Helga that he would not blame the infant for her death and that he would see to the children. It was a promise he had kept. Because he saw so much of her in the children, they were all that mattered to him now. He taught Karl to hunt when he should have been teaching him how to care for the sugarcane that was their livelihood. He regaled Heidi with stories of her mother's good nature and played games with Franz and Monika when he should have been poring over the plantation's ledgers. The cane suffered; and so did the house.

The final blow had struck when the spring floods burst through an unmended crevasse in the levee and flooded not only his cane fields, but his neighbors' as well. His guilty conscience urged him to borrow money against Magnolia

Manor to recompense them for their losses and to pay the bills at home. All had been fine until the bank began to press him for the money. For the first time since Helga died, Conrad had looked around and realized that he had allowed the plantation to fall into a terrible state of disrepair.

Fear and panic had stricken him then. He had walked the floors for weeks, searching for a way out of his financial quagmire. He hardly slept, and ate only when Heidi told him he was going to become ill if he didn't. He knew it would take a miracle to pull him out of the mess, but since Helga's death, Conrad had little belief in miracles. He figured that the only way he could get his hands on a large sum of money was to win it, and he had never been much of a gambler.

Nevertheless, here he sat, three hours into a poker game with strangers and losing steadily. Conrad realized that he shouldn't have had so much to drink before he'd come, but quaffing one glass of beer after another was the only way he could keep his courage bolstered. The liquor-induced fog surrounding him lifted as the night progressed, and his sobriety increased in proportion to his losses. Accompanying his clearer thinking was the growing concern that he was in over his head.

Though gambling wasn't his forte, he wasn't stupid. He had always been able to read people with a fair amount of accuracy. Early in the game he realized that the governor's cousin had the unfortunate habit of knuckling his mustache when he had a good hand, and the Boston banker was a careful player. No one would win much from him.

It was the Englishman who worried Conrad. It was rumored that Nathan Rambler was the son of a duke. Rumor also claimed that Rambler was as skillful with his sword as he was in his gambling. So far, rumor appeared founded in truth. One by one Conrad had watched the players drop from the game until no one was left but himself and Rambler, who won hand after hand. He was indeed skilled, Krueger thought, or Luck, that fickle lady, was smiling on him.

Conrad watched in disbelief as his opponent clenched his cigar between his teeth and, squinting against the smoke, drew the pile of bills and coins to him.

"Wh...what are you doing?"

"Perhaps we should call it a night," Rambler said. "I'm exceedingly weary, and I have a very impatient lady waiting for me."

Conrad looked at the stacks of money, much of it his, lying on the table. He pulled a monogrammed handkerchief from his breast pocket and mopped at his perspiring face. "B...but I've lost so much money."

"A good reason to stop," Rambler said, placing the Havana in an ashtray. He scooted out his chair and rose, arching his back.

"If you don't quit now, you might not get out of here with your shirt," the governor's cousin said with barely concealed sarcasm.

Conrad didn't notice. "You've got to give me a chance to get part of it back!"

"You've had several chances, Mr. Krueger." Rambler began to pick up the money and put it into his pockets. "Maybe tomorrow will be better for you."

"Wait!" Conrad blurted. Even he heard the desperation in his voice. "Just one more hand. Double or nothing."

At the moment, the five thousand dollars represented a fortune. Conrad silenced the voice of his troublesome conscience that asked him where he was going to get another five thousand dollars in the event he lost this hand, too.

He wouldn't think about that now. Instead, he looked into the gambler's implacable blue eyes. Not a flicker of emotion showed. Conrad watched Nathan Rambler slowly draw the money out of his pocket, sit back down and tap the ash from his cigar.

"Your game, then, Mr. Krueger," he offered, ever the gentleman.

"Double or nothing," he said again. "One hand of five-card stud—all the cards dealt up since there will be no additional betting."

Rambler considered the deal momentarily; then he placed the cigar between his lips and broke the seal on a new deck of cards. He slapped them down on the table.

Obviously Rambler didn't want to deal the cards. Under the circumstances, Conrad didn't, either. He pushed the deck toward the banker. "Will you deal, sir?"

"Certainly."

The cards were shuffled, and Conrad cut the deck. His first card was a two of hearts. Rambler's was a seven of spades.

"The seven is high," the banker said.

The second turn of the cards gave Conrad a five of clubs and Rambler a queen of hearts.

"Queen high."

Luck was still with the Englishman. A rivulet of perspiration trickled down Conrad's spine. A four of clubs was placed next to his five. Nathan Rambler was dealt a king of diamonds.

"King high."

Conrad ran a finger beneath the limp fabric of his once-stiff collar. Dear God, what had he done? he wondered as a fourth card was tossed his way. A three of spades. The collectively indrawn breaths were audible. It took him a second to figure out what had surprised them, and when he did, he gave a small gasp himself.

"Mr. Krueger has a possible straight," the banker said in a voice that mirrored his own surprise.

Conrad glanced at his opponent. Nathan Rambler, who

looked completely relaxed, took another draw on the fine Havana. The banker dealt him an eight of diamonds.

Conrad's mind reeled. For the first time, he had a chance to win. There was only one draw left for each of them, and he had the best hand by far. He had six chances to beat Rambler. If he drew an ace, he would have a low straight. A six would give him a straight on the high end. If he drew a two, three four or five he would have a pair, which would also beat Nathan Rambler's king. A smug smile twitched at Conrad's lips. The tables had turned. Luck was no lady. She was a two-timing tramp, and it looked as if she had just turned her back on Nate Rambler.

The banker started to flip over the last card.

"Wait!"

All eyes turned his way.

"I know there wasn't supposed to be any more betting, but if you agree, I'd like to sweeten the pot a little."

Rambler's eyes narrowed. "What do you have in mind?"

"I'd like to bet my plantation."

There was no discretion in the gasps this time. Nathan Rambler simply flicked the ash from his cigar.

"If I lose on the turn of this card, I'll give you the deed to Magnolia Manor—three hundred acres of prime sugar land. The house itself is just five years old, and it sits in one of the prettiest parks on the Bayou Lafourche."

Nate Rambler didn't look impressed. "I'd rather play for money."

The light of conquest gleamed in Conrad's blue eyes. He could smell victory. "You didn't mind upping the pot as long as the cards were in your favor," he said with a bit of sarcasm. "Do you bet only on sure things?"

Nate Rambler ground out his cigar. "I don't need a plantation."

"But you would like to own your own gambling den, I

hear," Conrad prodded. "If you win, the land would be worth a lot of money. You could always sell it."

For the first time that evening, Conrad imagined he saw a ghost of emotion in Nathan Rambler's eyes. "What do you think your plantation is worth, Mr. Krueger?"

"Twenty thousand ought to do it." If Nate Rambler agreed to put up money in equal value of the plantation and lost, all Conrad's problems would be over. Twenty thousand would get him out of trouble with the bank and give him a nice little nest egg. If he lost, he would lose his home, but chances of that happening were strong anyway.

Conrad preferred not to think of the bank taking over or the fact that if Nate Rambler did win, he would get not only the plantation but the debts that went with it. He pushed the thought aside. He couldn't think of unfairness just now. He had to strike while the iron was hot.

After several seconds of staring at the landscape across the room, Nate Rambler nodded. "All right, Krueger. I'm a gambler, and you're right. I do want to put in my own place." He held out his hand, and the two men shook on the bet.

"Ready?" the banker asked. Both men nodded.

A card came sailing across the table and landed near Conrad's others. For a split second, he couldn't believe what he was seeing. A jack of spades. No help. Silence filled the room.

Conrad stared at the cards. For a moment he couldn't breathe, couldn't think. His euphoria faded like the lonely whistle of a distant train. Reality came rushing back, and the bitter taste of failure rose with the nausea in his throat. It didn't matter what Nate Rambler's last card might be.

"It seems you win again, Mr. Rambler."

Rambler didn't reply. He was busy searching for a match.

Conrad used the edge of the table to help him get to his

feet. "The deed is in the bank vault." It wasn't really a lie, he told himself. "If you'll give me your place of lodging, I'll have the papers delivered as soon as the bank opens tomorrow."

"I'm at the St. Louis."

It didn't escape Conrad that Nate was staying at one of the finest hotels in New Orleans. Without another word, he nodded and left the room.

Chapter Five

The New Orleans, Opelousas and Great Western railroads did not make a direct connection between New Orleans and Thibodaux. To satisfy the townsfolk who didn't want the belching, noisy trains keeping people awake and dirtying up their city, the railroad crossed the Bayou Lafourche three miles south of town. Nate had left New Orleans on the train that morning. His problem was how to finish his journey to the plantation, which was still nine miles away.

Even though it had been three weeks since he'd won Magnolia Manor from Conrad Krueger, Nate could still recall the quick rush of relief he'd felt when he realized he'd won. The gamble had been all too real that night. If he'd lost, there was no way this side of hell he could have come up with twenty thousand dollars.

Nate's relief at winning had been short-lived. It hadn't taken long for the bank to inform him of the outstanding note against the plantation's acreage. They had made it known that he couldn't get a clear deed and resell the place until the debt was satisfied. Paying off the note had taken a considerable bite out of his savings and made selling Magnolia Manor imperative. The decision to take a look at the plantation wasn't a pleasure trip. He needed to know what he'd won so he could decide on a fair asking price.

"You looking for a way into town?"

Nate turned toward the sound of the creaking voice and confronted an old drunk with greasy white hair and rheumy eyes. Nate's inbred fastidiousness caused him to recoil a step. The only thing worse than the drunk's reprehensible appearance was his breath. Though it was an hour before noon, the man had a good start on his drinking.

"Actually, I'm not going to Thibodaux," Nate told him. "I'm going south, to Magnolia Manor."

The old man swayed like a willow in a breeze, scratched his head and looked at his grimy fingernails as if he expected to see something there. What that something might be, sent Nate back another step.

"That'd be the Krueger place."

"That's right."

"Alvin Sturges," the vagrant said with a rolling belch.

Nate cringed. "I beg your pardon?"

"Alvin Sturges." The man gave Nate a look that seemed to ask if he might be a little slow. "He owns the livery stable out back."

"Oh. Thank you." Nate dropped some loose coins into the fellow's outstretched hand, careful not to touch him.

Alvin Sturges did indeed have a horse. Nate could either rent the ancient gelding or buy him, depending on whether or not he wanted to bring him back within a reasonable time. Assuring Mr. Sturges that his business would keep him in the area only a couple of days, Nate rented the horse and set off down the road toward Raceland.

The hot September day was waning when he reined the horse to a standstill at the end of the lane that led to his new acquisition. Krueger was right. The house, which he was approaching from the back, did have one of the prettiest parks Nate had ever seen. Instead of the orange and lemon trees so common to the yards that bordered the bayou, Magnolia Manor and its outbuildings sprawled amongst a natural grove of live oak and magnolia trees. Nate had never seen magnolias before he'd come to Louisiana, but he thought the large, waxy-petaled flowers were some of the most lovely he'd ever beheld. The place would be breathtaking in the spring.

Weary from his journey, he started down a narrow road that divided the fields of thickening cane. A half-finished building stood at his right. It looked as if Krueger had started building a mill and abandoned the task midway. Tools had been left scattered about to rust in the weather, and weeds had reclaimed the area that was to have been the floor.

A few yards past the fields, Nate entered the main street of the slave quarters, where the aroma of frying johnnycake and boiling turnips set his stomach to growling, reminding him that he hadn't eaten since early morning. Women with babies clamped to their hips and small children clinging to their dresses came to the open doors to watch his progress toward the big house. Larger children peeked out of windows and from behind the corners of the small structures, which were in dire need of whitewash. Being the object of so much curiosity made Nate uncomfortable; he was glad to leave the quarters behind.

He guided the old horse past the greenhouse, the stables and the dovecote, noticing that they too could use some sprucing up. The house proper, built in the popular Greek Revival style, boasted a deep *galerie* that surrounded the entire edifice and protected the rooms from the sweltering sunshine. Wisteria vines had gained a foothold on several of the Ionic columns, crawling and sprawling in abandon over the sloping rooftop.

There was no sign of life around the house. Nate was beginning to think Krueger had already left the premises, when a Negro woman with a brightly patterned *tignon* wrapped around her head stepped out of the house toward the kitchen.

"Excuse me!"

The woman, small, wiry and well past her youth, looked up as Nate pulled he horse to a stop.

"Is your master here?" he asked, dismounting.

"Nah, sir," she said with a cautious shake of her head.

"Will he be back soon?"

"Nah, sir, I don't 'spect he will."

Nate swore. He should have written and told Krueger he was coming. "I'm Nathan Rambler. I've come all the way from New Orleans to see Mr. Krueger. Can you tell me when you expect him?"

"Fact o' the matter is, Mr. Krueger ain't comin' back."

"He's already gone, then?"

"Yassir," the woman said with a slow nod.

Nate fought the frustration filling him. "It's important that I speak with him. Can you tell me where he's gone?"

The Negress pointed to the small cemetery across the way. "Master Krueger, he done dead."

"Dead!"

"Yassir. After he come back from N'awlins he called all the children in and told 'em what he'd gone and done. It was eatin' on him right bad. Well, suh, he moped aroun' here until last week, and then he took his old shotgun to the stable and shot hisself."

A jolt of surprise coursed through Nate. "Shot himself! But...why?"

"I can't rightly say. Maybe 'cause he done lost everything that meant somethin' to him. I heard him tellin' young Karl that the shame was jest more'n he could bear. Course, he ain't been the same since Miz Helga died. He jest kinda let things go aroun' here. Fact o' the matter is, I think he was jest lookin' for an excuse to go be with her."

Nate hardly heard the woman's rambling dissertation. He was too busy recalling how nervous Krueger had been during the game and how sure he'd been that he would win that last hand. And because he hadn't won, he was dead.

Just as Nate couldn't imagine a title meaning more than flesh and blood, he couldn't imagine someone killing himself over a piece of land and house—or a woman, either, for that matter. On the heels of that thought came the realization that his chosen profession had some very serious hazards...and consequences.

"Are you that Englishman that won the plantation?"

The question drew his attention back to the situation at hand. "I am."

"I suppose you're the new master, then, ain'tcha?"

Nate opened his mouth to deny the statement and realized with another bit of surprise that she was right. He did own the place. All the paperwork was in his breast pocket. In a manner of speaking, he was the new master. Of course, he hastened to assure himself, that didn't mean anything—not really. But if the Negroes wanted to think of him in that light until he sold the place, what harm could there be?

"Yes, I suppose I am."

The woman nodded. "Uh-hum. I'm glad you come, then. You shore got a lot to do."

"A lot to do?" Nate echoed. "What do you mean?"

Surprise and a hint of irritation filled the old Negress's dark eyes. "Why cold weather's comin' on, and ain't nobody in the quarters got their winter clothes and such yet. Miz Helga always took care of us right good, but I had to remind Master Conrad when it was time to do everything."

Nate glanced toward the quarters. The shabbiness of the small shacks struck him again. He realized with something of a shock that he was responsible for these people now. Responsible for their shelter and the clothes they put on their backs. Responsible for every bite they put into their mouths and for caring for them when they became ill. It was a staggering bit of reality for a man who had only recently taken charge of his own needs.

He nodded in stunned acquiescence. "Uh..." he paused. "I'm sorry. I don't know your name."

"It's Sadie, Master Rambler. I help out in the house."

"I'll see that everything's taken care of first thing tomorrow, Sadie."

"That's good," she said with a nod. "Now what you got in mind for the cane?"

Nate frowned. "The cane?"

"Why, yassir. September's almost gone. We're supposed to start harvestin' at the end of October. Course," she said with a doleful shake of her head, "they ain't as much as usual. Been nigh onto fo' years since Master Conrad replanted."

Harvest cane? Nate stared at Sadie, his mouth hanging open. All he knew about sugar was that he put the brown granules into his coffee in the mornings and that *tafia,* his favorite alcoholic beverage, was made from it.

"B...but I don't know a thing about sugarcane. We don't grow it in England, you know."

"Thas all right. Old Jim and Levi will help you. Fact o' the matter is, they jest need someone to...oh, oversee things, I s'pose. Those field hands ain't about to listen to one of their own tellin' 'em what to do."

Nate just stared at her. His stomach churned, and it had nothing to do with the fact that he was hungry. He—Jonathan Garrett Ramble, who had never picked anything more than a wild berry—was responsible for harvesting three hundred acres of sugarcane. He felt like laughing. He felt like weeping. And he thought that he might never play another hand of poker in his life.

"Who are you?"

The angry words penetrated Nate's stupor. A young man

of approximately fifteen years stood on the bottom step, his chin thrust out in a belligerent manner.

Nate held out his hand. "Nathan Rambler."

The boy's face paled, then contorted with fury. "You!" he spat.

He coiled his hands into fists and hurtled himself at Nate. "You took away our land, you sorry bastard," he ground out between clenched teeth and ineffectual blows that Nate did his best to deflect. "You stole our land and then you killed my father!"

Chapter Six

Startled, and beginning to get angry himself, Nate fought to pin the boy's arms to his sides. "Stop it!" he commanded in a voice so much like his father's it shocked him.

The boy, no doubt the "young Karl," Sadie had mentioned, glared up at him, hate and pain in his eyes. Any other time, Nate might have related to the emotions, but at the moment, he was too furious. He had made the journey from New Orleans, intending to make a leisurely survey of his new property. What he'd found were the problems Conrad Krueger had left behind.

He shook the youth, who was struggling to free himself. "I'll let you go if you promise not to attack me again."

Krueger's son made a sound that sounded like a growl, but he stopped fighting. Breathing a sigh of relief, Nate eased his grip on Karl's sturdy wrists and stepped away. The boy stood in a quite acceptable military pose.

"I'm only going to tell you this once, young Mr. Krueger, so you had better listen carefully," Nate said, pacing back and forth in front of the youth. "First off, I did not steal this land. I won it fairly, a fact to which several people can attest. I didn't even want to play for your damned plantation, which these same people can also tell you, but I'm a gambler, and your father insisted. He'd been drinking, and—"

The shattered look on the young man's face halted Nate's diatribe. He could remember the feelings of betrayal accompanying those instances when he had learned his parents were not infallible, but mere mortals encumbered with faults and failings just like everyone else.

"He'd already lost heavily," Nate said in clipped tones.

Nate wanted to tell Karl that his father had played gamely. That taking a chance on the cards had required guts, and that, under the circumstances, he'd taken the only chance he had. He wanted to tell the boy that he admired his father for taking that chance, but the closed look on Karl's face prohibited further explanations. Nothing Nate said, nothing but time, would ease the boy's pain. Karl was still grieving over his double loss. He certainly wasn't in any frame of mind to listen to a man he considered his enemy.

"I will be glad to explain it in some length if you're ever of a mind to listen. But for now, suffice it to say that I had the better draw of the cards."

The boy didn't answer. Instead, he whirled on his heel and sprinted toward the barn.

The tension holding Nate ebbed, and he drew a deep breath. Slaves to care for, cane to cut, and one irate young man with a chip the size of the Louisiana Purchase on his shoulders. Could there possibly be anything else? He turned to Sadie, who was wringing her hands.

"Is there anything else you should tell me, Sadie? Any other problems your master left behind."

"No, sir," Sadie said. "No more problems. Just the children."

"Children?" Nate asked blankly.

"Yassir. What you gonna do about the children?"

"Do about them?"

"Why, yassir. There's three more besides young Master Karl."

Three? Nate blinked. "Three?"

"Yassir. Three. And not a soul in this world to take them in, 'ceptin' their Uncle Penrod, but ain't nobody seen hide nor hair of him since the missus passed." Sadie imparted that particular bit of information rather matter-of-factly. "I was wonderin', master, sir, jest what you're plannin' to do about the children, anyway?"

What did *he* plan to do with four children? Why was it his responsibility to see that they were taken care of? They didn't go with the plantation like the Negroes and the sugarcane, did they?

"They're good children," Sadie said. "There's Heidi. She's growing into quite a young lady, now. And Franz. He's...let's see, 'bout eight, I 'spect..."

She reminded Nate of a parrot Raoul had bought from some sailors. Once you got the bird talking, it was hard to shut him up. The only difference was that Sadie's dialogue wasn't peppered with the bird's colorful curses.

"And Monika, the baby. Miz Helga died deliverin' her. I was right there with her, and a terrible time—"

"Please," Nate interrupted, his mind reeling with all he'd heard the past five minutes. "Can we talk about this later? I'm rather...weary."

"Tired, are you?" Sadie said. "Why you're plumb peaked lookin'. Probably starvin', too." She started for the house. "Come on inside. I'll finish dinner while you freshen up."

"Thank you," Nate said, and stumbled up the steps after her.

Thirty minutes later, he sat at the table with Conrad Krueger's three youngest children, trying to fathom the mess that the turn of a single card had landed him into and doing his utmost to think of something to say to ease the silence that seemed to grow with each slow-passing moment.

To say that the children were uncomfortable was an understatement. They appeared frightened out of their wits. Nate wondered what he had done to make them look as if they feared he might take off their heads at any moment. In truth, he was as uncomfortable as they. It wasn't every day that a bachelor, whose only care was deciding what game of chance he wanted to participate in, was encumbered with the running of a plantation, a passel of slaves and four orphans.

He didn't want this responsibility; nevertheless, he *felt* responsible for having in some way contributed to the children's misfortune. Nate sipped his chicory-laced coffee and tried to set aside his resentment long enough to concentrate on how the Krueger children must be feeling.

What would his reaction be if fate took away his father and his home—the only life he knew? After a moment's consideration Nate decided he knew exactly how the Krueger children felt. When his father had accepted the Queen's terms to obtain his title, hadn't Nate been robbed of the very things a simple card game had taken from these children?

"Heidi," he said at last.

Her head came up sharply, like a wary doe sensing danger. "Sir?"

"Why does your brother blame me for what has happened here?"

A blush crept up over her fair cheeks, and Nate thought she was well on the way to becoming a lovely young lady.

"He says that you are a professional gambler and that Father should have known better than to play cards with you. He thinks you took advantage."

"I am a professional gambler, but I try hard not to take advantage of anyone who doesn't understand the rules."

"What does it matter? Father is gone, and we have lost our home," Franz said. His young voice was unsteady, but his gaze was not.

Monika's large blue eyes filled with tears. "I miss Papa."

"Don't cry, baby," Heidi said, her chin quivering in her effort not to give in to her own tears. "Papa has gone to heaven to be with Mama."

"I don't want him to go to heaven. I want him to come back so I can sleep with him when I have a bad dream."

Three pairs of eyes stared at Nate with complete condemnation. He gave a surreptitious sigh. He knew he had been irresponsible and perhaps even callous in the past, but he was not uncaring. The shy glances of little Monika, Franz's efforts to maintain a stiff upper lip and the quivering lower lip of twelve-year-old Heidi tugged at the strings of his heart, strings he hadn't known he possessed.

His hunger fled, and irritation fed his restlessness. Abruptly he shoved back his chair and strode from the room. As he passed through the door, he heard Franz say, "You've gone and done it now, Monika. You've made him mad. He'll probably send us to the nearest orphanage first thing tomorrow."

Nate started to turn back and tell Franz he was wrong, but his frustration kept his footsteps aimed for the back door and the kitchen. He couldn't turn these children over to an orphanage any more than he could let a year's worth of cane rot in the fields or a bunch of slaves go into the winter without proper clothing.

Damn it! He would do his duty by the plantation's slaves and crop. And he would search for Uncle Penrod—whoever and wherever the wretched man might be. But until the missing relative was found, he had little choice but to take responsibility for the care of the children himself.

At the sound of his footsteps, Sadie looked up from the cake she was slicing. "Is something wrong, Master Rambler?"

Master, Dear God, if he never heard that word again it would be too soon! "It's Nathan, damn it," he said more sharply than he intended. "Or better yet, Nate."

"Yassir, Master Nate," she said, her eyes widening at his obvious anger.

His long legs carried him into the room. "Who would I see around here if I wanted to make arrangements to have a governess sent here for the children?"

"Governess?"

"You know." He waved a hand vaguely. "Someone to care for the children. Someone to teach them."

"Ah. A teacher," Sadie said with a nod. "Might be you could talk to Father Menard about gettin' one of those nuns to come from N'awlins."

"Father Menard?"

"Yassir. He lives in Thibodaux, but he makes a pass through here every now and again. If anyone would know how to help you, it'd most likely be him."

"Fine, then. I'll look him up when I go to Thibodaux tomorrow to see about the clothes and things."

"That'd be real kindly of you, Master Ra—" she caught herself "—Master Nate."

Nate went back into the house, feeling somehow that in the short two hours he'd been there, his entire life had changed. He tried to comfort himself with the knowledge that the changes would be temporary, a few months at the longest. He would get in the cane and spruce up the place. It would be time well spent. By spring, he would have things in hand. The plantation would fetch a better price when the magnolias were blooming and the grass was green. Then Rambler's gaming den would become reality, and he would see the culmination of his dreams.

Chapter Seven

Late October...

The sound of weeping woke Lisette from a restless sleep and a dream where Henri lured her innocent sister deeper and deeper into the swamps. Disoriented, she opened her eyes and pushed herself to one elbow. She heard the whistling of the wind and the creaking of the house that told her a storm was brewing. Then she heard the sound again. It was the sound of sobbing, and it came from Silvie's room.

Lisette's heart sank. The reason for her sister's tears was obvious. She could have taunted her with "I told you so," but she wouldn't. The misery in Silvie's eyes the past few weeks was enough to still any harsh words Lisette might have uttered.

Drawing on her wrapper in the darkness, Lisette went to the doorway that connected the two bedrooms. She entered without knocking and crossed to the bed, which was bathed in the soft glow of candlelight. Downstairs, the grandfather clock chimed eleven.

"Silvie?"

Silvie sat up in the rumpled bed. "Oh, Lisette!" she wailed, holding out her arms the way she had so often as a child. "You were right. Henri is a beast! I should have listened to you and not my heart. I—"

"Shh," Lisette said. She pushed aside the mosquito *barre* and climbed into her sister's bed. Drawing her into a close embrace, Lisette ran a comforting hand over the tangled softness of her sister's hair. "Shh. It's going to be all right. I promise. It will hurt for a while, and then the hurt will go away, and you'll meet someone wonderful and be happy forever."

Silvie drew back, her eyes awash with tears. "I only wish it were true."

"It can be."

"No," Silvie said with an emphatic shake of her head. "It can't. Everything is ruined. Everything!"

"Ah, *petite,* it seems that way, I know, but things will look better soon."

"They won't look better," Silvie wailed, "and I certainly won't."

A chill that had nothing to do with the October night shivered through Lisette. "What do you mean?"

Two fat tears rolled down Silvie's cheeks. "I'm *enceinte.*

Dear Mother of God! Silvie carried Henri Duschene's child?

"He said I was beautiful and that he cared for me."

Silvie gave an angry swipe at her tears. Her laughter was bitter, so unlike her usual carefree giggle it frightened Lisette.

"He didn't care for me. He cared for himself. And when I gave him what he wanted, he was finished with me."

Lisette felt a sudden need to soothe her sister's smarting heart. "Perhaps he needs some time to sort out his feelings. I'm sure that when you tell him about the baby, he'll do the honorable thing."

Silvie shook her head. "No! I told him today, and he just shrugged and said that it was my problem. Can you guess where he is tonight?"

"No."

"He's gone to call on the widow Benoit."

Knowing him as Lisette did, Henri's interest was understandable. Patrice Benoit was a young, wealthy widow whose husband had died the previous year. "I'll speak with him."

"You'll be wasting your breath."

"I'll make him see that he's brought shame to this house—"

"No!" Silvie's voice halted Lisette's speech.

"No, Lizzie," she said, suddenly sounding more wise and grown-up than her older sister. "It is I who have brought shame to this house."

Lisette was still pondering her sister's predicament when she heard Henri's footfalls on the stairs some two hours later. She must speak to him. Surely she could make him understand that what he had done was sinful, shameful. Silvie was little more than a child, while he…he was a man full grown, and as such, he should have known better. He should have had more control.…

She sat up in bed and shivered at the chill ushered in by the howling of the wind. Thunder rumbled and the glass at the windows trembled. From the hallway, she heard the murmur of voices and realized that Silvie must have heard Henri come home, too.

As she listened, trying to decide whether or not to interfere, the voices grew louder, easily distinguishable over the sound of the storm. Suddenly she heard Henri swear and her sister cry out.

Dear God, was he hurting her?

Fumbling with a match from the matchbox, Lisette lit

the candle sitting on a nearby table. Her hand shook as if she had the ague. She scrambled from the bed and donned her wrapper for the second time that night. Then, lifting the heavy brass candlestick, she started for the door.

Neither Silvie nor Henri was making any pretense of hiding their anger or bitter feelings. Henri accused Silvie of being a child and strangling him with her constant demands. Silvie screamed that he was a selfish bastard and a rutting pig. As Lisette stepped through the portal, she saw Henri strike her sister across the cheek. The blow sent Silvie reeling against a table that held three flickering tapers.

"In the name of God, stop!" Lisette cried. "She's carrying your child."

Henri rounded on her, his nostrils flaring, his black eyes filled with fury and his hands curled into loose fists. In that one instant, she wondered how anyone could have ever thought him handsome.

"Then I would say that this little...altercation is between her and me, *n'est-ce pas?*"

Without waiting for an answer, he buried his hand in Silvie's hair and yanked her to her feet. Smiling a sick smile, he backed her toward the stairs. "No one will be the wiser if you have a little accident, now, will they?"

Silvie looked over her shoulder at the stairs falling away behind her. "Lisette!" she screamed.

He was mad, Lisette realized suddenly. Utterly mad. Giving no thought to her own safety, she raced toward Silvie, her bare feet flying across the plank floors. The candle guttered out and, gripping the brass candle holder tightly, she swung it at Henri's head. He turned at the last moment, and the blow landed against his shoulder, eliciting another curse.

Releasing Silvie, he made a vicious swipe with his arm that knocked Lisette off balance and sent the candlestick thudding to the floor. Silvie screamed again. With Henri's attention focused on Lisette, she scooted out of harm's way.

His hand caught Lisette across the cheek with a resounding smack that sent fireworks exploding in her head. Reeling with pain and dizziness, she was only partially aware that he was swearing at her. Every epithet was punctuated by a bone-jarring shake that rattled her brain.

Gathering what she could of her scattered wits, Lisette raised a small fist and rained a series of blows on his chest. They had the same effect as a moth battering the glass globe of an oil lamp. She felt his fingers close around her throat and his thumbs push against her windpipe. Hate and rage contorted his features. He would kill her, she thought numbly. Kill her with no remorse and with Silvie watching.

Lisette struggled to get a decent breath of air and rasped her sister's name from her burning throat. But Silvie didn't appear to hear. She only stood there, her hands pressed against her lips, her eyes wide, poised to run should Henri turn on her again.

The edges of darkness began to close in; still Lisette clawed at the hands choking the life from her. As the blackness gathered her closer, she began to think that perhaps it wasn't so bad after all. She would find rest in the darkness…and freedom from the pain…. Her knees gave way, and she crumpled to the floor. Miraculously Henri was not strangling her anymore.

From a faraway place, she heard him yelling. Forcing her eyes open, she saw that he was advancing on Silvie again. *Please, God. Please…* Exerting a maximum of effort, Lisette pushed herself to her knees and, reaching for the newel post at the top of the stairs, struggled to her feet.

"Henri." She pushed the word from her burning throat.

He pivoted on a well-shod heel, surprise on his face.

Had he thought her dead, then? Deliberately Lisette stepped in front of the stairs. "If you…hurt her, I will…kill you. I...promise." Speaking was agony, but she had never been more serious.

Henri gave a low growl of fury and rushed at her. Lisette's heart beat wildly in her chest, but she forced herself to stand her ground until the moment he stretched out his arms to shove her down the stairs. Ducking her head, she dropped to the floor. The momentum of his attack sent him sailing over her head. His handsome face wore a look of surprise as he uttered a hoarse cry and went tumbling down...into the same darkness that claimed Lisette.

Chapter Eight

"Wake up! Oh, Lisette, please wake up!"

Silvie's feverish plea penetrated the gray veil of unconsciousness separating Lisette from reality. Fighting the darkness, she forced her eyelids open. Pale and frightened, Silvie leaned over her. Behind her stood Dodie, the black woman who had cared for her and Silvie all their lives.

"Are you all right, child?" Like Silvie's, Dodie's face mirrored her concern.

"I'm...fine." The band of pain circling Lisette's throat made speaking an effort and brought back a vivid memory of what had happened to cause the pain. Henri. Choking her...trying to kill her and Silvie. Filled with sudden panic, Lisette struggled to rise.

"Gently, Lisette," Silvie cautioned, helping her to a sitting position.

Lisette looked from one to the other. "Henri...is he... dead?"

Dodie shrugged. "If he ain't, he can't be too far from it."

A sick feeling settled in the pit of Lisette's stomach. Dodie held out a cup half-filled with amber liquid.

"Here. Drink this. You gonna need it."

The smell of Henri's brandy made Lisette's stomach churn even more. "I can't."

"You got to. You got to get yourself awake and see 'bout gettin' to your Aunt Charlotte's in Baton Rouge."

"Why?"

"'Cause if that man dies, I ain't wantin' either of you to have to tell the law what happened here tonight. I'll jest pour a little o' this here liquor on his shirt and in his mouth and everyone will think he tripped on the stairs."

"I don't understand," Lisette said, raising a hand to her throbbing head. "Why shouldn't we tell the truth? Henri was trying to kill us."

"I know. But if you tell the truth, everyone on the bayou will find out about Silvie." Dodie's full lips flattened in anger. "And that man has caused this family enough grief."

Silvie gasped. "You know about the baby?"

Dodie's hand was gentle on Silvie's hair. "I know. I been knowin' what was goin' on for a while now. Ain't much goes on in this house I *don't* know about, child," Dodie said with a sad shake of her head. She looked at Lisette. "Do you think you can get up?"

She nodded, and Dodie and Silvie helped her down the stairs. So not to mark the baby, Silvie looked away when they passed Henri's body, but Lisette saw the pooling of blood beneath his head.

Her own head was still throbbing, but the brandy had burned away some of the cobwebs. Lisette sipped at the drink and tried to figure out what to do. Dodie was right. If they stayed and tried to prove that Silvie was Henri's victim, the whole world would find out about the baby.

Where could they go? Aunt Charlotte's was out of the question. They would be miserable there. Holier-than-thou Aunt Charlotte would never let Silvie live down her mistake, but if they went somewhere else—to New Orleans or

Shreveport—Silvie could claim a dead husband, and no one would be the wiser.

The problem was getting there. Each month, she and Silvie were given a piddling amount for "pin" money, but Lisette doubted that between them they would have enough for one train ticket. Then she remembered that Henri kept money in a leather bag in the back of a desk drawer. Anxious to investigate, she stood up. Her head spun, and she grabbed the back of a chair to steady herself.

"Where are you going?" Silvie asked.

"To see if I can find some money. You start getting some things together. Not much. Just a change of clothes. We can get more when we get wherever we're going."

Silvie grew pale. "I can't go back upstairs. I can't look at him."

"I'll get the clothes, then," Lisette said. "You see how much money is in Henri's desk."

She returned ten minutes later, carrying two small bundles. Besides the clothes they would wear, she had selected the barest of personal items—an extra change of clothes, brushes, two small mirrors, the rag doll Silvie still slept with and Lisette's favorite lilac soap.

By the time she reached the bottom of the stairs, Henri had been moved to a downstairs bedroom. The only reminder of the accident was the spot of blood that a young black girl was scrubbing away.

Suppressing a shiver, Lisette met Silvie in the dining room. "How much money did you find?"

"Five dollars."

"What!"

Silvie nodded. "He played cards the other night. He must have lost." Her eyes were wide and frightened. "What are we going to do? We can't start over with five dollars."

"I know." Lisette chewed her bottom lip. "His pockets! He must have money in his pockets."

"Lisette! You can't take money from a dead man!"

"We aren't sure he's dead."

Silvie looked as if she were about to swoon. Lisette shoved a plain cotton dress into her sister's hands. "Here. Get dressed, and take a sip of that whiskey," she commanded. "I'll be back in a moment."

Dodie was removing Henri's clothes when Lisette entered the bedroom. A red stain had already seeped through the white cloths binding her stepfather's forehead.

"How is he?"

Dodie grunted. "He sorta come 'round when we carried him in here. I think he may have some broke ribs, but he ain't as bad as I first thought." She shrugged philosophically. "Maybe one of them ribs punctured his black heart."

"Dodie!"

"I'm sorry, child, but after the way he killed your momma, nothing is too bad for him."

Everyone in the house knew that Henri had made Elizabeth's life hell, and it was true that his philandering ways had broken her heart. Remembering, Lisette hardened her own heart and checked Henri's pockets. To her dismay, she found only another two dollars. Where could they go on seven dollars that Henri wouldn't find them? She wasn't aware that she'd spoken aloud until Dodie answered.

"I don't know, child, but like Father Menard says, God will take care of you. Come on, now. Let's go out into the kitchen and fix you some victuals to take along."

Lisette followed the old black woman out of the sickroom, grateful for her support. She knew if Elizabeth was still alive that she too would tell her to put her trust in God. But Lisette wasn't certain God heard her prayers anymore, and despite Father Menard's claims, she didn't know how God could protect them from a vengeful Henri.

"What about the nuns?" Dodie said as she slathered a

thick slice of bread with butter and piled it high with smoked ham.

"Nuns?"

Dodie nodded. "Father Menard is always talking 'bout those nuns in New Orleans—you know, the ones who take in orphan girls."

"The Ursulines?" Silvie said, making a moue of dismay. "I can't imagine living in a convent with a bunch of stuffy nuns."

But Lisette thought it was a wonderful idea. What better place for them to go? Even if Henri pulled through and suspected they were there, the nuns would offer no information to strangers...especially if they were told how he had taken advantage of Silvie.

"It's a wonderful idea! We'll be safe there until we can figure out what to do. By the time the baby is born, we should have it all figured out."

"I don't want to live in a convent!" Silvie snapped, her willfulness surfacing even in the wake of the accident.

"It will only be for a few months."

"Lisette!"

"Shh," Lisette said. "Let me think."

She paced the width of the kitchen and back. "Perhaps we should split up, just in case Henri recovers and starts looking for us. I'll go with you as far as the outskirts of Thibodaux, and—"

"I don't like going by myself," Silvie said.

"Neither do I, but I don't know what else to do. We'll be less likely to draw attention if we go to New Orleans separately. When we get to Thibodaux, I want you to find Father Menard and tell him what has happened. He'll see to it that you get to the Ursulines safely."

"What about you?" Silvie asked. "Where will you be?"

"I'll get on a boat at Thibodaux and go down to Golden

Meadows. I'll stay with Tante Mabel a few weeks, and then I'll come up to New Orleans and get you."

"And then what?" Silvie asked.

"I don't know, *petite,*" Lisette said, taking her sister's hands in hers. "We'll figure it out later."

Silvie's eyes glistened with unshed tears. "You always know what to do."

Lisette smiled. She wasn't so sure.

"I'm sorry I let him hurt you," Silvie said. "I just…couldn't seem to move. I was so afraid."

Lisette squeezed Silvie's hands. "I know. But it's over, and we're both all right."

"I'll find some way to make it up to you, Lizzie," Silvie said fervently. "Someday, somehow, I'll find a way to make it up to you."

Chapter Nine

Though Lisette and Silvie left Belle Maison before dawn, they didn't reach Thibodaux until almost noon. The storm had passed, but morning sickness and blisters followed the rain, and by the time the town came into view, they were both cold and exhausted.

Because she had insisted that they hide in the brush whenever they heard a buggy or horse approaching, Lisette was relatively certain no one had seen them on the road. An old drunk had happened to look up from his bottle as they'd slipped past the train station, but Lisette took comfort in the thought that if his memory had any correlation to his sobriety and if someone did ask, he wouldn't remember seeing them.

All in all, it had been a wretched morning, and the worst was yet to come. She and Silvie still had to say goodbye.

"This is as far as I go."

Silvie turned. There was fear in her eyes, but behind it was the barest flicker of something else. Lisette felt a weary smile tug at her lips. In spite of the circumstances, in spite of everything, Silvie was excited about going to New Orleans and being on her own. Lisette wished she had a little of her sister's adventurous spirit.

"Will you be all right?"

Silvie nodded. "How will I find Father Menard?"

"Ask at the General Store. They'll know how to locate him." Lisette pressed a handkerchief into her sister's hand. "This is some money to tide you over until you get to the convent. They'll take care of you once you get there."

"What about you?"

"I have enough to get me to Tante Mabel's." Lisette crossed her fingers behind her back as she told the lie. She wasn't expecting a baby and could get by with far less food than her sister. She gave Silvie a fierce hug and pushed her away, toward the store. "Go," she said. "Go."

"I love you, Lisette," Silvie said.

"And I love you, *petite*." Without another word, Lisette spun on her heel and started off toward the bayou, where keelboats and flatboats and paddle wheelers sat waiting to carry their cargo down the bayou to the gulf. She didn't look back, afraid that if she did, the tears burning her eyes would fall.

Lisette stared dejectedly at the modest-looking paddle wheeler that delivered passengers and cargo up and down the bayou and gave a sigh of defeat. Though the boat wasn't as large or as fine as some she'd seen, she knew she didn't have enough money to book passage. And though she'd been brought up to be trustworthy and honest, there was no choice but to stow away.

Getting on board was easier than she'd expected. She simply waited until there was no one around, slipped on to the boat, and hid among some crates and barrels on the deck near the kitchen. Waiting in the cramped quarters until the boat left a loading platform would be the hardest part. Once they were on their way and darkness settled, she could stretch her legs.

Heaving a weary sigh, she rested her head on her arms

and breathed a prayer of Thanksgiving. If the good Lord was with her she would not be found.... "What are you doing there?"

Though the gentle voice matched the soft thrum of the steam engines and the rocking of the boat, it woke Lisette. Disoriented, she opened her eyes and glanced around, realizing that the day had vanished while she slept. The trees lining the banks were dark shadows that slipped by as the boat churned down the misty bayou. The moon, a silver disk that hung low in the darkening sky, raced alongside the boat. From the other end of the paddle wheeler came the sounds of laughter, singing and the music from the calliope.

She hadn't awakened when the boat left Thibodaux! Obviously the sleepless night and the walk from Belle Maison had worn her out—not to mention the ordeal with Henri—but how had she slept through the noise and gaiety?

"Well, child? Can you speak or not?"

The question drew Lisette's gaze to a plump wrinkled face framed by the white linen wimple and black veil of an Ursuline nun. Guilt settled like a lump of cold dumplings in her stomach. She was on the boat under false pretenses, which, since she'd been caught hiding amongst the kitchen supplies, the nun had no doubt figured out. What was the good sister doing milling about this part of the boat, anyway?

"Come," the nun said, holding out her hand. "I'm Sister Dominique. Won't you tell me who you are?"

Lisette put her hand in the aging nun's and felt her worries fade somewhat. "Lisette. Lisette Ant..." Under the circumstances, she thought better about telling her real name. If one was to be punished for sinning, one might as well make it worthwhile. "Lisette Angelou, Sister."

"You haven't a ticket, have you?"

Lisette shook her head and squeezed the nun's hand.

"Please don't tell the captain. I don't have enough money for a ticket, and I must get to my aunt's home in Golden Meadows."

"Hmm." Sister Dominique peered at Lisette over the wire rims of the thick glasses perched on the tip of her short nose. "Are you running away from your family?"

Lisette's stomach churned. "No, Sister. I have no family."

She consoled herself with the knowledge that it was not quite a lie. She had no one but Silvie. If Sister Dominique had asked if she was running away from her *home,* her answer would have been a lie.

"Hmm," Sister Dominique said again, piercing Lisette with a penetrating gaze.

"Well," Lisette said. "I do have a stepfather, but he...he has taken to...beating me." Henri had tried to kill her. Surely God would forgive her for not telling the whole truth to a stranger.

"He beat you?" Sister Dominique clucked in sympathy. "How awful! You're wise to seek sanctuary with your aunt, though it's terribly foolhardy for a young lady to travel alone. Come along, now. I'll take you to my room and get you something to eat."

She started off at a swift pace. Old habits died hard, and Lisette was accustomed to giving the clergy the respect that was its due. Obediently she fell into step beside the nun, who, like herself, was not very tall.

"It's a good thing for you that I stepped out for a breath of fresh air," she said. "No telling what might have happened if one of the crew had discovered your hiding place."

"I know, Sister," Lisette said. "I'm very grateful."

Sister Dominique's room was small with rather spartan furnishings. Lisette thought that perhaps it was normally used for one of the crew. A worn carpetbag holding an extra habit sat opened on the narrow cot. A sliver of soap and a rosary lay on top of the blanket. Evidently the nun had been unpacking before she went out onto the deck.

Sister Dominique took off the glasses and tossed them onto the bed. "I'm not used to traveling," she said, rubbing her eyes. "I'd gotten a bit queasy and decided a turn about the deck might do me some good."

"Where are you going?" Lisette asked politely, sensing that the nun was filled with excitement.

"To a plantation called Magnolia Manor. I'm to instruct the Krueger children. Do you know them?"

"No, Sister." For once Lisette could answer truthfully. She didn't know them, but she had heard Henri telling one of his friends about Conrad Krueger's loss of the plantation and his subsequent death.

"Well, Father Menard made it sound like an adventure, so here I am."

A bell of warning sounded in Lisette's brain. "You know Father Menard?"

"Not personally. Do you? I understand he's started many missions in the area."

"I've heard of him," Lisette said, crossing her fingers behind her back. "But we've never met."

"I see. Well, he approached Mother Superior, and she told me about the position at Magnolia Manor. There are four children aged four to fifteen, and I have always preferred country living to the city." She smiled again. "Just listen to me chattering on, when I know you must be starving."

"I am hungry, but I would really like to wash up and change my clothes." She pointed to the half dozen apples sitting on the wash stand. "Would you mind if I had one of your apples?"

"Of course not. There are clean cloths by the basin. I'll just go speak to the captain."

Lisette started to protest, but the nun held up a warning hand.

"We can't have you stowing away like this. I'll pay your passage to Golden Meadows."

Touched by the gesture, Lisette said, "But, Sister, I can't pay you back."

"I don't expect you to. I do expect you to help someone else who is in need."

Lisette felt like crying again. "Yes, Sister. I will."

"Good, then," Sister Dominique said briskly. "Have your apple. I'll bring back something else. There's fresh water in the pitcher."

"Thank you."

When the nun was gone, Lisette thanked God for sending Sister Dominique to her aid. Then she stripped down to her pantaloons and chemise and poured some water into the plain white ceramic bowl. The water was cool, and it felt marvelous to rid herself of the dust. Refreshed by her sponge bath, she sat down on the edge of the cot and sank her teeth into the juicy apple. It was delicious, tart and crisp, just the way she liked them. She was finishing the last bite when a giant shudder shook the boat and a loud *kaboom!* rent the air.

The blast knocked Lisette and Sister Dominique's glasses from the bed. Screams of pain and cries of panic echoed through the night. Only when Lisette felt the boat list to one side did she realize what had happened. The steam engine had blown up—a common enough occurrence—and the boat was sinking. Lisette's own panic began to rise.

If the boat was sinking, she had to get off. Where was Sister Dominique? Should she wait for her or see if she was on deck? Lisette grabbed the glasses that lay near her and struggled to her feet. Reaching for the carpetbag, she scooped up the nun's possessions and stuffed them inside. Saving the nun's belongings was the least Lisette could do to repay her kindness. Not bothering to dress—she'd heard that the weight of wet clothes could drag a person down—she muttered another prayer and headed for the deck.

Bedlam ruled. Fire blazed from the engine room, and passengers were running and screaming and leaping into the water with no thought to the dangers hidden there. Lisette looked out at the murky waters glittering in the moon and firelight. The shore looked so far away.

Unbidden, came the memory of her lies to Sister Dominique. Not only had she lied to the nun, but she had taken Henri's money and perhaps his very life. Lisette looked back at the fire and cringed from its heat. Should she jump or go down with the boat? Either way, she was afraid of the outcome. She didn't swim, but drowning would be preferable to dying in a fire—wouldn't it?

She started to leap and realized that even if she drowned she wouldn't escape burning. Somehow she was certain that the fires of hell would be far hotter than those on the boat.

She heard a scream and saw a man run to the rail, his shirt ablaze. Lisette clutched the carpetbag in one hand and slipped the rosary over her head. Without another thought, she took a deep breath and flung herself into the dark waters below.

Chapter Ten

The cold water snatched Lisette's breath as she plunged down, down into its murky depths. Part of her brain told her to release the carpetbag; another part refused to allow her fingers to let go. She clung to Sister Dominique's belongings like a talisman that she hoped would ward off the evil around her.

She held her breath and kicked her legs frantically in an effort to climb out of her watery grave, fearing all the while that it was an impossible task. After what felt like an eternity, she broke surface and dragged a deep breath of the chilly air into her starved lungs.

Slinging her dripping hair from her face and fighting to keep her head above the swirling waters that were quickly sweeping her downstream of the sinking vessel, Lisette tried to gauge the distance to the tree-lined shore. Too far, she thought as a sob of despair clawed its way up her throat. It was too far for a person who couldn't swim. A piece of flotsam banged her shoulder, causing her to go under again. Lisette flailed her arms and got her head above the water as another piece of wreckage swept by, within arm's reach.

She lunged at the board and held on to it for dear life, kicking her legs in an effort to push herself toward the opposite bank. Slowly she closed the distance between herself and the safe haven of the land. When she felt her bare feet touch the muddy floor of the bayou, she gave a sob of relief and splashed her way to the dry grasses bordering the water's edge.

Shivering, her teeth chattering, she sank to her knees. Lisette wasn't certain if the reaction came from fear or from the bone-chilling waters. She began to cry then, great gulping sobs that gradually eased her fears.

Her tears had tapered to an occasional sob when the sound of something rustling in the nearby brush raised the fine hair on the back of her neck. She clutched the rosary hanging around her neck and cocked her head, but all she heard was the soft soughing of the wind through the trees. Grabbing a sturdy branch she saw silhouetted in the moonlight, she peered into the trees.

As she stood there waiting for more calamity to befall her, Lisette realized that she was freezing. She knew she should get out of her wet things, but what could she put on? An owl hooted; she whirled around, stumbling over the carpetbag.

Lisette frowned. She vaguely remembered bringing the bag with her, but she couldn't imagine how she'd managed to hold on to it. She did recall seeing Sister Dominique's clothing—dry clothing—inside the carpetbag. She unfastened the valise and pulled out Sister Dominique's spare habit. Though it wasn't completely dry, it was far drier than Lisette's own chemise and pantaloons, and would give her far more protection from the chilly night air.

With her teeth still chattering, Lisette said a prayer for Sister Dominique, wherever she might be, and asked forgiveness for what she was about to do. Then she removed her wet things and donned the habit as quickly as her numb fingers allowed, even going so far as to drape the veil over her wet hair to ward off the cool breeze. A blanket would have been a welcome addition, but the habit afforded some warmth.

Lisette picked up the limb and settled herself against the rough bark of a tree. She drew her legs up beneath the habit and clasped her arms around them, wondering if Silvie was resting well in Father Menard's care and wishing she was in her warm bed.

As soon as the sun rose, she would try to find her way to a house and see exactly where she was. Then she would set off for Golden Meadows once again. A coyote's howl sent a shiver of apprehension through her. Lisette felt to make sure the limb was nearby and dashed an errant tear from her cheek.

Knowing Henri as she did, one thing was certain: if he recovered from his fall, there was no doubt he would place the blame on her and Silvie. And if he decided to come looking for her, she knew she was not nearly far enough away to escape his wrath.

Nate climbed out of the saddle with a groan. He hoped Sadie had the midday meal ready and that there was an abundance of it. He was forever hungry and figured that he'd put on at least a stone, weight he could certainly use with his height. His craving for food was most certainly due to his participation in physical labor for the first time in his life. Not only was he hungry all the time, he was exhausted from helping Levi repair the shingles at the quarters. Every muscle in his body ached, and his once-smooth gentleman's hands were riddled with scrapes and cuts.

Wearily he looped the reins over the hitching post near the back porch and winced at the sight of his most recent injury. The thumb of his left hand sported a blue fingernail, the result of a misdirected hammer. He took small solace in the knowledge that the thumbnail was no more blue than the curses that had scorched the air as he had hopped around on the roof, holding on to the battered appendage. He hadn't gotten any relief until Sadie drilled a hole in the injured nail with a pocketknife. Now she said he might lose the damned thing...lovely thought.

The three weeks since he'd arrived at Magnolia Manor had been rough. Sadie roused him out of bed at daybreak, fed him a breakfast that would have filled Goliath and then sent him out with Old Jim and Levi. Nate was only glad his friends weren't there to see him working—and looking—like a common laborer.

As he'd promised, he had taken care of the slaves' winter clothes. Their cabin roofs had been repaired, and he had seen to it that each home received a fresh coat of whitewash. He was currently in the process of seeing what repairs were needed to get the plantation back in top condition. A thorough perusal of the plantation ledgers confirmed his fears. Not only was there much to be done, there was damn little money to do it with since he'd paid off the debts against the place. On top of that, he still had the dratted cane harvest to get through.

Nate gave the horse a drink of water.

The only bright spot on his horizon was that the nun, Sister Dominique, should be arriving any time, any minute, in fact, and he could hand over the responsibility of the Krueger children to her. It was a task he would relinquish with thanksgiving.

Actually, with the exception of Karl, who still spoke to him only when he had to, Nate was finding the children quite...tolerable. Heidi was shy but helpful, Franz was wary but polite, and Monika flashed her dimpled smile at him more often than not.

Indeed, when he had awakened that very morning, he was surprised to hear the sound of someone snoring gently. Lifting his head, he had seen Monika curled up on top of the covers at the foot of his bed, her thumb in her mouth.

His first reaction had been anger. Damn Conrad Krueger anyway! Wasn't it enough that he'd left a passel of brats to care for? Must Nate sacrifice his privacy, too?

He'd started to wake Monika and tell her to get back to her bed, but then she'd smiled in her sleep, a sweet curving of her lips around her thumb, and his irritation had vanished like the darkness outside his window.

He'd leaped from the bed and dressed, curiously unsettled by the tender feeling the small girl's smile engendered. It wasn't that he disliked children. They were fine as long as they stayed away from him. His brother had three of the creatures, and a lot of rowdier hellions was not to be found.

But these children were different, Nate thought as he gave the horse's neck a pat and started up the steps to the house. He felt sorry for them and their situation, but he knew they neither wanted nor needed his pity. Other than Karl, they were handling the death of their father and the invasion of their home by a stranger with enviable grace.

Nate was almost to the door when he heard a flurry of hooves from the direction of the bayou road. Turning, he saw three men racing through the narrow street of the slave quarters. What could have happened? he wondered. And worse, did it affect him? He sighed, longing for the days when he had nothing to worry him but which cravat to wear for his night-on-the-town.

The men reined the horses to a stop, and Nate recognized one man as his neighbor, Maurice Hempstead. The other two were strangers.

"Good morning, gentlemen. Get down and come in. I'm about to have lunch, and I'd be happy for you to join me."

"Thank you, Rambler," Hempstead said, "but we can't stay. We wondered if you'd heard about the explosion."

"Explosion?"

"It was a paddle wheeler coming down from Thibodaux," Maurice said. "Full of people. We're trying to organize a search party to look for survivors, and we came to see if you could help."

Nate's heart sank, and he found himself wondering what other surprises the good Lord might have in store for him. There was no doubt in his mind that the boat that had exploded was none other than the one bringing Sister Dominique.

Lisette awoke to the angry chattering of a squirrel. Opening her eyes slowly, she looked up into the swaying branches of a pine tree. Daylight had arrived. If the sun was any indication, the day was half-gone, and neither the coyote nor whatever it was that had been slinking through the brush had gotten her.

She started to sit up and realized she was still clutching the branch in her hand. She tossed the stick aside, and, obviously rotten, it broke into three useless pieces. So much for her protection.

Lisette stood and gazed at the churning waters of the bayou, offering a prayer of thanksgiving for her safety and shivering at the memory of how the cold water had dragged her down when she'd leaped from the boat. Taking a deep breath, she added a prayer for Sister Dominique.

She wouldn't think of that. She would think of what she was going to do next. Shielding her eyes from the sunlight, she looked up and down the bayou to see if there were any signs of civilization or survivors. There was no indication that the paddle wheeler was anywhere nearby, no sign of a living person.

She was wondering which direction she should go, when she heard a man's voice call out and another answer. Henri! she thought on a wave of panic. Then she realized that if Henri was as badly hurt as Dodie suspected, there was no way he could be behind the search.

Search. That was it. The men were searching for survivors of the explosion. Relief eddied through her like the ripples lapping the water's edge.

"Hey!" a voice called. "I see someone!"

Lisette turned toward the man who sat astride a bay horse. He waved to her and, though she was glad to be found, she instinctively drew the dark veil closer around her face.

The quartet reined their horses to a stop and dismounted. Lisette ducked her head so they couldn't get a good look at her face.

"Are you all right, Sister?" The voice was gravelly, and belonged to the middle-aged man who had first seen her.

Sister? Lisette's first thought was to blurt out the truth, but something silenced her. Of course, they would think she was a nun, since she was wearing a nun's clothing.

"I'm...fine."

"Thank God!"

The fervent comment caused her to glance up from beneath her eyelashes. For an instant, her gaze collided with eyes as blue as the bachelor's buttons that grew in the back gardens. The quick look was enough to imprint the man's looks indelibly on her mind. He was tall with broad shoulders and narrow hips. Below a shock of blacker-than-the-pits-of-hell hair his face was incredibly masculine, incredibly attractive, despite the strong aquiline nose. He had lean cheeks boasting twin creases and a day's growth of beard. This was a man used to getting his way. A dangerous man. Lisette's heartbeat stumbled, then galloped on.

"Thank God, you're all right, Sister Dominique."

Sister Dominique? Lisette looked up sharply.

He moved to stand within a foot of her and extended his hand. "I'm Nathan Rambler. You'll be working for me and taking care of the Krueger children."

Chapter Eleven

With her stomach churning in apprehension, Lisette made an adjustment to the white wimple framing her face and donned the black veil. Clad in the full dress of an Ursuline nun, she folded her hands, put on her most pious expression and regarded herself in the mirror of the marble-topped washstand. To her own eye, she looked exactly like what she was: a young woman pretending to be something she wasn't. At least the nun's garb hid the ripening bruises circling her throat.

Impulsively she rummaged around in the carpetbag for the glasses she had rescued from the floor. Setting them on the bridge of her nose, she tried the posture again, squinting to see her reflection through the thick lenses. Better. Definitely better, she thought, before the glasses slipped. Well, at least she could see over the tops, and she supposed they would do, since she had to try to play the part of Sister Dominique.

No, she corrected herself. With Henri's retaliation a very real possibility, she couldn't play the part of Sister Dominique, she had to become the nun—at least until she could figure out how to get to New Orleans and find her sister...or until Sister Dominique was found. Lisette hadn't intended to live a lie, but when Nathan Rambler had mistaken her for the nun, Lisette hadn't known what to say—or do—so she had let him believe what he would. She had donned what she hoped was the mien of a woman of God, and let the handsome sugar planter set her on his horse.

All had been well until Nate Rambler had climbed up behind her and taken the reins in his hands. His arm had rested against her side, and every step of the horse had caused her back to brush his chest. A bevy of tumultuous feelings had assaulted the fortress of her heart. Her breath had grown short and shallow. She felt as if she might swoon and had wondered if this, then, was that wonderful feeling Silvie and her mother had experienced.

Though she was frightened of her wayward yearnings and of the unknowns the future might hold, Lisette was beginning to believe that Nathan Rambler's misconception was the providence of God. By staying at his plantation under the guise of a nun, she could maintain the secrecy of her whereabouts. Everyone in the area knew a nun was expected at Magnolia Manor, and though there was danger in hiding so near to Belle Maison, Lisette felt that if she stayed out of sight when visitors came to call, she could make the deception work, at least for a while. She could certainly teach four children.

A knock sounded, and Lisette jumped. "Yes?"

The door opened, and Nate Rambler stuck his head inside. Once again, she was struck by his astonishing good looks.

"If you're ready, I'll take you to meet the children."

"I'm quite ready, thank you." He held open the door, and she preceded him down the stairs.

The four Krueger children stood in a row, their hands at their sides as if they were prepared for a military inspection. It was obvious that they were as ill at ease as she was, though she tried not to let her discomfort show.

"This is Sister Dominique," Nate said. "She has come all the way from New Orleans to give you your lessons." He started with the youngest child, a blond cherub with rosy cheeks and dimples. "This is Monika."

"I'm too little for lessons," Monika said, and promptly poked her thumb in her mouth.

Lisette couldn't help smiling. "Perhaps we can find something else for you to do, then," she said.

"This is Franz, who claims to like history."

"So do I, Franz," Lisette said as Franz gave her hand a vigorous shake.

Nate stopped in front of a pretty girl approaching the brink of womanhood. "This is Heidi, the lady of the house."

Heidi Krueger blushed and smiled, and Lisette knew that Nate Rambler had made a conquest.

"I'm Karl."

The clipped comment drew Lisette's attention from Heidi to a young man, who, like his sister, was on the threshold of adulthood. Karl Krueger, a wide-shouldered, stocky individual, held out his hand, completely ignoring Nate. Lisette cast a quick glance at Nate over the tops of her glasses. Red suffused his neck and face. Humiliation at the boy's audacity?

"I hope you'll be happy here at Magnolia Manor," Karl said.

"I'm certain I shall be."

"Karl," Nate Rambler interrupted. "Why don't you take the children outside? Sister Dominique and I have things to discuss."

It was Karl's turn to grow red. The look he gave Nate could only be described as one of loathing.

"Certainly. Come, children. Let's leave Mr. Rambler and Sister Dominique alone."

When the room was empty, Nate invited Lisette to sit

down. He, however, clasped his hands behind his back and paced the length of the parlor. She couldn't help noticing how the fabric molded the muscular strength of his legs or that the lacing of his white shirt had come undone to reveal a tangle of crisp black hair.

"I'll be going into Thibodaux sometime soon. I was wondering what you might need."

She pulled her gaze from his chest and looked up over her glasses. "Need?"

He gave a vague wave of his hand. "Things for teaching. Personal things. You must have lost some of your belongings when the boat went down."

"Of course! If Father Menard could see about getting me a...change of clothes I would be most grateful."

"Of course. In the meantime, please feel free to ask Sadie to take care of your things at night."

"Thank you."

With the niceties out of the way, Nate launched into an account of what she could expect from her charges.

"Excepting Karl, you will find that the children are not hard to deal with. Franz is simply a boy. And Monika and Heidi are quite pleasant."

"And what is Karl's problem?" Lisette asked.

Nate stopped his pacing and stared out a nearby window where the children ran through the fallen autumn leaves. "He resents the fact that I'm here and his father isn't."

Lisette had heard about Conrad Krueger's loss. She had also heard of his death. "Have they no family?"

"An uncle who can't be found."

"I see." She could sympathize with the children, especially the older ones, but they should be thankful that Nathan Rambler was taking care of them, instead of sending them to an orphanage.

"Enough about the children," Nate said. "Tell me more about yourself, Sister Dominique."

Lisette felt the blood drain from her face. She tried to smile. "I'm afraid there isn't much to tell."

"Do you have a family?"

"Um...only a sister and an aunt or two."

"Oh? And where are they?"

Lisette realized that Nate Rambler was merely trying to make polite conversation, but his questions made her very nervous...and increased her guilt.

"My aunts live in Golden Meadow and Baton Rouge, and my sister is in New Orleans." She hoped.

"What made a...pretty girl like you become a nun?"

The fact that Nate Rambler thought she was pretty distracted her from answering right away. She looked at him and saw a smile toying with the corners of his finely shaped mouth. Was he *flirting* with her, even though he thought she was a woman of God?

She looked down at her hands clasped tightly in her lap. Her first impression had been correct. He was a dangerous man. She would have to be very careful to hide the fact that his smiles made her heart beat faster. She raised a steady gaze to his.

"A love of God, Mr. Rambler," she said. "A love for my fellow man, and the desire to help those less fortunate than myself."

Nate was quiet, thoughtful, for a moment. "Well, Sister, you've certainly come to the right place." He straightened his broad shoulders. "When do you plan to start lessons?"

"I thought perhaps tomorrow. I assume they have books and slates."

"They do."

"Good." Sensing that the interview was over, Lisette stood.

"If you think of anything you need, please let me know. I want your stay at Magnolia Manor to be comfortable and pleasant."

"Thank you Mr. Rambler. I'm sure it will be."

Chapter Twelve

Nate left for Thibodaux a week after Lisette's arrival at Magnolia Manor. It had been a week of adjustment, a week of observation, and a week spent in careful consideration of the strange situation in which she found herself.

The children's lessons were no problem. Conrad Krueger's offspring were smart, attentive and gave her no trouble as far as discipline. Even the defiant Karl offered his full attention during the hours set aside for learning.

However, Lisette did encounter small uprisings outside the schoolroom. It wasn't that the Krueger children were bad; it was just that she hadn't had much practice dealing with children. Monika was an angel, but she tended to cling—when she wasn't getting into things better left alone.

Franz was rowdy and rambunctious, forever getting into, onto or out of things he had no business getting into, onto or out of. They both needed a good spanking, but Lisette didn't feel that it was her place to mete out that kind of punishment. Heidi was changing, growing into a young lady, and her emotions went up and down like a seesaw.

Then there was Karl.

From the first day she'd come, Karl had made his dislike of Nathan Rambler clear. He talked back. He refused any overtures of kindness from Nate. He seldom joined in any discussions, and if he could find a way to sabotage a project his benefactor was working on, he did.

Lisette had overheard Nate ask Karl if he would like to make the trip to Thibodaux with him. Karl had declined, saying that he'd not be seen passing time with a man of Nate's ilk. Curious, Lisette had asked Sadie what had caused the bad blood between the two.

"It's 'cause Master Nate done win the plantation from Master Conrad. You shoulda seen Karl fly into Master Nate the first day he come here—a hittin' and accusin' him of cheatin' his daddy."

"Did he?"

"Cheat? Why, I couldn't say. All I ever heard Master Conrad say was that Nathan Rambler was a professional gambler and a ladies' man. But that don't make him a cheat, now, does it?"

"No..." Lisette agreed. But it did make him a man to stay clear of.

"Why, he don't even really want this place."

"He doesn't?" Lisette asked in surprise.

"No, ma'am. He don't like bein' tied down to no daily routine." Sadie chuckled, and the sound seemed to roll from her very soul. "Said he just as soon eat a bucket o' worms. All he plans to do is fix things up and sell out so's he can put in his own gambling den."

Lisette grimaced in distaste. If what Sadie said was true, the new owner of Magnolia Manor was cut from the same bolt of cloth as Henri. It was no wonder Nathan Rambler could make her heart flutter like a Fourth of July pennant! Being able to turn young ladies' knees to jelly was an ability born and bred into men like him and her stepfather—indeed it was a prerequisite to their kind.

"So you don't blame Mr. Rambler for anything, not even Mr. Krueger's death?"

"Master Conrad was just lookin' for an excuse to join Miz Helga," Sadie said with a sad shake of her head. "Losin' the place in a card game was as good as any, I 'spect."

"Do you think Karl will ever change the way he feels?"

"I couldn't say," Sadie had told her. "He's a good boy, but he's got a stubborn streak a mile wide in him. All we can do is hope and pray."

Pray. It was something Lisette did often and fervently. She prayed for the safety of Sister Dominique, Silvie and herself. And she prayed that she would hear something about Henri's condition. Asking for information about him was out of the question. It would only draw attention to herself. She would just have to make the best of things and take one day at a time.

One day at a time. Every day at Magnolia Manor was a test of her endurance. Believing Conrad Krueger's claim that Nate was a gambler and a womanizer was easy. But she couldn't help waffling between pique that his flirting was aimed at anything in skirts and relief for finding out the truth. If the truth was supposed to set men free, perhaps knowing the truth about Nate Rambler would free her from the traitorous feelings his nearness roused.

Nate was gone four days. The time away was spent with Raoul, who brought a Thoroughbred all the way from New Orleans to Thibodaux. The stallion, called Iron Warrior, was reputed to run like the wind, and Nate hoped the animal would make him a lot of money. He was already planning a race meet at Magnolia Manor and intended to invite everyone in the area who thought they had a horse that could compete.

Despite his much needed break from the plantation's problems and routine, Nate was almost back home when he realized, with a bit of a start, that he was anxious to be back. He rationalized his feelings by telling himself that there was still much to be done, especially with the upcoming race.

Honesty made him admit that work wasn't what drew him. Though he couldn't deny it, he was ashamed to admit that hardly an hour passed that the young nun he had found on the bank of the bayou didn't slip into his thoughts.

Sister Dominique intrigued him, from her pretty face to the wary glances she gave him over the tops of those thick-lensed glasses. Of course, he couldn't tell much about her body beneath the bulky black habit, but she was short, and if the shape of her hands was any indication, she was slender.

She was conscientious and kept up with the children admirably—thank God. Quiet spoken, she maintained control with a pointed look or a firm command, something Nate himself wasn't able to do. Karl wouldn't heed him if he was cautioned to watch out for a snake a foot away. And how could he be firm with Heidi, who walked a narrow line between laughter and tears? Franz needed a good belting, but Nate knew he couldn't do that or he'd have Karl to deal with. Monika could defuse his anger with a smile.

Thinking about them brought a smile to his own lips. He wasn't even aware that he urged Iron Warrior to a faster gait.

It was midafternoon when Nate approached the house. The late-October sun shone down warmly, and leaves drifted to the ground in lazy spirals. It was a perfect Indian summer day, and he suspected there wouldn't be many more before the autumn rains set in.

As he broke into the clearing at the back of the house, he heard a shriek and saw a black-clad figure round the corner of the kitchen. Thinking something was amiss, he clucked to his mount and cantered toward the building, which was separated from the main house. He had closed no more than half the distance, when he realized that the person in black was Sister Dominique and that Franz was in close pursuit.

He pulled the horse to a halt and watched as the nun, her skirts raised to her knees—her very pretty knees—skidded to a stop beneath the big live oak near the kitchen.

"Oley, oley in free!" she called, her laughter carried on the gentle breeze.

"No fair! You cheated!"

"Cheated!" Sister Dominique chortled, throwing her arm around Franz's shoulders. "How dare you accuse a nun of cheating?"

"You went to hide before Franz began counting," Karl said.

Nate watched the exchange in bewilderment. He hadn't much experience with nuns, or any holy people for that matter, but they'd always appeared a staid lot, as if they were afraid a smile might crack the pious looks off their faces. Sister Dominique was different. He'd sensed it from the beginning, and her actions today only verified his feelings. He would never have imagined that a nun would behave like...like such a hoyden!

"Look! It's Nate!"

Monika's joyous cry halted the good-natured arguing, and every eye turned his way. The sudden change in the older children's actions would have been comical if it hadn't been so sobering. The moment they saw him, their laughter dried up like puddles in the sun, and they became models of propriety. Sister Dominique smoothed her wrinkled habit and straightened her veil as he dismounted.

Monika, the only one who was genuinely glad to see him, threw her chubby arms around his leg and looked up at him with a dimpled smile he couldn't help returning.

"Did you bring me a present?"

"Monika!" Karl snapped. "It isn't nice to ask for presents. Leave Mr. Rambler alone."

"She's fine," Nate said, bending down to pick her up. "Now why would you think I'd bring you a present?"

Monika wound her arms around his neck and thought about it for a moment. "Because I'm the baby, and I'm spoiled."

Nate laughed. Obviously Monika had heard the phrase from one of the older children. He glanced up and saw a smile on Sister Dominique's lips, as well. She really had lovely eyes without the glasses, he thought. Large and long lashed and a deep chocolate brown.

Sister Dominique realized he was looking at her, and her smile fled.

"Did you?" Monika pressed, placing a plump hand on his cheek and forcing his attention back to her.

"Did I what?" Nate asked, her question forgotten as he'd gazed into the warm depths of the nun's eyes.

"Bring me a present?"

"I did."

Monika squealed with glee. "What is it? Show me!"

"Actually, I brought everyone a present." Nate placed her on the ground and opened one of his saddlebags. "Ribbons for Monika's curls—"

"But I wanted peppermint," she interrupted, her bottom lip protruding in a pout.

"And peppermint sticks." He gave her the presents. "Checkers for Franz." Nate handed a box to the boy and a flat parcel to Heidi. "Fabric for a new dress for the lady of the house."

Franz smiled, and Heidi tore open the brown paper wrapping to reveal a folded square of cobalt-blue fabric. "It's lovely, Nate. Thank you."

"My pleasure." He turned to Karl, who was rubbing a gentle hand over Iron Warrior's neck. "I brought bay rum for Karl, so he can make a suitable impression on the young ladies."

As Lisette expected, Karl refused to take the proffered bottle.

"I don't want your damned bribes," he said, turning and running toward the house.

Stunned by his actions, the other children looked after him. Franz was the first to move. Without a word, he dropped the checkers to the ground and followed his brother. Heidi's lips trembled as she handed Nate the dress material. Even Monika seemed to know something serious was afoot. She gave the gifts a longing look, and handed Nate the bundle of ribbons. Clutching the candy to her chest, she followed her siblings inside.

Without a word, Nate stooped and retrieved the presents, tossing them onto a pile of leaves Levi planned to burn. Then he went to the saddlebags and turned with two small squares in his hand.

"I brought you a gift, too, Sister," he said with a bitter smile. "Of course you know it's a bribe."

He saw the longing in her eyes as she looked at the bars of soap.

"What could you possibly be bribing me to do?" she asked.

Nate offered her a reckless smile. "Why I'm a terrible person. A gambler. A killer. A faithless womanizer. I'm bribing you to share my bed."

She gasped, and he was immediately filled with penitence for his crude outburst. He pressed the soap into her hands. "I'm sorry," he said, all vestige of laughter gone. "I'm bribing you to stay until I can find somewhere to send the children."

"I'll stay, Mr. Rambler," she told him with a lift of her chin. "I really have no choice." Her voice trembled, but he couldn't deny her composure.

He gave a short mirthless laugh. "Neither do I."

"Sadie told me how you got possession of the plantation and the responsibility of the children."

"And what's your opinion, Sister?" he asked with a mocking smile. "Do you think I cheated Krueger out of his plantation and cost him his life?"

"I'm not in the business of passing judgment, Mr. Rambler. I'm here to teach the children."

"A compromising stance," he murmured. "But what do you *think*, Sister?"

A delicate blush colored her cheeks.

"I think that at some time in his life every person gets backed into a corner. And I think we often make decisions that affect not only our lives but the lives around us. Conrad Krueger had problems he couldn't deal with. If he hadn't lost the plantation to you, he would have lost it to the bank, no doubt with the same end result. Give Karl some time."

Nate hadn't considered that possibility, yet it only marginally eased his guilt. He cast another look at the house and plowed his hand through his thick shock of black hair. "Time? For what? To figure out how to stick a knife in my ribs while I'm not looking?"

"Have you explained your side of the story to him?"

"He won't listen."

Sister Dominique raised a compassionate gaze to his. "How do you know unless you try?"

Nate stared into her eyes for a moment; then he turned and swung up into the saddle and walked the horse slowly toward the barn.

Lisette watched him go, her own feelings in a muddle. One minute it was easy to believe the claims she heard about him; the next, she wasn't quite so sure. There had been a look of total bewilderment in his eyes as he watched the children throw his gifts and kindness back in his face.

Bewilderment and...pain—which he'd done his best to hide beneath a facade of sarcasm. One thing was certain: the Krueger children were loyal to each other. Even Monika.

Lisette reclaimed the gifts from the pile of leaves. There was no use throwing perfectly good items away, especially when the children would no doubt accept them at a later date.

She looked at the soap he had given her, her first gift from a man. A real nun wouldn't have accepted the present—a sign of vanity—but her soap had been lost in the explosion, and she did love this one small extravagance. She brought the soap to her nose and breathed in the sweet fragrance. How had Nate known lilac was her favorite? And why had he gone to the trouble to buy it for her?

Chapter Thirteen

Nate closed the plantation's ledger and stood, arching his back against the ache of a hundred abused muscles. Ignoring his rumbling stomach, he lit a Havana cigar and poured himself a generous splash of Krueger's fine bourbon—his third since he started the ledger entries—before reclaiming his place in the burgundy leather chair and swinging his feet to the gleaming desktop.

He squeezed the bridge of his nose between his thumb and forefinger and gave a great sigh. Perhaps if he drank enough, it would dull the memory of the children refusing his gifts and the shock in Sister Dominique's eyes when he'd said he was bribing her to share his bed. He could still see the stain of embarrassment that reddened her cheeks and the surprise in her pansy-brown eyes.

Why had he made such an asinine comment? The last thing he needed was to alienate the good sister. Swearing at his stupidity, Nate downed a healthy swallow of the liquor, grimaced and set his booted feet to the floor.

Restlessness sent him to the window that overlooked the back of the house. Strange. The evening meal was far past, and Sadie should have retired for the night, yet there was a candle still lit in the kitchen. Perhaps she was making some sort of preparations for tomorrow's meal.

Nate's stomach growled again, another reminder that he hadn't joined the children at the dinner table. Maybe he would go down and see if there were any leftovers to keep his hunger at bay until breakfast. He finished the bourbon much too fast—there was no sense wasting it—and set the glass on the desk, acknowledging that he was the tiniest bit pickled. He should have known better than to imbibe so freely on an empty stomach.

Nate made his way through the lower level of the house and stepped outside. The chill night air felt good against his face, and he felt somewhat less raddled. He was about to step onto the kitchen's porch when the silhouette of a woman shone through the feed-sack curtain and stopped him dead in his tracks. The figure wasn't tall and skinny and wizened, like Sadie. It was short and curvaceous.

Soused though he was, he knew the body belonged to Sister Dominique. Still, being a Ramble, no force this side of hell could have prevented him from tiptoeing to the window and peeking through a crack in the curtain...just to make sure.

The sight he beheld stole his breath and made his heart race. It was, indeed, Sister Dominique, who was just stepping into the bath. She had dragged a washtub near the fireplace, whose flames sent flickering light through the kitchen. Near the galvanized tub sat a ladder-back chair with a towel and night clothes draped across it.

She was submerged in the tub, her back to him and her ivory legs drawn up against her breasts. Her hair, which he'd never seen, was a rich tobacco brown that matched her eyes. It was coiled atop her head to keep it out of the water. Several wavy tendrils had come loose and lay damply against the wet curve of her back. For long moments, he watched as she scrubbed herself with a cloth and the soap he'd brought her.

Finally she stood, and water sluiced down over the rounded curve of her buttocks and her thighs. She bent at the waist to reach for the towel, and Nate was granted a glimpse of one gently rounded breast before she turned and gave him her back once more. Like a man in a daze, he watched her blot the moisture from her body and step out of the tub. When she turned to reach for her gown, his breath threatened to choke him.

She was gorgeous. Built on a dainty scale, she was put together in a way just shy of perfect. Her waist was small, her hips narrow, her legs slim. Her breasts were full and rounded and tipped with rosy areolae that were puckered from the bath. His own body tightened in response.

She lifted the gown over her head and let its voluminous folds drift down over her. His breath trickled from him in sweet relief that was tinged with regret. She took the hairpins from her hair, which slipped over her shoulder in a silken swath. It was lustrous and wavy and grew to just below her breasts. Nate could almost feel it against his lips and pictured it twined around his sweat-slick body.

He watched her slide her feet into her slippers and begin to gather her belongings, the towel, the soap…her habit. Reality hit him like a sickening blow to the stomach. She was a nun. And he was despicable.

Disgusted with himself, he pushed away from the outer wall and hurried back through the darkness to the house. It would never do for her to find him there. She would be embarrassed. Mortified. She might even decide to leave.

Dear God! Nate thought, as he let himself into the house and took the stairs two at a time, what kind of crazed maniac was he anyway? She was a nun, a woman of God. How could he have stood there and watched her like that? How could he have felt those shameful feelings for her?

Nate was nothing if not honest about his feelings; he did not even attempt to deny that what he felt for Sister Dominique was lust, pure and simple. Not so pure, perhaps, but lust, nonetheless. He'd never professed to be religious, but he'd never thought of himself as perverted, either. Yet, weren't his feelings for the beautiful young nun the worst kind of perversion?

Reaching the sanctuary of his room, he fell across the bed, breathing heavily. He threw his forearm across his eyes and tried to force his body to normalcy. It was useless. Pictures of Sister Dominique in all her naked glory paraded through his mind. He was hard-pressed to recall when a woman had affected him so.

Perhaps it was the fact that she was unattainable that made her so desirable. Weren't the things he had always wanted the most those he knew he couldn't have?

Unfortunately, the recognition of his feelings was not enough to quench his desire or his resolve. From that night on, he stood at the window of the kitchen, smoking and watching the good sister's nightly ritual. He fancied he could smell the lilac scent of her soap and pretended she was in his bed, in his arms.

And hated himself for his fantasies.

Chapter Fourteen

"Where in the hell did they go?"

The question, yelled in rage, preceded the crack of the whip. Blood welled in the newest cut in Hank's back, but the young man didn't cry out or answer. Dodie stood in the shadows of the barn, a shawl thrown around her shoulders, wringing her plump hands while Henri supervised the whipping of her son. Hank wouldn't talk. How could he when he didn't know anything?

In the month since Lisette and Silvie had fled Belle Maison in the middle of the night, Henri had made slow but steady progress. While the broken ribs were painful, they were healing, and though the gash on his head had kept him mostly unconscious for more than a week, that too got better with each passing day.

After the way that devil man had treated her babies, it had been a great temptation for Dodie to give him a big dose of laudanum and be done with it, but her fear of being found out was stronger than her hate. She was old, and she just wanted to finish out her few remaining years in peace.

Dodie didn't like the way Henri looked at her these days, as if he were trying to get into her head and see what was going on inside. When he had asked her where his stepdaughters were, she had told him she didn't know. She had stuck by her claim of not having heard what went on because she'd been with her daughter and her family in the quarters that night. She had told Henri that when she'd come into the house early that next morning and found him at the foot of the stairs, she'd gone to get help.

She knew he didn't believe her, and she knew Hank was reaping the punishment that should be hers and well might be, even yet. Henri figured she knew where the girls had gone, and he hoped she would tell the truth to save her son.

Dodie hardened her heart as the whip cracked again. Every lash Hank received ripped at her heart, but it was time to put an end to Henri Duschene's cruelty. Hank's back would heal, but Elizabeth Antilly would never laugh with her daughters again.

One of the field hands cut Hank down, and Dodie gave a sob of relief. When she passed Henri to get to her boy, he gave her a cold, cruel smile. Dodie dropped her eyes so that he couldn't see the hate residing there. She wouldn't tell him where her babies had gone if he cut her to ribbons with a whip.

Henri Duschene was a bad man, and he had hurt too many people. Her precious Elizabeth and Silvie. There was no doubt in Dodie's mind that Lisette would have been next. No doubt what her punishment would have been.

Henri's nostrils flared as he drew in a shallow and still-painful breath. Not wanting to watch Dodie's tender ministrations to her son, he turned and went back to the house, leaning heavily on his cane. His head throbbed, and he couldn't straighten up yet, but he knew that, with the fall down the stairs, he was lucky to have escaped with his life. Just yesterday, Dr. Morrison had told him how fortunate he really was. The injury to his head had been quite serious, and the fact that he had come so far in the space of a month was nothing short of a miracle.

When the doctor had questioned him about what had happened, Henri had explained that his stepdaughters, who were trying to regain control of the plantation, had accosted him in the dark, pushed him down the stairs and robbed him of the money in the desk.

The tale had instigated a visit from the parish sheriff, who had assured Henri that no stone would be left unturned in finding the two girls. Sheriff Purcell said he would question the neighbors and see if any of them had seen Lisette or Silvie on the day in question. He would check at the train station and with the captains of the various boats who put into Thibodaux on a regular basis.

But the lawman's assurances were not enough. After several days of consideration, Henri was convinced the girls would head to New Orleans and the Ursuline convent. Where else could two unchaperoned young women go to find sanctuary? Henri himself had drafted a letter to the Pinkertons, soliciting two of their best agents for the job of locating his stepdaughters. His next move had been to question Dodie. When she refused to talk, he had taken the whip to her son. That hadn't worked, either.

The old woman was loyal; he'd give her that. She had taken care of Silvie and Lisette since they were born, and they were like her own. He had often felt she cared more for Elizabeth's girls than she did her natural children. Hell, hadn't she just let her own son take a beating to protect them?

Henri pushed open the door to his study with the tip of his cane. He was convinced that Hank had no idea of where the girls had gone, but nothing this side of hell would make him believe Dodie's innocence. He eased into the chair and poured himself a stiff drink to combat the pain raging in his head. In a matter of minutes he was feeling better and able to think about his next course of action.

The Pinkertons were on their way. The sheriff was doing his part. He himself would put out the word that he was looking for two thieving runaways. He would offer a substantial reward for information leading to their capture. If anyone had seen them, they would step forward. Then he would track down Elizabeth's brats and make them pay for what they had done to him.

Chapter Fifteen

Nate was dreaming. He knew it was a dream, but he gave himself over to it, anyway. He was outside, lying along the slope of the bayou. Spring was here—the birds were singing and wildflowers littered the lush green of the grass growing beneath him. Sister Dominique was beside him, but she wasn't wearing her black nun's habit. She wasn't wearing anything.

He reached up and drew her down until their lips met, softly at first, then harder. She tasted like wild honey and sweet woman. And when he touched her breasts, Nate thought he would die. He groaned and pulled her closer....

"Nate."

She was calling his name, but how could she be calling his name when she was kissing him?

"Nate. Wake up. You're scaring me."

The urgent words were accompanied by the gentle tapping of hands against his cheeks.

"Go away," he mumbled, brushing the hand aside and struggling to keep the fantasy.

"You're mean!" The hurt cry banished the last of the dream. Monika. Nate pushed himself to one elbow. Monika stood on the stool beside the bed, a single fat tear slipping down her sleep-flushed cheek.

"Monika!" he cried, reaching out and brushing away the tear with his thumb. "What's the matter?"

"I came to wake you up, and you told me to go away." Her bottom lip trembled.

"I'm sorry, sweetness," he said, reaching out and pulling her up beside him. "I was asleep. Dreaming. I didn't know it was you." He smiled at her. "I'd never tell you to go away if I *knew* it was you."

"Promise?"

"Promise."

"Was your dream a bad dream?"

"No," Nate said, recalling the feel of Sister Dominique's mouth against his. "Well, perhaps," he amended.

"I thought it was a scary dream. You were making awful sounds. *I* was scared."

Scary dream? Awful sounds? Nate's lips twisted in a wry smile. "I'm sorry, sweetness," he said. "I never meant to frighten you."

"I know." Monika smiled her forgiveness and added a redundant, "It's morning."

Nate rubbed a hand over the stubble on his chin. "So it is."

"I'm hungry. Are you?"

He was hungry all right, but it wasn't a hunger that could be appeased by food. He was woman hungry. Why else would he dream of making love with a nun?

"Nate?"

"Hmm?"

"Why don't you marry Sister Dominique? Then you could be my father, and she could be my mother."

Nate's heart ached for the child and her loss. It must be hard on her. It must be hard on all of them. "I can't marry Sister Dominique."

"Why not? Don't you like her?"

"Of course I like her, Monika, but she's already married. To the church."

The reminder sat in the pit of Nate's stomach like a green persimmon. Memory of his dream ate at him, riddling him with guilt. He had to get out of the house, had to get away from her, from them all, before he went mad.

As usual, Lisette joined the children for breakfast. More often than not, Nate gulped his meal and left them sitting there. It was as if he couldn't bear to be around them. She understood how he felt. He was putting forth a great deal of effort to make his integration into the household smooth, but the children were slow coming around. This morning, neither he nor Karl was at the table.

"I really would like a new dress for Christmas," Heidi said, toying with the piece of ham on her plate.

"Me, too," Monika added.

Lisette slathered a biscuit with butter. "Why shouldn't both of you have one?"

Heidi frowned. "I don't have any money and, even if I did, there's no one to take me to town to buy one."

"Why can't we make you a new dress?"

"Make a dress?"

Lisette smiled over the tops of Sister Dominique's glasses. "You're a good hand with a needle, Heidi, and my sewing is far better than my embroidery. I can't think of any reason why the two of us shouldn't be able to turn out something you'd be proud to wear."

Heidi's smile brightened the gloom of the day. "What about material?"

Lisette smiled in return. "It just so happens that I have the fabric Mr. Rambler brought you from Thibodaux."

Heidi's happiness vanished. She looked at Franz, as if asking his permission since Karl wasn't there.

"I think you should have a new dress," Franz said. "And the color would match your eyes."

"If Heidi gets her present, may I have my ribbons back?" Monika asked.

"Of course you may. As a matter of fact, I was wondering, Franz, if you'd like to open up the checkers. All this rain is so dreary, and I'm tired of sewing and reading. I'm ready for a bit more excitement."

Franz managed to stifle his grin of pleasure, but he couldn't hide the joy in his eyes. "I'm sure he won't mind...since it's for you, Sister."

"Good, then."

"Do you think I could have Karl's bay rum?" Franz asked. "He doesn't want it."

"I don't see why not," Lisette said.

"Nate bought good presents, didn't he?" Monika said. "Did he bring you one, Sister?"

"Indeed, he did. He brought me my favorite soap, though I can't fathom how he knew I liked it."

"I told him," Heidi confessed. "You'd mentioned that yours was lost in the explosion and when he asked me what I should bring you, that's the first thing I thought of. I hope you don't mind."

"Not at all. I've enjoyed it very much."

Heidi looked relieved. "Do you think Nate will be angry if I use the material?"

"He certainly won't be."

The comment came from Nate himself, who was dressed in work clothes. His firm jaw was freshly shaven, and his dark hair was combed away from his face. Lisette knew it was only a matter of time before it fell back over his forehead. He looked very handsome. Very much a man. A small sigh escaped her.

"I bought the fabric for you, and I want you to have it," he said, sitting down across from Lisette.

Heidi's adoring look was her thank-you.

"Where's Karl?"

"Perhaps he's sleeping in," Lisette suggested. "It's certainly a good day for it."

Nate agreed, though he avoided looking at her.

"Nate didn't sleep well," Monika said. "He had bad dreams. Didn't you, Nate?"

Nate glanced at Lisette and, if she didn't know better, she would have sworn he blushed.

"Nightmares," he said. He took a swallow of his coffee. His eyes widened and teared. Obviously the coffee was too hot to drink. When he was finally able to speak, he let loose with a curse.

"Not in front of the children, Mr. Rambler, please," Lisette reminded.

Heidi smiled. "You sound just like Mama. She was always after Daddy about cursing in front of us."

"I told Nate I wanted him to marry you, Sister, but he said you were already married."

The sound of a chair scraping across the floor drew everyone's attention to Nate.

"Excuse me," he said, tossing his napkin onto the table. "I'm not very hungry, and I have things to do." He turned on his heel and left them sitting there staring after him.

Surely he realized Monika's comment was innocent, Lisette thought, watching him leave. She took a sip of coffee and wondered who—or what—had put the cocklebur under his saddle blanket.

Chapter Sixteen

Nate left the dining room and donned a coat, his mood fouler than the rainy day. He was sick of being cooped up inside with people who didn't give a tinker's damn about him, and he was sick of the rain. It was time—past time—to start harvesting the sugar, but it had been so wet the last week that the chore had been put off. The weather had been so bad that there was nothing much to do but go over the accounts and pace.

He knew his irritability stemmed from more than just a delayed sugar harvest. He also had to deal with the everyday running of the estate: hours spent over columns of numbers, grain to harvest, and fodder to put up for the stock. Those tasks—tasks he'd never had to deal with before—and a growing guilt over his reprehensible behavior made him short with Sister Dominique and cross with the children. Knowing he was dooming his soul to a fiery hell, he sought the kitchen window each night while she bathed, drawn like the moth to the proverbial flame.

He couldn't remember ever wanting a woman the way he wanted this one, and he'd never wanted a woman he didn't wind up having. Any female in skirts had been fair game, no matter their social status or their marital status—as his dalliance with the duchess had proved.

But this was different. As low as he'd sunk, he knew he would never make a move toward indulging in his desire for Sister Dominique. She wasn't just a woman. She was an institution. The church. He had to stop the madness that drove him to the kitchen each night. He was courting disaster...and perhaps his own destruction.

His guilt was so great he could hardly bear to be in the same room with her. Each time he looked at her bundled in her heavy robes, he pictured her as she stepped from her bath, her skin rosy, her cheeks flushed, her hair in loose waves from the steam.... This morning the children's innocent comments and the lingering memory of his dream had made things even worse.

Calling himself a dozen kinds of fool, Nate stopped by the kitchen and snatched up a teakettle full of hot water. He would go to the barn and fix Iron Warrior a breakfast of hot bran—anything to escape the boredom of the house.

The barn was dark and gloomy. As Nate's eyes adjusted to the semidarkness, he breathed in the combined scents of straw, damp earth and manure that saturated the heavy moistness of the air. They were familiar smells, smells he associated with years of pleasure.

The sound of a low whinny echoed throughout the barn.

"Easy, boy. Easy."

The soothing words came from the stallion's stall. Carrying the kettle, Nate rounded the corner to see Karl with a currycomb in his hand. Nate stopped in surprise. Though he wasn't a mean horse, Iron Warrior was high-strung. It took a man with considerable skill to ride him, and he wouldn't let just anyone into his stall without causing a ruckus. Yet here was Karl, grooming him. Nate remembered that Karl had been petting the horse the day he'd refused to accept the bay rum. He must like animals. It was obvious he had a way with them.

Watching the boy with the horse, it occurred to Nate that he might have stumbled across some common ground on which he and Karl might meet. He would have to play his hand with the utmost skill.

"He's magnificent, isn't he?"

Karl looked up, guilt and a hint of defiance on his face. When he saw nothing but a smile on Nate's features, the tenseness in the bay's stance relaxed. "He is that."

"You're out early," Nate said, struggling to find something else to say. "We missed you at breakfast."

Karl shrugged. "I was tired of being cooped up. I haven't done much to work up an appetite lately."

"Me, either."

Wonderful, Rambler. You've exhausted two topics of conversation in as many seconds.

He plunged his hands into his coat pockets. "You like horses, then?"

"Yes." Karl looked askance at him. "I hope it's all right that I brush him."

Nate grinned. "I have no quarrel with it if he doesn't. You've a nice touch. He isn't usually so calm around strangers."

"My father..." Karl looked at Nate, a defiant gleam in his blue eyes. "My father said I had the gift for getting along with animals."

"It appears he was right. Have you fed him yet?"

"No. I wasn't sure what you wanted him to have or how much to give him."

Nate was impressed that the boy realized how important the feeding schedule was. "With the race coming up, I have him on a special mixture."

Karl left the horse and followed Nate to the wooden barrels that held the feed. "We're—I mean you're still going to have the race next Saturday?"

"If it clears up by tomorrow, it should be dry enough, don't you think?"

"If the sun comes out." Karl peered over Nate's shoulder. "What do you feed him?"

"Three scoops of whole oats. One of crimped corn. Half a scoop of maize. A scoop of bran. A handful of salt—that's really important in the summertime. It helps a horse sweat. If they stop sweating, you've got trouble. Remember that."

"Yes, sir."

"Then I put a lot of molasses in it."

"Why?"

Nate thought about that a moment. "I dunno, lad. Because he likes it, I suppose." He picked up the teakettle and poured hot water onto the grain. "And last, some hot water."

"What's that for?"

"You like a hot meal when it's cold, don't you?" Nate said, stirring the mixture with a broken axe handle.

"Yes."

"So does a horse. A hot bran mash is good for them, the same way a shot of good whiskey is good for a man." He set the bucket aside. "We'll just let it cool a bit."

"Is what he eats important to the outcome of the race?"

"You're damned right it is. He's got to have the best if he's to give us his best."

Karl nodded. After a considerable silence, he spoke up. "I'd like to take care of him for you."

The offer took Nate by surprise. What was the boy's motive? Did he think to sabotage the race by doing something to the stallion? A close look into Karl's eyes found no obvious ulterior motive.

When Nate didn't answer, Karl must have realized what

was going through his mind. He blushed. "Nothing's changed between us, Mr. Rambler, and I'm not doing this for you. I'm offering because I love the horse, and I'd really like to take care of him."

"Nate," Nate said.

"What?"

"Call me Nate. You're almost a man. And a man generally calls his peers by their given names."

Looking embarrassed, Karl nodded and thrust his hands into his pockets.

"If I let you do this, I expect it done right. He's to be fed twice a day. I don't want him fed early or late. Do you understand?"

"Yes, sir."

"He's to be galloped every day it isn't raining. You do ride, don't you?"

Karl looked insulted. "Of course."

"I want him groomed as soon as he's cooled out, and I want his hooves picked."

"Yes, sir."

"No sloughing off. No excuses for not doing the job. If I find out you're not doing what I asked, I'll take over his care myself."

"Yes, sir."

"You can start this afternoon. Let me know if you run into any problems."

"Yes, sir!"

Nate adopted an air of nonchalance. "If you do a good job and I like the way you work him, I might let you ride him in the race."

Karl's stoicism slipped enough to let a joyous light into his eyes.

"And if we win, I'll give you part of the purse." Nate held out his hand. "Deal?"

Karl placed his hand in Nate's, and they shook. "Deal."

* * *

"Come in, come in," Henri said to the drably dressed man standing in his doorway with rain dripping off his derby. Arnold Massey, the Pinkerton agent, was of average size and average looks. His hair, suit and eyes were brown. There was not a single distinctive thing about him in manner or looks—which made him an excellent choice for his job.

Leaving his wet things in the hall, he followed Henri into the study and accepted the proffered chair.

"Would you care for a drink, Mr. Massey?"

"No, thank you, Mr. Duschene."

Henri poured himself a whiskey and sat down behind the desk that had once belonged to Etienne Antilly. "It's a nasty day, isn't it?"

"Very."

The amenities satisfied, Henri smiled. "I trust you've brought me news to brighten it."

The man nodded and took a small journal from his breast pocket. "Some good. Some bad. We spoke with dozens of boat captains and workers, and didn't find out a thing. Sheriff Purcell had already talked with the people at the train station, but we followed up ourselves and found one person Purcell hadn't approached."

"Oh?"

"The drunk who helps at the livery stable on occasion."

"A drunk!" Henri looked skeptical.

"I'll be the first to admit that his word might not count for much, but he does say he remembers seeing two girls pass by the station just about daybreak one morning—which morning, he couldn't say. His statement puts your stepdaughters in a position where it's quite possible that they boarded a train for New Orleans, just as you thought."

That was good, Henri thought. Very good. "How soon can you find out?"

The Pinkerton agent replaced the book in his breast pocket. "As soon as I can figure out how to get the information I need out of a Catholic nun."

Chapter Seventeen

February 1853

Bored beyond belief, Lisette paced the confines of her room. The holidays had come and gone and, even though they had celebrated their first Christmas without their father, the Krueger children had made it through the season admirably. Each passing day brought a measure of acceptance to their lives.

Lisette had seen Nate Rambler conquer a multitude of responsibilities and undergo tremendous changes during the past four months. For the most part, the children consented to his presence in their lives, and Lisette had witnessed a reluctant bond developing. He was firm but fair and, though he was sometimes short with Karl, his gruff exterior couldn't hide the genuine feelings reflected in his eyes.

Nate had let Karl ride the stallion in the October race, partly because the younger man was only a fraction of his own weight and partly because it seemed politic to do so. It turned out to be an excellent move; Iron Warrior won. As he had promised, Nate gave Karl a fair percentage of his winnings—a considerable sum for a fifteen-year-old—

hoping Karl would recognize that Nate was a man of his word. While the two could not be called friends by any stretch of the imagination, their relationship had mellowed to one of politeness and perhaps a mutual respect.

The day after the race, they had started harvesting the sugarcane, and Lisette's suspicion that Nate was a man who didn't give up easily was reinforced. The fact that he knew nothing about the dangerous job of getting the sugarcane to the mill hadn't stopped him. He learned fast, and he didn't mind getting his hands dirty. He worked the men eight full hours and was with them every step of the way. He seemed determined to prove the duties he had inherited weren't too much for him…including the children.

She had watched him play checkers with Franz, had listened to him read to Monika. She had heard him tell Heidi that when the time came for her to show herself, he would have to beat off the suitors with a stick. Legal or not, whether he liked it or not, and for all intents and purposes, Nathan Rambler had become a stepfather to the children Conrad Krueger left behind.

Her own feelings for the master of the house had become more complicated with the passing of each day. With the exception of mealtimes, she went out of her way to avoid the hardworking hardheaded Englishman who was too often in her thoughts. Suppressing her growing attraction had become harder with each slow-passing winter day.

Part of the problem was that she had too much time on her hands. In comparison to Nate's, her own duties were easy. She and the children had become used to each other's ways and, since their daily routine was fairly simple, Lisette was left with hours of emptiness. If she was at home, she would be running the house, which had never failed to keep her mind or her hands occupied. Because her status at Magnolia Manor fell somewhere between hired help and guest, she had no say in the management of the house, which left little to do but ponder the cryptic words Dodie had uttered the night of Henri's accident, brood over her future and pace.

There was no way to stop the worries, but she could put a stop to the boredom. Resolutely she turned toward the door. She wouldn't worry about Henri and the possibility he might have harmed her mother and might do the same to her. She would go to the kitchen and demand that Sadie allow her to help with the evening meal. Her mind might be in turmoil, but at least she could keep her hands busy.

Sadie was ironing and glad for the extra pair of hands. She armed Lisette with a crock of apples and a knife. Lisette set to work while Sadie and the other cook chattered about the weather, about who was sick in the quarters and when the next baby might be born. The lull of their voices and the monotony of paring the fruit was mesmerizing. Lisette soon felt her worries vanish. She grew sleepy, and her greatest concern was keeping the ruby-red skin intact through the paring of an entire apple.

"Did you hear what Mr. Hempstead said 'bout that ruckus up near Thibodaux, Sister?"

The unexpected question jarred her from her trance. She placed a freshly peeled apple in a bowl of water to keep it from turning dark and stifled a yawn with the back of her hand. "I didn't know Mr. Hempstead was here."

"Yassim. He come just after breakfast. Said the sheriff stopped by his place askin' if he'd seen a couple of girls."

Lisette's heart stumbled, and she felt the blood rush to her face. She hoped Sadie and Lottie didn't notice. She forced a steadiness she didn't feel to her voice and picked up another apple. "What girls?"

"Some planter's lookin' for his stepdaughters. Seems they almost killed him."

"Almost..."

Thankfully Lottie and Sadie took Lisette's inability to finish her comment as a sign that she was properly shocked.

"They pushed him down the stairs and robbed him."

"How...terrible," Lisette managed to say. "He... doesn't have any idea where they've gone?" she asked, hoping the question was logical, under the circumstances.

"No one has seen hide nor hair of them, but he's got Sheriff Purcell out lookin'. Hempstead said that Mr. Duschene swore he was gonna git them girls if it was the last thing he did."

The last of the cane had been shipped down the bayou to the mill, and Valentine's Day was upon them. Nate was busy replanting the ratoons in the fields that had been neglected the year before and making repairs to the house and the outbuildings. According to Sadie, he was doing everything possible to increase the plantation's value. When spring arrived, he planned to sell out to the person making the highest offer.

Lisette looked around her. Time was passing, and warm days had already set the crocus and daffodils to blooming. Spring was just beyond the horizon. The children would probably go to an orphanage. Nate would go back to New Orleans, and Lisette Antilly would soon be homeless, no closer to finding out the truth about her mother's death or locating her sister than she'd ever been.

She had spent the past few days worrying about the news that Henri was actively searching for her and Silvie and worrying about her precarious position. Good heavens, she was posing as a nun, seven short miles from a man who wanted her dead! The whole thing was tantamount to thumbing her nose at him. Like a bear, she had gone to ground for the winter, and like the bear, she would soon be forced to come out from the safety of her den. Though the February days held the promise of spring and new beginnings, Lisette felt her uncertain peace could be shattered at any moment.

Sweet Mary, how had their lives gotten in such a tangle? She wondered if Silvie had made it to the convent and if she had any idea that Henri was after them. Lisette considered and discarded a dozen ways to warn her sister, even as her thoughts took her back to the night of the accident time and time again. She replayed every word, every action, every nuance of speech. And, as she had all winter, she mulled over Dodie's strange comment.

"*...after the way he killed your mama...killed your mama...killed...*"

Had it been a poor choice of words, or had Dodie been trying to tell them that Henri had had a hand in their mother's death? At the time, Lisette had assumed Dodie meant that Henri had broken her mother's heart, but after surviving his serious attempts to harm her and Silvie, she was haunted by the nagging possibility that there might have been more to her mother's death than anyone knew.

She told herself not to be ridiculous, that Dodie's comment had been just a figure of speech. Her mother had died of gastric fever. Lisette could still recall Elizabeth's last weeks: the weight loss and vomiting. The clammy skin. And finally the coma.

But the possibility that Henri might be to blame wouldn't leave her alone. While she couldn't imagine how he could have been responsible for her mother's illness, it was becoming harder and harder to convince herself that he could be innocent of anything.

Lisette knew she would never rest until she knew the truth, and Dodie was the one person who could help her. Hadn't she told Silvie she knew everything that went on in the house? The problem was, talking to Dodie would entail going back to Belle Maison, and that was not only foolhardy, it was madness. How would she get there? What kind of excuse could she give Nate for wanting to go? He was no fool. He would see through any ruse she might come up with. And even if she could get away, how could she talk to Dodie without running into Henri? It was an impossible situation, and common sense told her not to act until she was forced to. But the more she thought about it, the more certain Lisette became that she had to find a way....

Then, an idea came to her from nowhere. In less than two weeks Nate was holding his first race of the year. There would be dozens of people in attendance. The men would be drinking and playing cards far into the night. It should be easy to slip out, and if she was a little late getting back, well, perhaps they would all be too potted to notice.

"Mr. Massey to see you." Dodie made the announcement and stepped aside for the Pinkerton agent. Henri rose from his desk and shook hands with the visitor.

"I have good news, Mr. Duschene, very good news, indeed," Massey said, a genuine smile toying with the corners of his lips.

"Good. I was beginning to think I was paying you for nothing." Henri made the statement, a subtle reminder to Massey that he and his partner, Donaldson, hadn't brought any valid information since the fall.

"These things take time, Mr. Duschene. Locating a missing person in a city the size of New Orleans requires skill and tact. We don't want to be too obvious and scare away the quarry."

"I understand," Henri said, but he didn't. "What do you have for me?"

"We've located one of your stepdaughters."

"Only one?"

"I'm afraid so."

"Was she at the Ursuline convent?"

"For a time. The young girl who finally gave us the information said that she showed up alone, and that she didn't stay long. They sent her out to the French Market one day with another nun, and she evidently got lost in the crowd. They couldn't find her, and she never came back."

"And you don't know where she went?"

"Ah, but we do." There was an air of smugness in Arnold Massey's tone. "It took a lot of time and man-hours, but we finally located her just last week."

"Where?"

"She's at a bordello in the Irish Channel."

"A bordello!" It must be Silvie. There was no way the virtuous Lisette would stoop to prostitution. But pretty, not-so-bright Silvie would be easy prey to the gaiety of New Orleans. She wouldn't see past the music and the fun. He could almost feel her slender throat in his hands. "Silvie," he murmured with satisfaction.

"From the description and the daguerreotype you gave us, we believe it is Silvia, yes." He closed his journal. "Shall we bring her in?"

"No. Not yet."

"Begging your pardon, Mr. Duschene, but why not?"

"I know Silvie. If she leaves that bordello, she won't go far. But her sister is different. Lisette is the most clever by far, and finding her will be difficult, unless..."

He let the sentence trail away, and the agent looked at him expectantly.

"Unless she goes to Silvie herself."

"So you want us to watch the whorehouse?"

"Precisely. Lisette is the older, and she feels responsible for her sister. If we wait long enough, she'll come looking for Silvie, and when she does, you nab them both."

Chapter Eighteen

Lisette wrung her hands and paced the length of her room, her veil flying out behind her. Though she had a cough and her throat felt scratchy, tonight was the night. She had sneaked carrots and sugar cubes from the kitchen to give to Iron Warrior, and she had confiscated some of Karl's clothes to wear on her excursion to Belle Maison. There was nothing to do but wait until it was safe to leave. Safe! No matter how long she waited, it wouldn't be safe, but heaven knew when she'd have another opportunity.

Nate's big race was tomorrow, and planters with horses competing in the event had been arriving for hours. The downstairs was filled with laughing, drinking men. Sadie had fed them a short while ago, and the poker playing was scheduled to begin at any time. Once they became immersed in their whiskey and their games, Lisette would slip away. She glanced at the clock on the mantel. Half past six. Why wouldn't the time go faster?

Someone rapped sharply on the door. Placing a hand over her racing heart, she said, "Yes?"

"It's Nate, Sister. May I come in?"

Relief left her weak; nervousness left her shaking. She clung to the post of her bed. "Yes. Please."

Nate stepped into the room, and Lisette could no more stop staring at him than she could stop her next breath. His tight pants were tucked into the tops of expensive leather boots. A paisley vest in navy, maroon and gold topped a ruffled shirt, worn beneath a black frock coat. A black string tie completed his ensemble. He looked every inch the successful planter, every inch the successful man. Awareness and excitement stormed her crumbling defenses.

Sweet Mary. It was as if she were seeing him for the first time. He was so tall and fit, she thought, as he took a step nearer, swaying a little in the process. And so—drunk? Perhaps drunk was too strong a word, she amended, but there was little doubt he'd made several trips to the liquor cabinet. Otherwise he wouldn't be looking at her as if—Lisette swallowed hard—as if he wanted to…strip off all her clothes and…

"I hate to bother you, Sister, but it's Monika. She's sick." Nate's apology interrupted the shameful turn of her thoughts.

"Monika? What's the matter?"

Without waiting for his reply, Lisette headed for the door. His hand curled around her upper arm and drew her to a stop. They stood so close she could see the flecks of midnight blue in his eyes and count the fine lines radiating from their corners. She clenched her hands in an effort to refrain from pushing that stubborn lock of jet-black hair away from his furrowed forehead.

"She has a fever," he said at last, slowly, as if he were having a hard time remembering what they were talking about.

Lisette caught a whiff of *tafia* that lingered on his breath and the scent of cigar smoke that clung to his clothing. A wave of dizziness swept through her. Giving a slight shake of her head, she tried to recall what they were talking about.

Something important. But she couldn't think. All she could do was stand there and tremble.

"Fever," she gasped, remembering at last. "Monika has a fever?"

Nate released her arm and took a step back. "I think so. She...she says her stomach—" his gaze dropped to Lisette's middle, and she pressed her hand there "—hurts. Heidi couldn't find you, so she came and got me."

Lisette's face flamed with guilt. Heidi must have come looking while she had been in the kitchen filching carrots and sugar cubes.

"I'll...go check her." She bolted from the room, her face flaming and her heart pounding a crazy, erratic rhythm. Nate Rambler at close quarters was far more than her faint heart could bear.

Nate took a faltering step toward the door. He wondered if the awareness he saw in Sister Dominique's eyes was real or a hallucination brought on by too many glasses of *tafia.* Giving a small shrug, he followed her.

When he arrived at Monika's room, Sister Dominique was sitting on the edge of the bed, smoothing back the child's tousled hair.

"How is she?"

Engrossed in her ministrations, the nun didn't look up. Instead, she dipped a cloth in a basin of water and wrung it out. "She does have some fever."

"Is there anything I can do?"

Sister Dominique placed the cloth on Monika's forehead. "I don't think so. She may just be catching a cold. I've been fighting one for two days."

There was a definite huskiness in her voice, Nate thought. Feeling helpless and inadequate, he shifted his weight from one foot to the other. "I'll go back downstairs, then. If you need me, send Franz or Karl down."

Sister Dominique glanced up, and there was a soft smile on her face. "Thank you."

The innocence of that smile made Nate feel like a gauche schoolboy...and filled him with shame. Turning on his heel, he left the room and bounded down the stairs as if the hounds of hell were nipping at his heels. What he needed was another *tafia,* he thought. Something to make him forget the smell of lilacs that clung to her slender body. Something to blot out the way her hair fell forward and formed a backdrop for the purity of her profile. Anything to make him forget what a lowlife he was...

The *tafia* didn't help. Neither did the gambling. Nate couldn't keep his mind on the game and lost the first dozen hands. Instead of concentrating on the cards, his thoughts were filled with Sister Dominique and what an important role she had come to play in his life...in all their lives.

He was beginning to realize that before fate had landed him at Magnolia Manor his life had been lacking. The past four months had been illuminating in several ways and, though he hadn't wanted the responsibility of the plantation or the children, he knew he had grown from the experience.

While he had once shunned any form of physical labor and thought that one could get joy only from the pursuit of women and frivolity, he had learned that there was satisfaction in hard work and pleasure in simple things. Things like knowing that he had completed a worthwhile task. Things like familiar faces at the dinner table, infectious smiles and the feeling that he belonged.

Lord, Nate thought, swallowing another sip of his drink. He was certainly waxing sentimental. Or was it philosophical? And whatever it was, was it a sign of getting old, or drinking too much? He pushed back his chair and stood, swaying from the effort.

"What's the matter, my friend?" Raoul said.

"I need to go outside and clear my head."

"Not a bad idea, but I think you're quitting because you're losing your shirt, don't you, Henri?" Raoul directed the question to one of Nate's weekend guests who had a horse running against Iron Warrior.

There was no humor in Duschene's smile. "It is hard to keep throwing good money after bad."

"Indeed." Nate made a small bow—a mistake considering his inebriated state—and left the room, glad to get away from the noise and the smoke.

He had never met Duschene before that afternoon. He was an acquaintance of Hempstead's who supposedly had a good horse, and since Nate saw no reason not to take the man's money, he'd told Hempstead to invite his friend to come along.

Nate couldn't say he was impressed with the fellow. From what he had observed, Duschene was arrogant and something of a braggart. If his tales were true, women swooned at the mere sight of him. But if the story that his stepdaughters had tried to kill him was true—and the scar on his forehead was fair proof that it was—there were at least two women he hadn't impressed.

Nate made his way none too steadily to the porch. He leaned against the railing and struck a match on the sole of his boot. Holding the flame to the tip of a Havana, he drew deeply on the fragrant tobacco. The liquor had muddled his head, and the cold night air did little to clear it.

He tilted his head back and looked up into the clear, inky sky; he could count every star. Before he'd come to Magnolia Manor, he'd never paid much attention to the world around him. It had taken misfortune and adversity to steer him away from his pursuit of a worthless life. And it had taken four orphans and a nun with the mouth of a courtesan to show him the truth about human relationships. He didn't want to think of what would happen to them when he sold the plantation...and if he couldn't find their Uncle Penrod.

Dear God! He *was* getting maudlin. Or soft. And neither would do. Nate straightened his shoulders. There was no room in his life for sentimentality. He hadn't asked for any of this. The Krueger children were not his affair, and neither was a nun with a body made for sin.

Damn it! *No more liquor, Rambler. No more thinking about things you have no business thinking about...no more dreams about a woman you can never have.* What in sweet hell was the matter with him? What kind of man would even think such thoughts about a nun?

Nate ground out his cigar and scraped his fingers through his hair. In truth, he was ashamed of what he'd done. And that shame had grown daily until just before Thanksgiving when he'd stopped his nightly trips to the kitchen window.

Instead, he had taken to watching Sister Dominique at odd times. There were many nights he had peeked in as she readied the children for bed. He had heard her encouraging Karl to give a valentine to the daughter of a neighboring planter. He had heard her explain the changes taking place in Heidi's body. And he had heard her calm Franz's fears after a particularly scary dream.

Monika was told stories or read fairy tales. The younger children were kissed good-night, and the covers were tucked beneath their chins. It was obvious that they loved her and just as obvious that the feeling was returned. Which left him where he'd always been: outside the love. Excluded from the caring.

It was a feeling he'd never grown accustomed to, one he didn't like. Driven by the sudden need to be amongst them, Nate decided to check on Monika.

The door to her room was open a crack, and he pushed it wider. A lamp near the bedside was turned low and illuminated the immediate area. Sister Dominique sat in a rocking chair near the bed, the child cradled in her arms. The gentle squeaking of the rocker was a soft accompaniment to the lullaby that floated through the semidarkness of the room.

To combat the spinning of his head, Nate leaned against the door frame. At some time since he'd left her, she'd changed into her night clothes. It occurred to him that, in her gown and wrapper, Sister Dominique didn't look like a nun. She looked like the Madonna. Like a mother. Like a real flesh-and-blood woman, a woman meant to have a husband and rock her children to sleep.

It was a damned shame it would never happen.

Guilt followed the sacrilegious thought. Who was he to judge whether or not Sister Dominique was wrong to devote her life to God instead of a man and family? Hadn't she proved she was perfect for her vocation every day she had spent with them? It was he who had entertained the carnal longings, not her.

The *tafia* had turned his mind to mush. One minute he was a puddle of sentimentality; the next he was filled with improper thoughts; and the next he was squirming with guilt. But the drink had made one thing clear: He couldn't go on living with the constant, nagging shame for his thoughts, for his actions. He had to rid himself of it once and for all.

Pushing himself away from the doorway, he set an unsteady course across the room. Sister Dominique looked up, and he thought he detected an uncomfortable look in her eyes.

"How is she?" he asked, his words slurred and soft.

"Better. She had a sick stomach, but I think I got the fever down."

"Good." Nate knelt beside the chair and was assaulted

by the scent of lilacs. The few coherent thoughts that had evaded the fog of liquor fled. He forced himself to look at the child instead of the woman. Monika was asleep, her thumb, as usual, in her mouth. "She's asleep," he said unnecessarily.

"So is my arm."

He glanced up and met the nun's smiling gaze. A wave of light-headedness that had nothing to do with his liquor consumption washed over him. He rose quickly, another mistake. "I'll take her."

He reached down and slipped his arms beneath the sleeping child, trying not to think of how his fingers brushed the soft fullness of the woman's breast, trying to ignore her sharply indrawn breath. He placed his small burden in the center of the bed and pulled up the quilts. When he turned, Sister Dominique was so close he could feel her warmth.

She brushed a lock of blond hair away from Monika's cheek. "Thank you."

"You're welcome."

"How did you do?" she asked, straightening.

"Do?" Nate's mind was blank.

"Your card game. Did you win?"

"No," he said with a shake of his head. "I lost. I lost a lot."

"What about the race?" There was a gleam of genuine interest in her eyes. "Do you think Iron Warrior is the best?"

She was being nice. Why was she being nice? "He's a fine horse and I have a fine rider."

"Giving Karl responsibility for Iron Warrior has been good for him. Thank you."

Nate cringed. He didn't want her to thank him. He didn't deserve her thanks. "Sister, I have to talk to you."

"I thought that's what we were doing."

He took a deep breath. "No. I mean I have something to confess. I want to make a confession."

"You want to make a confession? But you aren't Catholic, and there's no priest."

Nate shook his head, determined to go on. "I know. It doesn't matter. I want to make my confession to you."

"To me?" Her eyes widened. "B...but I don't take confessions. Only priests—"

"You're a nun, aren't you?" he interrupted.

"I..." Sister Dominique looked as befuddled as Nate felt. "Well, yes, but—"

"Then let me tell you, please."

He knew his tongue was running away with him, knew the drink had given him Dutch courage. He didn't care. All he knew was that his confession would bring respite from his guilt.

"All right," she said at last. "If it's so important to you."

Relief flooded him. "It is. Thank you." He indicated the rocker. "Sit, please."

Sister Dominique sank down into the rocking chair and clenched her hands in her lap.

Nate sat down on the edge of Monika's bed, placing his hands on his knees and letting his head fall forward. When he spoke, it was to the floor, and his voice was barely audible, even to his own ears.

"I've sinned, Sister," he said, and felt the tension binding him ease. "I've sinned against you."

Chapter Nineteen

He's drunk, Lisette. He has no idea what he's saying.

"You've sinned against me? How?" His confession overcame the embarrassment she felt at being caught in a compromising state of semiundress.

Nate raised his head and met her curious gaze. Despite the bleary aftereffects of the liquor, there was true remorse in his blue eyes. "I..." He swallowed. "One night I...was going to the kitchen for something to eat, and...I saw you...when you were...taking your bath."

Shock rendered Lisette speechless. A hot blush crept into her cheeks. Feeling strangely vulnerable in her gown and robe, she crossed her arms over her tingling breasts. The man was three sheets to the wind, and the drink had no doubt triggered some latent sense of guilt. She recalled a similar feeling the time she had walked in and caught her parents in their undergarments. What Nate had done was nothing that should make him feel this bad, was it?

"It's all right," she told him in a voice designed to placate. "It was an accident. You shouldn't upset yourself this way. Now why don't you go to your room and try to get some sleep, Mr. Rambler? It's obvious that you've...had a bit much to drink. You'll feel better about everything in the morning."

Nate leaped to his feet so quickly Lisette shrank back in her chair. He plowed an unsteady hand through his already mussed hair, struck a weaving course across the room and came back to stand before her. She looked up into his determined face.

"It wasn't like that," he said.

"What do you mean?"

Reaching down, Nate grabbed her shoulders and hauled her to her feet.

Lisette gasped in surprise. A thrill of fear scampered down her spine, and a feeling of déjà vu swept through her. Henri holding her...Henri...shaking her...

Then she looked into Nate's eyes. The pure agony she saw there banished the terrible memory of her stepfather, and her fear drained away. Nate wanted forgiveness, and sweet heaven, if it was in her power, she would grant it. She would do anything to erase that look of torment from his face.

Without thinking of the consequences, Lisette placed a hand on his chest. He closed his eyes, and she felt a shudder ripple through him. "I don't understand."

He released her and took a step backward, as if he couldn't bear her touch. He held up one finger. "Only the first time was an accident, Sister, but once I saw who it was...what you were doing, I stayed. After that, it wasn't an accident."

The confession spilled out of him in a drunken rush.

"A...after what?" Lisette asked, though she already knew what he was going to say.

"After that first time, I watched you every night."

As soon as the words left his lips, Lisette could see the relief on his face. Propriety demanded that she be shocked, affronted...scandalized, but living a lie didn't put her in a position to cast stones.

"Every...night?" she asked on a gust of breath.

He nodded. "Until Thanksgiving."

"I see." An undeniable excitement spiraled through her. She clasped her trembling hands together and took a step away. Nate's fingers curled around her arm. She looked at the hand, so strong, so tan...and wondered how it would feel against her skin....

"Do you...forgive me?" he asked in a faltering voice.

Her gaze flew to his. "What?"

"Am I forgiven?"

"God...always forgives those who are truly penitent."

Nate waved aside God's forgiveness. "I'm not worried about Him, Sister. What about you? Do *you* forgive me?"

"Oh...of course," she said.

He exhaled a great sigh of relief and offered her a weak smile. "Thank you."

Lisette returned the smile in kind. "Can you rest now?"

He looked thoughtful for a moment, blinked as if he were surprised, and nodded.

Lisette took his arm. "Then come. I'll help you get settled."

In his room, Nate removed his boots and let Lisette help him off with his coat. She put the boots in the armoire and hung up his jacket. When she turned, he had removed his tie and unbuttoned his shirt. Wide-eyed, she watched him tug it from the waistband of his pants and strip it from his torso.

Life had not prepared her for the sight of Nate Rambler's bare chest. His body was covered with taut skin burnt to a golden brown from the hours spent roofing in the sun. Flat copper nipples peeked from a tangle of crisp black hair that sprawled over his chest and down the flat surface of his belly and, from the looks of it, to the hidden, forbidden portion of his anatomy covered by the black pants.

A tingling, aching feeling invaded her lower body. She longed to touch the smooth skin of his shoulder and wondered what the hair on his chest would feel like against the palms of her hands. As she stood there gaping, her hands clenched at her sides, he unfastened his trousers and peeled them from his long legs.

She must have made a sound, for he looked up, bewilderment on his face. It was obvious that in his inebriated state he had forgotten she was there, or if he hadn't, that her presence had little effect on him.

The surprise in his eyes softened and changed to a look of devilment. His mouth turned into a smile of cocky assurance. "Your turn now, eh, love?"

His British accent had never been more pronounced... nor had his masculinity, as he stood before her, as naked as the day he left his mother's womb. Lisette had never felt so near to fainting. She closed her eyes, but it didn't help. She could still picture every exciting inch of Nathan Rambler's body.

She heard him chuckle, heard the squeak of the bed and the rustle of covers. "You can open your eyes now." The threat of laughter was still in his voice.

Lisette complied and saw that he was in the bed, propped on one elbow, the quilts pulled midway to his chest. He wasn't smiling, but looked as if he might do so at any moment. She had to get out of the room. Nathan Rambler was detrimental to the resolves she'd forged since Henri Duschene had come into her life. She squared her shoulders.

"Good night, Mr. Rambler," she said in icy tones. Turning, she started for the door.

"No kiss, Sister?"

She whirled around. "I beg your pardon?"

The smile was back in his eyes. "When you tuck in Monika and Franz, you give them a kiss."

Horrified by his audacity, Lisette could only stare at him. Why, he was *teasing* her, she realized. He *liked* seeing her squirm. Drunk or not, if she could, she would take back her forgiveness! Gathering her dignity around her, she gave him a cold smile.

"One doesn't ask forgiveness only to deliberately go back into the same sort of sin, Mr. Rambler. Good night."

She escaped into the hallway and closed the door behind her. For a moment she just stood there, trembling, her icy hands pressed to her fiery cheeks. She had to find a way to get out of Magnolia Manor before she found herself involved in something she wasn't able to deal with.

She could no longer deny that she was drawn to Nate Rambler or that he was drawn to her—even if only in the basest of ways. Lisette was no fool. She knew that if Nate thought she was anyone but Sister Dominique, he would already have tried to get her into his bed.

Chapter Twenty

Pressing a kiss to Monika's cheek, Lisette pulled the blanket over the sleeping child's shoulders. She had slept in Monika's bed to be on hand in case she got sick again. Thankfully, she hadn't, and her fever had subsided toward morning.

Lisette rolled to her back and stared up at the whitewashed ceiling. She wondered if the master of the house was awake, and if he was, how he was feeling after his night of indulgence and confession. Her cheeks burned anew as she recalled his telling her that he'd sought her out specifically to watch her bathe...to see her naked.

Naked. A small moan of mortification escaped her lips. She had seen Nate naked, and the wretched man hadn't been the least embarrassed—which should, she thought testily, say something about his character. He was a worldly man, a man who gratified his every sensual whim, including the bedding of any woman he deemed fair game.

For the first time in her life, Lisette was becoming acquainted with the emotions and feelings that had ruled her mother's and sister's lives. While it was exciting, it was also frightening. She had determined that no man would charm her into doing his will, but Nathan Rambler was chipping away her resolutions the same way the Krueger children were making her take a second look at her decision not to deal with the heartache of having children.

A knock intruded on her thoughts, and Heidi poked her head inside.

"Good morning, Sister."

Smiling, Lisette held a finger to her lips. "Shh, and good morning," she whispered, climbing down from the bed.

"How is Monika?"

"Much better. I think a day of rest is in order, but she should be fit as a fiddle by nightfall."

Heidi looked relieved. "I'll tell Karl and Franz at breakfast. Did you know that Nate is having our breakfast brought above stairs so his guests can have the dining room?"

Lisette drew on her wrapper. "Really? What a thing to do!"

"Oh, I'm not upset. I rather like it. We're going to put a quilt on the floor and pretend we're having a picnic."

"That sounds like great fun," Lisette said. "Have you seen Mr. Rambler this morning?" she asked, trying to appear nonchalant.

"Only for a moment. He was growling at Sadie like a bear with a sore paw."

"I think perhaps Mr. Rambler indulged in too much *tafia* last night," Lisette said with a smile. "I imagine his head is hurting like the very devil."

Heidi giggled softly. "Serves him right. I'll be sure to tell Karl and Franz to stay out of Nate's way."

"That should be easy. You'll be outside most of the day, watching the race and eating all that wonderful food Sadie and Lottie have been cooking."

Anticipating the arrival of more people as the day progressed, Nate and Old Jim had set up tables on the back lawn. At noon, they would be laden with smoked hams, fried chicken, venison and a dozen different vegetables and sweets. The slaves had been given the day off and were having their own celebration in the quarters. There was an air of contagious festivity surrounding the running of the race.

"You're right. It's going to be a lot of fun. Karl says Iron Warrior is as ready as he can be. Will you be joining us?" As she spoke, Heidi's enthusiasm grew.

"I think it's best if Monika and I stay inside. We'll watch from the window."

Heidi nodded, but her disappointment was obvious. "If you'll excuse me, I'm going to go warn Karl about Nate."

She left the room, excitement illuminating her face. Not for the first time, Lisette thought that there had been too little of that emotion in the lives of the Krueger children. With Henri as a stepfather and master of Belle Maison, Lisette, too, had lacked excitement in her life. Despite her plan, which Monika's illness had thwarted, she had joined in the thrill of preparing for the race.

Lisette had been looking forward to observing the contest from a peripheral vantage place, but now it looked as if she would be spending the day inside with Monika. She consoled herself with the knowledge that there would be other days, other races, and then realized that she might not be there for them.

The abundance of men wandering around had necessitated that Lisette forgo her nightly bath, so she made do with a quick wash at the basin. Feeling refreshed with the scent of lilacs surrounding her, she donned Sister Dominique's attire. Since Monika was still sleeping soundly, Lisette decided to go to the kitchen and have Lottie make some broth for when the child awoke.

Downstairs, the guests were beginning to stir, though things were fairly quiet. A young girl from the quarters was serving coffee to two gentlemen with frowns etched into their foreheads and bags beneath their eyes—the result of too much liquor and too little sleep.

Outside, the birds were singing, and the sun was fast burning the chill from the early-morning air. A group of men were clustered near the finish line of the race, and Lisette had no problem picking Nate out from among the well-dressed planters. A breathless feeling took her, and she told herself that it was the promise of spring that made her heart and her step so light.

As she neared the kitchen, she spied a solitary jonquil that had pushed its way through the cold ground. She stooped to pick it up and was admiring its delicate beauty as she stepped onto the kitchen porch. Her hand was on the door handle when a man stepped through, almost knocking her down.

Hard hands gripped her shoulders. "Excuse me, Sister. I wasn't expecting anyone to be out here."

Lisette's blood ran cold. The voice sounded like Henri's. She glanced up over the tops of her glasses. It *was* Henri! Complete with an angry-looking scar on his forehead. What was he doing here? A dozen thoughts, none of them pleasant, darted through her mind. It was all she could do to keep from picking up her skirts and running back to the house.

Instead, a strong sense of self-preservation made her duck her head and murmur, "It's all right."

She had never been thankful for a cold before, but she was now. Perhaps he wouldn't recognize her voice with its husky deepness. With no desire to linger, she stepped through the open portal.

"Are you—"

"Henri!" one of the planters called. "Can you come over here for a moment? We need your opinion."

Lisette could have kissed the unknown man. She could feel Henri's vacillation between the need to try to talk away his clumsiness and the equally pressing desire to reaffirm his colossal ego with his peers.

With a hurried "Excuse me, Sister" he brushed past her and strode off across the yard, certain that his superior intelligence and opinion could not be done without.

Weak with relief, Lisette slipped through the door, clinging to it for fear her trembling legs couldn't support her.

"You all right, Sister?" Sadie asked, looking up from the bread she was kneading. "You're as white as a sheet."

"I...I'm not feeling too well," Lisette said, which wasn't totally untrue. "I...perhaps my cold is getting worse."

"Well, you git right back up there in that bed with the baby. I'll see to it that the children don't get into any mischief, and I'll bring the both of you something nice and warm to eat jest as soon as I get this bread to risin'."

Lisette nodded. Sadie's idea was excellent, a perfect way to stay out of sight until Henri left. "Thank you, Sadie, I think I will."

The moment Iron Warrior crossed the finish line Nate was bombarded with congratulations, curses and a small body that pushed through the gathering crowd and flung itself at him.

"We did it!" Franz cried, clinging to Nate's waist. Heidi hung back, a shy smile of pleasure lighting her pale blue eyes.

Nate wondered where Sister Dominique was, and then realized with a combined feeling of disappointment and relief that she was probably with Monika. His head still throbbed with a dull ache, and he burned with shame whenever he thought about Sister Dominique's knowledge of his transgression. He glanced toward the house and imagined he could see two figures silhouetted in the second-story window.

Karl, still astride the stallion, came loping up to the gathering, a wide smile on his face. As Nate made his way through the crowd of well-wishers, he couldn't help noticing that the lad, who had recently turned sixteen, was quite handsome now that he was filling out and his face was losing its youthful contours. No doubt courting was in the offing; Nate was glad he would be long gone when that day arrived.

"We won!"

"No, Karl, you won," Nate said, graciously giving credit where it was due. "You won yourself a goodly sum of money today, too, and you deserve it." He patted the stallion's heaving side. "Good work, boy."

"Why don't you children go on and play, so Nate can collect his due?" Henri Duschene's voice intruded on Nate's moment with Karl.

Anger flashed in the boy's eyes, but he controlled it, another sign he was maturing. "I'll go and cool Iron Warrior out. Franz, you and Heidi come and help."

Nate watched them go. For the next few moments, he was the recipient of hugs, slaps on the back and vociferous congratulations. The purse was handed to him, and all side bets were satisfied. Weary of the attention, he urged everyone to partake of more food and drew himself a glass of beer, hoping it would ease the persistent pain in his head.

"I hear you're selling the place."

Nate turned. Duschene, a glass of wine in hand, stood nearby, a pretty woman in a floppy-brimmed hat clinging to his arm.

"I hope to."

"I might be interested if the price is right," Duschene said, looking out over the fields of cane stubble.

Damn it! What was it about the man that grated so? "I haven't decided on an asking price yet." *But for you, sir, it will be higher than it would be for anyone else.*

"Henri," the woman said, her bold gaze raking Nate from head to toe, "aren't you going to introduce me to our host?"

Henri's lips tightened. "Allow me to introduce Patrice Benoit. Her late husband was the owner of Catalpa. Patrice, Nate Rambler, lately of New Orleans."

"Oh," Patrice drawled with a sigh that made her generous bosom heave. "I just love N'awlins. Where did you come from before that? You have the most *intriguing* accent."

"England," Nate said, squelching an ironic smile. Duschene was becoming quite undone over the woman's obvious interest. Though he couldn't have said why, Nate was anxious to get away from the gushing widow. A few months ago he would have found her interest flattering and probably would have returned it. Now, all he felt was a vague irritation that she made her feelings so conspicuous.

"If you'll excuse me, I must see how dinner is progressing." Nate looked at Duschene. "Are you staying over tonight?"

"I'd planned on it, especially if we can play cards again."

Duschene's smile bordered on smugness. He was no doubt thinking of Nate's losses the night before, losses that had lined his pocket.

"I don't see why we can't. There are several others I'm sure we can talk into joining us." Nate made a slight bow to the widow Benoit. "It was a pleasure making your acquaintance, madam. Perhaps we'll meet again." He made a sketchy salute to Duschene and started for the house to check on Monika.

He was tired—of bragging, hot-tempered men and fawning women. He was sick to death of hearing about how fast so-and-so's horse was, and who was the gossip of New

Orleans. Thankfully, most of the men were leaving, and Nate was glad. He was anxious for the weekend to be over. He would welcome the return to the sameness of his routine.

Chapter Twenty-One

The afternoon was waning, and the visitors who had flocked to Magnolia Manor for the day's festivities had started the long trek back home. Lisette had left Monika to play with Heidi and was almost asleep in her own bed when someone knocked at her door.

"Come in," she called, tucking back a strand of hair that had escaped the long braid hanging over her shoulder.

Nate, looking none the worse for his evening of debauchery, stepped through the opening. Her heart made its usual little flip, and Lisette pulled the quilts up to her chin.

Seeing that she was in bed, he stopped inside the doorway. "I'm sorry, Sister. I didn't mean to intrude. Are you ill?"

Lisette thought of Henri wandering around somewhere downstairs and her stomach churned. Ill? She was sick to the soul...and afraid. "I...must have caught Monika's fever," she said, avoiding the intensity of Nate's gaze.

"How is she?"

"Fine, the last I checked."

He shifted awkwardly and stared at his feet. If she didn't know better, she could almost think he was uncomfortable—a ridiculous state for Nathan Rambler. Then again, perhaps his guilty confession had left him feeling as vulnerable as it had her. She scoured her mind for a topic of common interest, one which would divert the focus of their conversation from her own tumultuous feelings.

"Heidi said Iron Warrior won again." It was the best she could do with the memory of his naked body uppermost in her thoughts.

Nate looked up and nodded.

Strange, but she'd never noticed how long his lashes were before, or how strong his jaw was. "Congratulations."

"Thank you, but I believe Karl deserves the congratulations."

"Perhaps." The conversation fizzled like fireworks on a rainy day, and another uncomfortable silence filled the room.

"Sister," he began, "about last night..."

Lisette saw the determination in his eyes and knew what was coming. She didn't want to think about last night. She had taken his *confession* for goodness' sake. She wasn't worried about *his* sins; the question was, would *she* ever be forgiven?

"No apology is necessary, Mr. Rambler," she interrupted. "Drink makes the strongest of men play the fool."

He cleared his throat. "Nevertheless, I want to apologize for my behavior."

The humility in his voice was unexpected, as was the lump that lodged in her throat. There was something about seeing a man like Nathan Rambler humbled that was disturbing, even while it was endearing. Though meekness wasn't a role he played well, it was comforting to know his heart could still be touched by the gentler emotions.

"Apology accepted."

Instead of replying, Nate neared the bed and reached out a hand toward her. Lisette's eyes widened, and then she felt him place his palm on her forehead. Her eyes drifted shut. His hand was warm, and his touch was tender, even though his palm was rough.

"You feel a bit warm," he announced. "Is there anything I can get for you? Tea? A toddy?"

"No," she said, urging a polite smile to her lips and hoping he didn't hear the breathlessness in her voice. "Thank you."

Nate thrust his hands into the pockets of his black frock coat and nodded. "Then I'll bid you good-afternoon and go play the part of host."

"Are your guests staying overnight?"

"Several are, yes."

Was Henri among those several? A thrill of fear whispered through her. She couldn't take a chance of running into him again. Covering her mouth, she gave over to a fit of fabricated coughing.

"You sound terrible," Nate said. "I'm going to have Sadie bring you up a hot toddy. No," he said, holding up a silencing hand. "I insist. I want you to drink every drop. It will make you feel much better, I guarantee."

"Very well."

"May I check on you later?"

The tenderness Lisette imagined she saw in his eyes melted the last stubborn bit of ice surrounding her heart. She knew she was a fool for allowing him to affect her this way, but nothing would ever come of it, so what could it hurt to allow herself this little indulgence?

"That would be...very kind. Thank you."

He gave her a parting smile and left the room. Lisette was hard-pressed to explain the aching sorrow that filled her when he was gone.

Lisette obediently drank the toddy Sadie brought her and was soon asleep. She awoke some time later to find that the fire was blazing in the grate. Funny. It usually burned down, and she had to get up and add wood. Raising herself to her elbows, she looked around the room and saw that Nate was sitting in the rocking chair by her bed, his feet resting on a small stool.

"What time is it?" Sleep and her cold lent a huskiness to her voice.

"Almost morning."

It hardly seemed possible that she'd slept with such soundness throughout the night. The toddy's work, no doubt.

"What are you doing here?"

"I thought someone should stay with you."

The thought of Nate watching over her while she slept was disconcerting...and touching. She recalled Heidi telling how her father had sat by her mother's bed for hours on end. Conrad Krueger must have loved his wife dearly. But Nate didn't—couldn't—love her; he thought she was a nun.

"Why?" she asked.

"Because I was worried about you."

Lisette blinked back the sting of tears. No one had worried about her since her mother died. "I'm fine."

"You didn't say anything earlier, but Sadie told me you'd been in bed all day."

"Yes, but—"

"Then you aren't fine. Did you drink your toddy?"

Lisette sat up and dragged her pillows behind her. "Yes."

"Good." He stood and reached for a thick mug sitting on the table beside him. "You were restless and coughing awhile ago, so I went down and fixed you another."

Lisette shook her head. "I don't want it. The liquor tastes terrible."

Nate sat on the edge of her bed. "Drink it," he said,

taking her hand and folding her fingers around the handle. "It's good for you."

She looked into his eyes for long moments. Perhaps it was silly. Perhaps she was crazy, but she had come to trust Nathan Rambler to do what was best. Besides, she could no more fight the gentle solicitation in his eyes than she could fight the heady feelings inspired by his touch. With a sigh, Lisette took a sip of the steaming drink. It was hot, sweet and spicy, with a strong taste of rum.

"You'll make me drunk," she grumbled.

"Sister Dominique drunk. Now that would be a sight," Nate said with a smile that stole her breath.

Unfortunately, the comment reminded her anew of her position at Magnolia Manor. She couldn't—mustn't—forget that she was Sister Dominique, not Lisette Antilly, no matter how much she might want to.

Wordlessly, sneaking peeks at him all the while, she finished her drink, wondering how she had let herself be drawn into Nathan Rambler's web, and how, under the circumstances, she could get out of it.

When the mug was empty, she handed it back. His hands curled around hers, and her lashes drifted upward. The look in his eyes started a giddy feeling inside her, or perhaps it was the rum doing what it did best. Her head swam, and the room seemed warmer. Her worries about sullying Sister Dominique's reputation vanished. An insidious warmth stole through her, leaving her weak and weightless and as malleable as a piece of warm wax awaiting the right hands to shape it. His?

He set the cup on the table and took her hands in his.

She shook her head in denial, but instead of releasing her, he carried her hands to his lips and placed one against his heart.

"See what your nearness does to me?"

Lisette quaked like a leaf in a high wind, and her own

runaway heart pumped a scorching heat throughout her body.

"You feel it, too, don't you?" Certainty that he was right shone in his eyes.

"I...should not."

At her faltering confession, Nate ducked his head and feathered a series of kisses along her jaw, his mouth moving inexorably nearer hers. She could feel the warmth and the strength of his body, could smell the mingled scents of tobacco and bay rum. She wanted to burrow into the haven of his arms and take refuge from the world outside her room. Just once, she wanted to revel in the knowledge that she had reduced a man like Nathan Rambler—a strong, worldly man—to sighs of passion and fulfillment.

The image brought Lisette's thoughts up short. Sweet Heaven! Nate Rambler was seducing her! He was drawing her into the midst of the very feelings that had condemned her mother and sister to enslavement. She brought her hands to his shoulders and gave a little push as his lips found hers.

The kiss was nothing but a light brushing of his mouth against hers, but it had the same effect as lightning striking dry grass. Flames of desire, hot and sweet, swept through her, stealing her breath and her reason.

"I...you...you mustn't. As a gentleman you must stop," she said, though her mind was so muddled that had she been pressed to offer him a reason, she couldn't have mustered one. All she knew was that she had to stop him and herself before the heat reflected in his eyes consumed them both.

"Please," she added, risking a peek at him from beneath her lashes.

Nate sighed heavily and released her. "You're right. I mustn't. But make no mistake about it. I'm not a gentleman, and the only thing stopping me is the black habit you wear."

Lisette took no comfort in the knowledge that she had been right. Quiet filled the room as she searched for some coherent thought among the chaos filling her mind. The fire spat and hissed, and from somewhere in the night, a horse whinnied.

To Lisette's surprise, Nate leaped to his feet and went to the window, where the black night sky was gradually changing to the charcoal gray of early morning.

"What is it?"

"I heard a horse," he said with a frown.

"So?" Lisette frequently heard the horses in the night.

"The stable is on the other side of the house." He started for the door. "I'd better make certain Iron Warrior hasn't slipped out of the barn."

Lisette watched him go, torn between irritation that his mind was so easily diverted and relief that temptation had been removed from her.

Chapter Twenty-Two

Nate stepped out the door and into the early-morning darkness. There was no sign of a loose horse where he'd heard the shrill whicker, so he headed toward the stable.

Shafts of light escaped through the cracks of the barn, slicing the shadows and striping a nearby oak with bands of silver. Someone was in the barn. What the devil was going on?

As Nate stepped inside and turned the corner to Iron Warrior's stall, he plowed headlong into Karl, who, lantern in hand, was leaving.

"Wh...what are you doing here?" Karl asked, apprehension lurking in his eyes.

"I was planning to ask you the same thing."

"I, uh..."

If ever Nate had encountered guilt, it was now. He fancied he could see the wheels turning in Karl's mind, gathering and rejecting ideas until he came upon the perfect lie.

"I thought I heard something. I came out to check."

"In your best clothes?" Nate didn't bother hiding his anger or his sarcasm. Had there been sufficient light, he knew he would have seen a flush suffuse Karl's fair face. As it was, the boy looked away with a heavy sigh.

"You took the horse out, didn't you?"

"Yes, sir."

"Where?"

"Oakley."

"Oakley? Good God! Oakley Plantation is better than five miles from here. What were you doing? Not matching Iron Warrior against your friends' horses, I hope."

Karl's head came up, and fire flashed in his eyes. "I'd never match him the same day he ran a race."

"No?" Nate shot back, as furious as Karl.

"No!" Karl snapped.

Nate started for the horse's stall, and Karl followed close on his heels. "Damn it, Nate, I take good care of that horse, and you know it."

Without answering, Nate snatched the lantern from his young charge and held it aloft.

Slinging his head in protest to the bright light, Iron Warrior snorted in irritation. Nate's sensitive gaze roamed the stallion, from his muddy hooves to his flared nostrils. There was a patch of wet hair where the saddle had sat, and perspiration streaked the animal's powerful neck. Nate turned to Karl, censure in his eyes.

"Is this how you take good care of him? You ride the hair off him, and then leave him in the stall without cooling him out?"

"I was trying to get inside before—"

"Before you were found out," Nate supplied. "God's blood, boy! This horse is worth a fortune to me, and I daresay he's been worth a pretty penny to you, too! Is this the way you repay him—by leaving him to catch his death and not giving him so much as a drink of water?"

"I did give him a drink!" Karl railed. "But I took out the water bucket because I was afraid he'd founder."

"How kind of you."

Karl matched gazes with Nate for long moments, but

Nate had no intention of backing down. Finally Karl nodded. "All right. I was wrong. It won't happen again. May I go now?"

Nate's laughter held no humor. "Go? The only place you're going is inside to change your clothes. Then you get your tail out here and take care of this horse the way he's supposed to be taken care of. The way you're paid to take care of him. And then," he said, grimly, "you're going to tell me exactly where you took my horse—and why."

Nate sat on an overturned bucket while Karl carried out his duties. To his credit, he did a smashing job of cooling out the horse and cleaning up both the animal and the stall. And he did it without so much as a word of complaint. It was plain to see that Karl knew he was in the wrong. Nate also saw that, despite his treatment of Iron Warrior the night before, the boy cared deeply for the horse.

Nate had no intention of letting Karl think his behavior was acceptable, but neither did he plan to remind him of it when things got rough between the two of them in the future—the way *his* father had. He and Karl had come too far since that first day.

He was a good lad, smart and hardworking, but he was approaching an age where trouble seemed to go out of its way to find good lads. Thinking back, Nate realized that his own problems had begun when he was about the same age as Karl. It must have something to do with one believing he was more of a man than one actually was.

Karl hung up the pitchfork and smothered a yawn. Iron Warrior circled the stall several times, then he folded his front legs and dropped down into the fresh hay Karl had used to bed his stall. He stretched out his legs, gave a deep sigh and closed his eyes. The fact that he chose to sleep lying down instead of standing up was a testimony to his weariness.

"Quite a nice job," Nate offered.

Karl looked at him in disbelief.

"I've never believed that you took anything less than the best of care of that horse," Nate said, "which is why your actions last night took me by such surprise."

"I never meant to harm him."

"I know that. And I don't believe you'd do it again, even if it meant getting caught doing something you weren't supposed to be doing, or...going someplace you aren't supposed to go."

A wry smile curved Karl's mouth and he gave a slow shake of his head. "You intend to exact your pound of flesh, don't you?"

"If possible. Come, Karl. Where were you?"

Karl scuffed the tip of his boot in the dirt. "I went to Oakley, just as I said. I went to see Sara Whittaker."

"Sara Whittaker! Do you mean that she met you someplace, and the two of you were together most of the night?" Nate asked, aghast at the possibilities that presented themselves.

"Yes."

"But why?"

"Why?" Karl ducked his head. "That's pretty obvious, isn't it?" he mumbled. "Sara is a pretty girl."

"God's blood, Karl! Do you realize that if word gets out that Sara has been sneaking out to meet you, her reputation will be in tatters?"

"How will anyone find out?"

"*I* found out, didn't I?"

"B...but, that's different," Karl stammered. "You're a man. You understand these things."

Nate scraped his hand through his hair, started to walk away and spun back around. "Oh, I understand, all right. I understand that you're thinking with a part of your anatomy that isn't located in your head."

Karl's blush was obvious, even in the gray morning light. "We didn't *do* anything except kiss."

"Why does that not relieve my mind?" Nate asked, rolling his eyes heavenward. He took Karl by the shoulders and sat him down on the bucket he'd just vacated. "Sit, my boy. We need to have a talk."

Nate paced back and forth, wondering how to approach the subject of Karl's growing urges. "Did your father ever talk to you about..." Nate paused and cleared his throat "...the birds and the bees?"

"Birds and— Oh. You mean the relations between men and women?" Karl shook his head. "No, not really."

Nate swore beneath his breath. Damn Krueger anyway! Had he done anything for his whelps but sire them? Nate recalled having this discussion with the duke and how it had felt to be on the receiving end of the lecture. With the weight of Karl's actions sitting squarely on his own shoulders, Nate felt—for the first time—a reluctant sympathy for his father. Instilling responsible behavior was not an easy task.

"All right, then," he said. "All right." He expelled a deep breath. "You're, uh, getting to an age, Karl, where you are...changing. You're becoming a man. And with these changes taking place, you may find that when you're with a young lady—especially, when you are *kissing* a young lady—you become...aroused."

He nodded. "Yes, indeed. I believe I love Sara."

Nate stifled an urge to throttle the boy for his naiveté. "At your age, the things you're feeling are most likely lust, not love. They are perfectly natural feelings, but they lead to other...things...things which should only be savored within the sanctity of marriage."

"Then you yourself have felt this...arousal before?" Karl asked.

Considering that he'd been seriously contemplating a

night in bed with Sister Dominique, Nate wasn't sure he'd ever felt like such a hypocrite. The thought resurrected his guilt for his actions and feelings toward her. Dear God, why must a nun, of all women, stir such tender yet wanton feelings inside him? And how could he lie to this boy who was looking at him as if he possessed the answers to his every question?

"Yes, Karl, I have felt it."

Karl considered that a moment. "You are seven and twenty and not married. Are you telling me that you have never—"

"I'm saying no such thing!" Nate snapped. Damnation! Why wouldn't the boy let it lie? Did all fathers go through such torment, preaching one set of values and practicing another? Again Nate plowed his fingers through his hair, the weight of his past sins weighing heavily on his shoulders. He sought his words with care. "There are women who...women who are willing to allow certain...liberties, in exchange for money."

"Harlots?"

Nate's mouth fell open. "Where in God's name did you hear about harlots?"

"I read it in the Bible," Karl said in complete innocence. "Papa explained what they were."

Thank heaven for the smallest of favors. "I see. Well, at any rate, if a man has...an urge, there are certain women—not all of them harlots—who will..." Unable to think of a delicate way of wording what he wanted to say, Nate swore roundly.

"Suffice it to say there are nice girls and not-so-nice girls. You do not sneak around and see nice girls at night, because if you do, and things get...out of hand, you may be forced into a marriage for which you have no liking." He sighed and sought to sum up the conversation.

"A gentleman takes responsibility for his actions, and

you must learn to think further than the moment at hand. You must consider how your actions affect the future. Do I make myself clear?''

Karl thought about that for a moment. ''Perhaps I was thinking about the future. There are worse things than being forced to marry Sara Whittaker. At least I would have a place to call home.''

''What are you talking about?'' Nate snapped. ''You have a home.''

Karl's steady gaze met Nate's. ''For how long? You own the home that was to have been mine, and you've made it abundantly clear that you plan to sell out come spring, which is almost here. What will happen to me and my brother and sisters then? Where will we call home? An orphanage?''

Nate was too surprised by Karl's outbursts to speak.

''Well, let me tell you this,'' the boy continued. ''I'll not be cooped up in an orphanage with strangers telling me what to do. What do you think I've done with the money I won riding Iron Warrior?''

Nate hadn't the faintest idea and said so.

''I'm saving it. I hoped to use it for a down payment.''

''A down payment? On what?''

''My home. I plan to make you an offer for the plantation myself.''

Nate couldn't believe what he was hearing. A sixteen-year-old boy wanted to buy a sugar plantation. What was it about owning a parcel of dirt that caused people to go to extreme lengths to keep it?

''Spend that money on yourself,'' Nate said in exasperation. ''You're still a boy. Material possessions shouldn't mean so much to you. You should own the land, the land shouldn't own you. That's what happened to your father.''

''What did happen to my father?'' Karl asked quietly.

"When you first came, you promised to tell me, if I wanted to hear. I do."

There was no denying the sincerity in Karl's eyes. The boy deserved to know the truth, and perhaps he had matured enough to take it. Leaning against the wall of the barn, Nate related how he'd come into possession of Magnolia Manor. When he finished, he waited for Karl to speak.

Now that he knew what was bothering the boy, Nate could see that Karl's actions had mirrored his uncertainty about who he was and what he and his siblings were supposed to do with their lives since a stranger had "won" their future and turned their lives upside down.

The winning of Magnolia Manor had turned Nate's life upside down, as well. He had gone from a life of negligence to keeper of hearth and home. He, who had never broken sweat in a day's work or taken responsibility for anything but his gaming debts, now had calluses on his pampered hands and could chop wood with the best of them. He, who had seen no hope in his own future or the good of mankind, now realized that the path to happiness lay not in the pursuit of pleasure, but the pursuit of personal relationships.

Conrad Krueger's children had taught him that. He had watched and been amazed at their love and support of one another. He had listened to their tales of their father's kindnesses and his caring for their mother, and he had come to one conclusion: Krueger might not have been a good gambler or a smart businessman, but there was little doubt that he had been a good father and loving husband, or that he had passed the importance of those qualities on to his children.

"Don't put your trust and your hopes into things, Karl. Put them in people. Things can't make you happy, but people can."

"People let you down. You can only count on yourself and the land. It never changes."

Nate thought of his actions toward Sister Dominique. As immoral as his life had been, he had always been careful not to step over an imaginary line...until she had come along.

"You're right. The land doesn't change, and I'm not saying you shouldn't want to hold on to what's yours. But I know for a fact that sometimes a person can't count on himself. Someday, Karl, you'll probably let yourself down. Just as I have let my ownself down."

Chapter Twenty-Three

Lisette awoke at noon, plagued by a mild headache, brought on, she was certain, by her unaccustomed imbibition of demon rum and aided by the nagging thoughts of Nate that paraded through her mind. Even though all his guests had departed earlier that morning, she intended to stay close to her room. She no more wanted to chance running into Nate than she did Henri.

She spent the afternoon playing with the children and going over her plan to visit Dodie later that night, after everyone had gone to bed. Her reaction to Nate's overtures earlier that morning made it imperative that she make the seven-mile journey as soon as possible. She had to find out the truth about her mother's death, so that the blame could be placed where it belonged—squarely on Henri Duschene's handsome, scheming head. The sooner she completed that task, the sooner she could take up her rightful residence at Belle Maison and leave behind the temptations Nate threw in her path.

Perhaps if she was back in her normal habitat she could summon the backbone that seemed lacking every time he came near her. She'd known from the beginning that he was dangerous, but she had foolishly believed herself above corruption by someone with such a dubious past.

Last night had proved her wrong.

Sweet Mary, she couldn't believe that she, who had seen the devastation left by men like Nate and Henri, could be lured so easily into the charming web they spun. It was bad enough that Lisette Antilly could be duped, but the fact that she had allowed him to compromise Sister Dominique—and the church—was unthinkable!

How could she have let him flirt with her so? How could she have sat there while he tried to kiss her, knowing that to give in to the desire coiling deep inside her was to give up her independence, her very will? Hadn't she learned anything from her mother's and sister's situations? Didn't she know that succumbing to those desires made one weak?

There was no place for weakness in her life. No place for a few moments of illicit love with Nathan Rambler, or any other man for that matter.

Love. Now why would that word enter her mind in the same context as Nathan Rambler? Her mouth twisted bitterly. Oh, she believed in love. Her parents had shared that rarest of emotions. But what she felt for Nate wasn't love. It was lust, the tender trap that had ensnared both her mother and her sister. Lust was a tool men like Nate Rambler and Henri used to their advantage. They marched right in and took what they wanted—never mind the broken hearts, the shattered dreams and the tattered egos left behind.

Lisette sank onto her chair and stared at the crackling fire. What she felt didn't matter. What mattered was that, despite her good intentions, despite her vows never to fall under the spell of a man, she had done just that, and there wasn't a thing she could do about it...except leave before he suspected.

But she couldn't leave until she had a place to go, and

that wouldn't happen until she got back her birthright and rid her life of Henri Duschene, which made the trip tonight so important. She had no choice. She had to get the matter of Henri settled and leave Magnolia Manor before she did something foolish.

Using soft words, sugar cubes and an overturned bucket, Lisette managed to saddle Iron Warrior. The stallion was wary of her, but he made only minimal protest as she climbed onto his back and walked him out of the barn. She knew he was hard to handle, but she'd heard Karl say that fearlessness and a strong hand were all that was needed to keep him in line. Perhaps the fact that she weighed so little compared to Karl and Nate helped the horse's acceptance of her.

The night was clear and cold, and Lisette was thankful for Karl's warm coat. The moon was waxing full, which meant staying to the roads would be easy. It would also make her progress noticeable to anyone else who might be traveling after dark. Her stomach churned at the thought of making the trip alone, but she had no choice. Her only consolation was that if anyone saw her and took pursuit, there was scant chance of them overtaking the stallion.

A sudden howling of a coyote drew a shrill whinny from the horse and caused him to sidestep. Lisette's heart took a tumble. What if Nate heard the sound as he had last night? She took a firm grip on the reins and leaned over the horse's back the way she'd seen Karl do. Smooching into the stallion's ear, she gave him a slight kick in the flanks.

To her surprise, he bolted forward. Only her determination not to be caught kept her in the saddle. He was fast. He was faster than fast. A pleased smile curved her lips as she skirted the quarters and headed for the road. The shanties were a blur in the night. Lisette knew he couldn't maintain this speed all the way to Belle Maison and back, but even so, she should be home before dawn, and Nate would be none the wiser.

Nate was making his daily entry in his journal and ledgers—and trying unsuccessfully to keep his mind on his work and not Sister Dominique—when he heard the horse whinny. Damning Karl for a fool, he leaped to his feet and headed for the door. Hadn't his talk with the boy accomplished anything?

As Nate stepped into the wide hall, Karl came bounding down the stairs. Nate looked up at him in disbelief. If it wasn't Karl on the horse, who could it be?

"I heard a horse," Karl said. "Do you think Iron Warrior got out?"

"I don't know. Let's check the barn."

A quick check of the stall proved that the horse was indeed gone, but there was no sign that he'd kicked open the door or worried the latch loose.

"The saddle's gone," Karl announced.

Nate swore and raked a hand through his hair.

"Do you think one of the slaves took him?"

"I don't know," Nate said grimly, "but I certainly intend to find out."

Thirty minutes later, both he and Karl were satisfied that none of the Negroes were missing. They trudged back to the house in silence.

"It must have been horse thieves," Karl said at last. "Some damned horse thief stole my horse."

"I was thinking as much myself," Nate said. "There's no other explanation. Everyone knows he's a valuable animal. It would be easy enough to take him up into Arkansas or over into Texas and sell him for a pretty penny."

"I know." Karl's curse blistered the night. "What can we do?"

They stepped into the comparative warmth of the house

and took off their coats. "Nothing tonight," Nate said. "I'll go into Thibodaux first thing tomorrow and talk to the sheriff. Perhaps he'll have some idea of how to pursue the search."

"Nate?"

The sound of Heidi's voice drew his and Karl's gazes toward the stairs.

"Yes, Heidi," Nate said with as much patience as he could muster under the circumstances, "what is it?"

"It's Sister Dominique."

His heart lurched. His first thought was that the nun's illness had grown worse. "What is it? Is she sick?"

Heidi's face mirrored her disbelief. She shook her head. "She isn't sick. She's gone."

Chapter Twenty-Four

Some two hours later, Lisette reined Iron Warrior to a halt at a spot far enough from the house that no one would hear their approach. She dismounted near a rotting stump and tied the reins to a sapling, praying that Iron Warrior wouldn't get fretful and pull free while she was gone. Plunging her cold hands into the pockets of Karl's coat, she started for the house, darting from shadow to shadow and ducking out of sight whenever she heard a strange sound.

Lamplight shone through the kitchen windows, and Lisette prayed she would find Dodie there, alone. She'd missed the old black woman who had raised her, missed her as much as she missed Elizabeth. The thought of seeing Dodie again lent eagerness to Lisette's step; she actually felt the burden she'd been carrying for so long lift a bit.

Slipping between some shrubs and sidling near the window, she peeked inside. The old black woman was sitting at the stone hearth using a small hatchet to splinter a piece of pine heart, which she dropped into the kindling bucket. She looked tired. And older than Lisette remembered. Satisfied that Dodie was alone, Lisette tapped on the window.

The aging Negress looked up, and when she saw Lisette

standing on the other side of the window, her eyes widened and a broad smile split her plump face. She laid the hatchet aside and motioned for Lisette to go to the door.

In a matter of seconds, she was being folded against Dodie's plump, shaking bosom. When Lisette got control of her tears, she pulled away from the comforting embrace and tried to smile. Dodie's eyes were still filled with moisture, but there was happiness behind the sheen of her tears.

"Lordy, child, but it's good to see you," she said, gripping Lisette's hands.

"It's good to see you, too."

"Where's Silvie?"

Lisette gave a small shrug. "I don't know for certain. When we left, we split up outside of Thibodaux. I gave her most of the money and told her to have Father Menard help her get to the Ursulines. I don't know if she made it or not."

"Well, Henri ain't found her, or we'd aheard about it. Speaking of bein' found, what do you mean comin' back here, anyway? Don't you know the master's got the sheriff *and* the Pinkertons out lookin' for the two of you?"

Pinkertons? Lisette's blood ran cold. Henri was serious about finding them. "The Pinkertons?" she said with a bravado she hoped hid her true feelings. "My, aren't we special?"

"Don't you be a cuttin' up like that, Lisette Antilly. This here's serious business."

"I know," she said, sobering abruptly. "Believe me, I know. But I had to come and talk to you. There are some things I need to know."

"I'll help you if I can, baby." Dodie gave Lisette a hard look and planted her fists on her ample hips. "You're lookin' awful skinny, child. And a little pale. You been eatin' right?"

Lisette smiled. "I've been eating just fine, but I'm starving right now. I don't suppose you have anything left from dinner, do you?"

"I might be able to rustle up somethin'. Take off your coat, an' I'll fix you a plate."

Dodie bustled around the kitchen, warming up the food while Lisette told her about her trip down the bayou, her meeting with Sister Dominique and the explosion on the boat.

"We heard about that but, Lord, I never dreamed you was on that boat."

"It was pretty frightening. I still don't know how I made it to land."

"It wasn't your time," Dodie said philosophically. "The Lord's got somethin' special in mind for you."

A picture of Nate flashed through Lisette's mind.

"What happened after you got outta the water?"

"A search party found me the next day," Lisette explained. "I'd put on the nun's clothes because mine were wet, and one of the men mistook me for the nun he was expecting from New Orleans."

"Why'd he need a nun?"

"He won the plantation in a card game, and when he got there he found four orphans. He needed someone to look after them, to teach them, so he sent for the nun. I thought it was a rather nice thing for him to do." Lisette was unaware that her eyes took on a dreamy softness as she spoke of Nate.

"That gambler done stole your heart, ain't he?" Dodie asked.

The bluntness of the question took Lisette by surprise. She summoned what she hoped passed for a carefree laugh. "Stolen my heart? Of course not. He's not the type who appeals to me at all. And he isn't the kind of man one falls in love with...not if one wants to avoid a broken heart. I don't intend to follow in *Maman's* footsteps, Dodie."

"The right kind of man won't break your heart, Lizzie. The right kind of man *is* your heart. Don't let what Henri did to your mama and Silvie stop you from lovin' if the right man comes along."

Dodie's words troubled Lisette. Was she right? Should she listen to her heart, which said that the tenderness and caring she saw in Nate's actions were real? Or should she listen to her head, which warned her not to trust any man?

Wearing a thoughtful expression, Dodie set the food on the table and seated herself across from Lisette, effectively interrupting her thoughts. "So you've been at that plantation house teachin' some children all this time. It wouldn't be Magnolia Manor, would it?"

Lisette nodded. "The Krueger place, near Raceland."

Dodie looked appalled. "Why, that's where Henri went on Friday. He just got home this mornin'."

"I know," Lisette said. "I ran into him. Literally. If I hadn't been pretending to be Sister Dominique, he'd have caught me out for sure."

Dodie shook her head, mumbling something about the good Lord looking out for fools and children.

"Don't fret. He didn't recognize me." Lisette took a bite of the chicken and dumplings. "Mmm, Dodie, no one can cook like you."

"Fancy talk ain't goin' to get you out of tellin' me why you risked comin' back here."

"I know. And I'll tell you soon enough, but right now, I just want to savor every bite."

Lisette finished her meal and pushed her plate aside. Then she rested her forearms on the table, wanting to know the truth but afraid to hear it.

"I came back because of something you said the night of the accident."

"What was it, baby?"

"You said something about Henri killing *Maman.* At the

time, I was so distraught that I thought you were talking about the way he broke her heart. But after I had time to think about it, I began to wonder if you really meant it."

Dodie carried Lisette's dishes to the dishpan and submerged them in the hot water. "I meant it. Every word."

"Why didn't you say anything?"

"What would I say? Who would I say it to? You? Silvie? She was a child, and you... Sweet Jesus, you was a doin' all you could to hold things together. Later...after your mama died, why, I figured you and Silvie had about all the misery a body could handle."

"You really believe Henri was responsible for *Maman's* death."

"I know he was." She wiped the plate and set it on the shelf.

"But...I thought the doctor said it was gastric fever."

"Might be that she had gastric fever all right. But it could have been because Henri gave it to her."

"What do you mean?" Lisette asked with a frown. "How could he have given her gastric fever?"

"He was poisonin' her, baby. He was givin' your mama arsenic."

"Arsenic? B...but isn't that what you use to kill mice?"

"It is, but Henri was givin' your mama a little dose when he took her tea in the mornings."

For a moment, Lisette felt as if her heart had stopped beating. "Are you sure, Dodie? I mean—how could you *know?*"

Dodie's weary smile was edged with bitterness. "I told you before. Ain't nothin' goes on in the big house that the house slaves don't know about. Nothin'."

Lisette felt like crying again at the thought that her beautiful, charming mother had been deliberately and systematically murdered by a man she loved.

"I'll go get Sheriff Purcell," Lisette said, dashing the tears away. "We'll have Henri behind bars by nightfall."

"How you goin' to do that?"

"I'll have the sheriff come out here, and you tell him what you told me."

Dodie shook her head. "No, child. That ain't never gonna work."

"Why?"

"It'd be my word against Henri's. Who do you think the sheriff's gonna believe—a slave or the master of the house?"

Lisette's heart sank. Dodie was right. "Then, there's nothing that can be done?"

"I reckon not."

"It isn't right!" Lisette cried, leaping to her feet. "It isn't right that innocent people have to suffer in the hands of men like Henri."

"No, it ain't."

"Well, I'm going to see to it that he pays, Dodie. I swear on the name of my mother, that I'm going to see that Henri Duschene gets exactly what he deserves!"

"How you plannin' on doin' that?"

Before Lisette could answer, the sound of approaching hoofbeats filled the silence of the room. Dodie's eyes widened, and she went to the window. "Oh, Lordy, it's Master Henri come back from Miz Patrice's place."

Lisette felt as if some giant hand were squeezing all the air from her lungs. She'd never considered that Henri might not be inside the house, asleep. Fast on the heels of that thought came the realization that her coming here had endangered not only herself but Dodie, as well.

"Dodie," she said in an anguished voice, "I'm sorry."

"It's all right, child. You get your coat on and slip outta here while he's gettin' his horse settled in."

Lisette snatched Karl's coat from the back of the chair

and thrust her arms into the sleeves. "What will you tell him about being out here in the middle of the night?"

"You don't worry about me, Lizzie. I been workin' Henri Duschene ever since he come here. One more fib ain't gonna make any difference." Dodie peeked outside. Satisfied that Henri was nowhere in sight, she gave her young charge a fierce hug. "I don't know how you're gonna put Henri away, but I'll be prayin' for you."

"Thank you," Lisette said with a watery smile.

She slipped out the door and off the porch, careful to keep close to the shadows of the building. Fear made her look toward the barn as she rounded the corner. Henri stepped out into the moonlight.

Hardly daring to breathe, she cast a longing glance at the woods that would hide her until she reached Iron Warrior. Unfortunately, reaching the safety of the woods meant she had to cross a vast expanse of lawn. With the moon lighting up the night, she would be as vulnerable as a mouse in a barn full of tomcats. She would have to stay put until she was certain Henri was inside. Keeping to the shadows, Lisette inched her way farther down the outer wall of the kitchen until she reached the back. She squatted near the window, where she had a view of most of the room.

As she dropped to her knees, the door opened and her stepfather sauntered in. His hair was mussed from the ride, and his cheeks were ruddy with cold. He really was a handsome man, she thought dispassionately. As she watched, she saw him lift his head and cast his eyes around the room, as if he were aware of something...someone nearby.

Lisette shrank deeper into the shadows.

"Evenin', master," Dodie said, her voice coming clearly through the closed windows.

"Evening?" Lisette heard Henri say. "Good God, woman, it's almost three in the morning. What are you doing out here, anyway?"

"You know how it is when you get old, master. Your bones get to achin' somethin' fierce. I couldn't sleep, so I come out here to make me a little tisane for the pain."

Henri didn't answer. Instead, Lisette heard the sound of his booted feet crossing the room to the window. His silhouette fell onto the dew-wet grass as he peered out at the darkness, almost as if he could feel her presence. Breathless, motionless, she waited for him to turn away.

When he did, she breathed in a sigh of relief. If Henri suspected that Dodie had entertained someone in the kitchen before his arrival, he would probably take a look outside. Lisette knew she had to chance covering the open ground before he started for the house.

Risking a peek through the window, she saw that his back was turned and he was even then reaching for the door latch. He was leaving! She took a deep breath, murmured a prayer and, crouching low, sped across the frost-covered ground. Safety was no more than a dozen steps away, when she heard Henri's hoarse cry of "Stop!"

Stopping was the last thing on her mind. She brushed past a bush and ducked a low-growing limb. A sawbriar vine scored her cheek and tangled in her hair, eliciting a soft cry. As she struggled to free herself, she heard the sharp retort of a pistol and almost instantly felt a white-hot agony score her side.

For a moment the shock and pain rendered her motionless. Henri had shot her! His name screamed through her brain. She couldn't let him find her. She had to get away, back to Magnolia Manor. The promise of finding safety in Nate's arms lent strength to her wobbly legs. With no consideration to her tender scalp, she pressed her hand to her side and wrenched her hair free of the vine.

It wasn't far to the spot she'd left Iron Warrior tethered. If she could just make it to the horse, she'd be fine. If she could make it to the stallion, he'd see to it that she got safely back to Nate....

Chapter Twenty-Five

The grandfather clock in the parlor struck three in the morning. Damn it! Nate plowed his fingers through his tumbled hair. Where could Sister Dominique have gone? He took another swallow of *tafia* and, with a curse, tossed the dregs into the fire. The alcohol hit the flames in an explosion of blue smoke, but Nate wasn't sure he'd ever feel warm again.

She was gone, and drinking wouldn't change the fact that he was the reason why. He conjured a picture of her face with its wide brown eyes and dimpled chin. If only she wasn't so pretty, so sweet and even tempered. If only she didn't smile at him the way she did—as if she were afraid to, as if...

As if what, Rambler? There's no use putting the blame off on the good sister. She left because of you.

True enough. If he hadn't tried to paw her like some callow youth with an itch in his britches, she would still be here. If he had, for once in his irreverent, irresponsible life, behaved as befitting his station, she might—

Egad! Nate realized with a start, he was starting to think like his father. At the thought of his father, a feeling of sadness filled him. He wondered suddenly what the duke would think of his new position as a landowner and the way he was managing his new responsibilities. Would he be pleased? Would he feel that his youngest son had finally grown up? Or after more than two years, would he care?

Nate wondered what it was about him that drew trouble like metal filings to a magnet. How was it that he managed to alienate everyone he loved? His parents, his siblings, Sister Dominique…

Sister Dominique?

The inclusion of her name among those he loved rendered him motionless, speechless. Dear God, he thought in amazement. He had done the unspeakable…the unbelievable. He had fallen in love—love, not lust—with the young nun who cared for his children.

His children? When had he begun to love the Krueger children? When had he begun to think of them as his? Yesterday, when he and Karl had had their man-to-man talk? The time Franz had climbed on his back and they had roughhoused in the parlor? Perhaps it had been the first time Heidi had smiled at him, or maybe it was because Monika trusted him to keep her safe.

When it happened didn't matter. What mattered was that he loved them…just as it mattered that he loved Sister Dominique. When had that come about? As he watched her tutoring the children in their daily studies, or when he'd seen her with her skirts hiked up, running from Franz?

He'd seen women more beautiful and definitely more glamorous. He'd met women who lived lives that were a counterpart to his. So why, out of all those he'd come into contact with, had his heart settled on the one who was as out of his reach as the stars studding the night sky?

Nate sank down into a chair, dropped his chin onto his chest and stretched his legs toward the fire. He built a tent with his fingers and rested them against his lips, staring at the flickering flames as if he might find an answer there.

* * *

The faint thunder of hoofbeats roused Nate from a light sleep. He opened his gritty eyes and stood, and his back screamed in protest. A chair was not the best place for a man his size to sleep. Rubbing his eyes, he went to the window and saw pink and mauve clouds streaking the gray sky. The new day had dawned while he slept.

He heard the horse again, nearer this time, and his eyes searched the area near the quarters. He spied a horse and rider heading toward the house. There was no mistaking Iron Warrior, though at this distance, he couldn't be certain the rider was Sister Dominique. A sigh of relief escaped his lips, and he turned toward the door.

To Lisette, the trip back to Magnolia Manor seemed to take aeons. She couldn't run Iron Warrior as much as she had on the trip to Belle Maison. The horse was tired, and not only was she exhausted, but she hurt like the very devil. Each time the horse's hooves hit the ground, she had gritted her teeth against the burning pain. She had lost some blood—not too much, but enough that she felt light-headed.

As Iron Warrior had carried her through the night, she had clung to the saddle horn and filled her mind with thoughts of the children, thoughts of Nate and of Silvie…anything to keep from dwelling on the fact that had it not been for Karl's heavy coat and the blessed cover of darkness, she might have been lying dead in the woods near her home.

Her luck, the same luck that had landed her on the boat with Sister Dominique, had not deserted her yet, but it was running out. She'd had two close calls with Henri, and the third, as they said, was the charm. It was foolhardy to believe that her assumed identity would protect her forever. Two encounters in as many days had proved that.

The closer she got to Magnolia Manor, the closer she came to losing consciousness, yet the clearer her thoughts became. She couldn't keep up the charade any longer. If what Dodie said was true, she had to find a way to put Henri behind bars. To do that, she had to trust someone enough to tell them what was going on, and the only one who could help her was Nate—the gambler who'd broken more hearts than she could imagine. Dare she trust him with her secret?

A wave of weakness washed over her, and her head lolled to one side.

"Love and trust go hand in hand, Lizzie."

The echo of her mother's words urged her to trust her heart. Elizabeth Antilly was right. She wouldn't fall in love with someone she couldn't trust, and Nathan Rambler had proved he was trustworthy in a dozen different ways. She had to tell him the truth about everything—her mother, Silvie, and the night Henri had fallen down the stairs. Nate would know what to do....

Nate hit the back door at a run, his long legs eating up the distance between the house and the barn. For an instant, the weathered gray structure blocked the horse and rider from sight; then they came careening around the corner.

He didn't know who he expected to see riding his horse hell for leather, but he hadn't expected it to be a woman whose long, chocolate-brown hair streamed out behind her like ribbons in the wind.

Nate grabbed the bridle and glared up at the woman whose memory tormented him day and night. His fury over her taking his horse warred with his guilt over how he had treated her and the overwhelming relief that she was all right. Yet all of those emotions paled beneath the purely carnal longing that swept through him as he stared up at her.

Her face was pale with weariness, and dark shadows smudged the delicate area below her eyes. The wind had tossed her hair into a wildness that sent his blood to singing. Her legs were encased in a pair of Karl's cast-off breeches that fit her slender thighs like a fine pair of leather gloves. Karl's coat hung from her slender shoulders, revealing a soft cotton shirt of purest white—no doubt pilfered from the drawer along with the breeches. The top buttons had pulled loose, and the soft swell of her breasts was as tempting as sitting down to a card game with a pocket full of money.

Nate's loins ached with longing. God help him, he wanted her, even though he knew his feelings would condemn him to an everlasting hell. He hid his feelings behind a facade of anger.

"Where the hell have you been?"

He thought her chin lifted a fraction. "I had to go to Belle Maison."

Belle Maison? Duschene's place? Why in the name of God would Sister Dominique go to see Henri Duschene? Nate wasn't aware he'd asked the question aloud until she answered.

"Because," she said in a voice hardly above a whisper, "that's where I live."

"Where you live? What in the devil are you talking about?"

Lisette didn't answer. Her eyes drifted shut, and she swayed in the saddle. Was she so weary, then? She drooped to one side, and slid from Iron Warrior's back. Nate caught her before she hit the ground. Panic, keen and piercing, knotted his gut. He lowered her to the grass and cradled her head against his chest.

"Sister Dominique." He tapped her cheek with his fingertips. "Sister Dominique, wake up."

Her eyelashes lifted slowly; beneath them, her brown eyes were hazy with pain.

"I'm not Sister Dominique."

"What?" Nate asked, his heavy brows drawing into a frown.

"I'm not Sister Dominique," she said thickly. "I'm Lisette." Her eyes rolled as she struggled to stay awake. "Lisette...Antilly. Henri Duschene's...stepdaughter."

Duschene's stepdaughter? The stepdaughter who had tried to kill him? Nate opened his mouth to ask her what in the devil was going on, but it was too late. Sister Dominique...Lisette Antilly...whoever the sweet hell she was, had lost her battle with consciousness.

Swearing roundly, he scooped her up into his arms. Standing with his burden, he started for the house. He was almost there when he looked down and saw that the coat had fallen open and a splotch of red stained her shirt. Only then, did Nate realize that the dampness he felt against his fingers wasn't perspiration. It was blood.

Chapter Twenty-Six

Nate carried Lisette up the stairs and into his room, where he placed her in the center of the feather mattress. She was hardly heavier than a good down-filled pillow herself. Retrieving a towel from the marble-topped washstand, he placed it beneath her injured side. Carefully he removed Karl's coat and tossed it to the floor.

Then he surveyed the evidence. The patch of blood was already drying around the edges. There were two holes in the shirt—one small and fairly neat, the other larger, more ragged. A bullet, he deduced, though the wound couldn't be a bad one, or she would be bleeding worse. Still, to keep down the risk of infection, it would have to be cleansed and dressed.

Giving no thought to her modesty, Nate tugged the blood-stained shirt from the waistband of Karl's breeches and, starting at the bottom, began to free the mother-of-pearl buttons. With each unfastened mooring, a bit more of Lisette Antilly was revealed: her flat abdomen, covered with the brown fabric of Karl's pants, her ivory midriff; the soft undersides of her breasts; and finally, her breasts themselves, not too large, but round and full nonetheless.

The subtle scents of lilac and warm woman wafted up to tease his nostrils.

Nate swallowed hard. Damn, but she was prettily packaged he thought, not for the first time. But it was the first time he'd been close enough to see the small mole that nestled close to the rosy areola of one nipple. He could no more stop himself from touching the small blemish than he could have stopped the next beat of his heart.

Her skin was as soft as the purest silk, and there was nothing that felt better against one's skin than silk...

The wound, Rambler. Keep your mind on the wound.

It was difficult, especially knowing that the desire he felt for her was no longer taboo. Reining in his licentious thoughts, Nate forced them to the problem at hand. He eased her arms from the shirt and aimed it in the general direction of the coat.

As he expected, the wound—a shallow groove about two inches long and situated near the lower rib—was superficial, though he had no doubt that it hurt like the very devil. Every step that Iron Warrior had taken would have aggravated it. Thankfully, for the most part, it had stopped bleeding.

Nate poured fresh water into the basin and carried it to the bedside. Dipping a cloth into the cool water, he blotted gently at the wound.

''What are you doing?'' Lisette murmured, without opening her eyes.

''Cleaning the wound.''

She forced open her eyes and raised herself to her elbows. Heat spread throughout her cheeks. ''I...I'm not dressed.''

A muscle in Nate's jaw tightened. ''There are worse things. Tell me—Lisette, is it?—who shot you?''

She collapsed against the mattress and tried to cover herself with her forearm. ''Lisette...Antilly. It was...Henri.''

"The hell you say!" The look in her eyes begged him to believe her, and for some obscure reason, he found he did.

She wet her dry lips with her tongue. "May I have a drink of water, please?"

Without answering, Nate went to the pitcher and poured some water into a glass. Sliding his arm beneath her, he lifted her upper body and held the drink to her lips, trying not to dwell on the soft mound of flesh pressed so intimately against his chest.

"Thank you," she said, when she had drained the glass.

Nate propped her up with pillows and took another look at her side. Satisfied that the wound was clean, he reached for a bottle of *tafia*. "You say Duschene shot you?"

"Yes."

"What were you doing there in the first place?" he asked, tipping the bottle and letting the fiery liquor run over the weeping flesh.

Lisette's back arched against the pain, and her cry of agony filled the room. Pressing her into the bed with the weight of his upper body, Nate clamped his hand over her mouth to stop her from waking the rest of the household.

"Shh. I'm sorry. Please, I'm sorry," he murmured, his eyes begging for forgiveness as they probed hers.

Dear God! He was so upset by the things she'd told him, so relieved that his feelings for her were not as terrible as he'd once assumed, that he'd given no thought to the effects of the alcohol on her raw flesh.

Her eyes were filled with tears that tore at his soul and vanquished all thoughts of her nakedness from his mind. "The wound," he explained. "The liquor will keep down the infection."

She nodded, and Nate removed his hand. Lisette sank her teeth into her bottom lip to hold back another groan.

He poured a splash of the liquor into her water glass. "Have a drink. It'll ease the pain."

Lisette latched onto the glass gladly. "You're always trying to get me drunk."

Nate only smiled at the testy tone of her voice. "Easy does it," he cautioned as she lifted the glass to her mouth. "It's potent stuff."

She sipped obediently at the drink, while Nate wound a long strip of cloth around her middle and knotted it fast. That he could keep his mind on his task and a look of nonchalance on his face with his hands so near her unbound breasts was a testimony to his years of card playing.

Finished with his task, his gaze sought hers. "So you're not a nun?"

The simple question brought a blush to her face, and she grappled to draw the towel up over her bareness. "No."

Nate knew there were more important issues at hand, things that needed clearing up—like what the hell she was doing riding around the countryside on his horse at night—but first, he had to settle this to his satisfaction.

"Why did you tell me you were?"

"I didn't. You assumed I was Sister Dominique. Under the circumstances, I didn't bother to correct you."

"You had her clothes." He feigned a thoughtful expression. "Let's see. You are most likely the stepdaughter who tried to kill Henri. Did you steal the nun's clothes?"

"How dare you!"

"Oh, I dare a lot, Lisette Antilly," he warned in a silky voice.

"I didn't steal her things. After I...left Belle Maison I stowed away on the boat."

"You what!"

"I was desperate. I didn't have any money. I'd given it all to my sister. Sister Dominique found my hiding place, and she had gone to find the captain and pay my passage when the engine blew. I tried to save her things. It seemed the least I could do to repay her kindness."

Nate stared up at the ceiling. His laughter was bitter, mocking. "So that's how you became a nun. God, I'll bet you had a good laugh over my *confession.*"

"No," she said, with a slow shake of her head, "I didn't. I knew you were feeling a great amount of guilt, and the thought of your watching me...was..." Unable to finish, she looked away.

Nate reached out and took her chin in a gentle grasp. He turned her face until she was forced to look at him. "It was what?" he asked in a soft voice. "Disgusting?"

She shook her head.

"Ridiculous?"

"No." The word was a wisp of sound.

"What, then? As exciting for you when you heard it as it was for me when I watched?"

"No!" she cried, but the blush that rushed to her cheeks contradicted her denial.

"You're lying." He rubbed his thumb over and inside her bottom lip, smearing the moisture over its soft fullness. "You liked it...Lisette. You liked it as much as you liked it when I kissed you yesterday."

His tone was as light as the finger he trailed down her throat to the edge of the toweling. "Do you have any idea what hell you put me through? A hair shirt would be preferable to the agony of knowing that I wanted a woman of the church."

His lips mimicked a smile, and he moved his hand to rest on her breast. A soft gasp of surprise escaped her, but she didn't try to stop him.

"I'm notorious for desiring the wrong women, but I'd never wanted a nun before. I'm no saint," he said, then tugged the toweling from her breasts, "and you're no nun, thank God."

He leaned forward until their chests touched and his mouth was a whisper away from hers. "There's no habit between us now, Lisette Antilly, and nothing this side of heaven—or hell—can stop me from kissing you."

His lips met hers as his fingers curled around her breast. Lisette drew in a sharp breath and was shocked to feel his tongue slip into her mouth. Nothing in her life had prepared her for the wave of emotions that battered at her fragile defenses. Nothing had prepared her for the feel of his rough palms against her flesh or the way his tongue stroked the virgin recesses of her mouth and laved the sensitive tips of her breasts, kindling a fire deep within. And nothing this side of heaven—or hell—could have stopped her arms from circling his neck or her lips from answering his.

He kissed her for hours, or was it only moments? Time was measured only by the sweet anticipation of where and how his lips would touch her next. No wonder mothers warned their daughters not to indulge in kisses. Kisses could lead to other things, things that Nate was doing to her. She lifted her hips, pressing herself against the heel of his hand, seeking a closeness she knew she couldn't find with the heavy fabric of Karl's breeches separating them. She groaned in desire and frustration and felt the buttons give beneath his clever fingers.

Every sense was heightened, and she knew that this moment would be etched in her mind until the day they laid her in the grave. The spicy scent of bay rum lingered in her nostrils, and if she wasn't already approaching delirium, she could get tipsy from the *tafia* on his breath. She could actually hear the frenzied thudding of his heart...or was it hers?

He slid his hand over the flat surface of her belly, covering her, his fingers stroking, seeking the heart of her desire where moisture gathered in anticipation of—what? What else could there be but this mindless madness?

He started to move away, and when she tried to hold him, he silenced her with a kiss. She was unable to think, unable to open her eyes. She heard the bed creak, heard the sound of clothing rustle and felt him peel Karl's breeches down her legs. He settled his body between her thighs, his weight a delicious burden.

There was a tentative probing and, unable to wait for whatever it was her body demanded, she thrust her hips upward. Pain—sharp, sweet, and tinged with an intangible desire for more—drew a sharp cry from her lips. Then the pain ebbed, and she felt Nate's fullness inside her.

Neither moved. A part of her recognized that he was allowing her time to get accustomed to the newness of their union. She felt strangely like crying. So this was the love that had changed her mother from a strong woman to a simpering shadow of herself. This was what Silvie was talking about when she said Henri's kisses made her feel so alive. Lust? Love? Whatever it was, it was marvelous.

Nate began to move against her, slowly at first and when she met him thrust for thrust, his body moved faster and harder. His breath rasped harshly in her ear, and she felt the dampness of perspiration beneath the fingertips that ranged from his muscular shoulders to his hard buttocks.

She felt as if she were racing to the top of a mountain whose peak stayed just out of reach. The harder she tried to get there, the more elusive it became. Nate breathed words of encouragement to her, while his body urged hers to an even faster rhythm. Lisette had never felt more alive, yet she was sure she was dying. Tomorrow might bring remorse, even shame, but at the moment there was nothing but Nate.

Just when she was certain that she could not draw another lungful of air, that she could not possibly bear another second of the exquisite agony, she reached the summit. Time, life, the world ceased to exist. For the beat of a heart, for the span of a second, she hung suspended and waiting; then she tumbled over the other side...and down...into a whirling abyss of feeling that transcended every emotion that had gone before.

Henri Duschene woke with a hangover and the nagging suspicion that there was something important right beneath his nose, something he couldn't quite grasp. He also suspected that that something had to do with Lisette and Silvie. The problem was that he couldn't concentrate for worrying about the prowler.

Who in the hell had been skulking around the night before? Though he'd risked the shot, he was not stupid enough to go after the intruder alone, on foot. Who knew how many of them might have been hiding in the woods?

Though there was no evidence that either Lisette or Silvie was in the vicinity, he had toyed with the idea that one of them might have been the nighttime visitor. He was about to confront Dodie with the question when she had come flying down the steps and thrown herself on him in a storm of weeping. Thank the good Lord he'd come home when he had. Here she was, an old woman stove up with the rheumatiz, and someone about to break in the place.

Henri had listened to her gratitude and drunk the tea she fixed him with weary resignation. Finally, pleading early chores, he had escaped the tiresome woman and gone to the house, confident that Dodie wasn't involved with whoever had been prowling around. The old woman's relief had been too real.

Chapter Twenty-Seven

Lisette awoke in slow increments. Sunlight shone through the window and lay warmly against her face. Her side throbbed like a sore tooth, and there was a matching ache between her thighs. Even her head felt as if a tiny blacksmith were in there pounding on little horseshoes. She moaned and rolled to her side, a mistake, as she quickly learned.

Exploring the area of pain, her searching fingers encountered the strip of material that bound her midriff. Except for the bandage, she was naked. Her eyes flew open. Her mind was filled with flashbacks of the gunshot that had grazed her and the wild ride back to Magnolia Manor… Nate wrapping the cloth around her, his dark head close, so close…Nate kissing her…his body's sweet invasion of hers.

Lisette shut her eyes tightly, as if doing so would stay the rush of memories crowding her mind. The ploy failed. All it did was resurrect another recollection: Nate, as naked as the day he was born, carrying her to her bed before the rest of the house awoke. Nate brushing her hair away from her face and murmuring soft words in her ear, telling her to sleep.

She pressed her palms against her hot cheeks. Dear God, what had she allowed to happen? She had let pain and a few swallows of liquor breach all her defenses. It didn't matter that she knew Nate was as unlike Henri as night was to day. He might be different, but he still wasn't the kind of man to fall in love with, and his actions the night before had proved he wasn't *that* different. If he was a real gentleman, if he truly cared for her, he wouldn't have taken her outside the bonds of marriage.

He didn't take you, Lisette. You gave yourself to him.

Though she knew the voice inside her spoke the truth, she didn't want to listen. She had let a man get close, too close, and she didn't need the problems loving a man brought.

Loving. The word silenced her thoughts and sent her heart to thudding. Had she done the ridiculous, the incomprehensible? Had she mistaken what she felt for Nate? Was what she felt for him love—not lust? The very idea sent her scrambling to her feet, despite the protest of her side. In love? With Nate Rambler? Impossible! Yet she had a vague recollection of the ride from Belle Maison and thinking that she could trust Nate with the truth because she loved him.

"Lisette?"

Nate! She reached for the wrapper lying at the foot of her bed and slipped her arms into the wide sleeves, her mind searching frantically for something to say. What did people talk about after they slept together?

"Lisette? Are you awake?"

"Y...yes. Come in."

The door opened, and Nate stepped inside. Lisette's breath caught in her throat, and she thrust a swath of hair over her shoulder in a gesture that betrayed her nervousness.

He must have been outside working. He was wearing

heavy denim trousers and a blue chambray shirt with the sleeves rolled up to the elbow. That untamed lock of dark hair fell over his forehead. There was tenderness in his eyes and a smile on his face.

Both filled her with dismay. Even if she was to acknowledge what she felt for him, would he do the same? Or would he, like Henri, use her until he tired of her, and then flit to another woman who caught his eye?

Nate took her shoulders in his hands and bent his head to kiss her, but Lisette turned away, and the kiss brushed her cheek.

He stepped back and lifted her chin until their eyes met. "Is something wrong, love?"

"No, not...really." She tried to smile. "It's just that... this is new to me, and I...I'm wondering if perhaps we made a mistake."

"Mistake?" Nate echoed.

She turned away and went to the window, holding tightly to the sill. "I...I'm just afraid that, because of the *tafia* I acted...wantonly."

"I see," Nate said after a lengthy silence. "If it weren't for the *tafia* you never would have succumbed to my crude advances. That doesn't say much for my technique, does it?" His laughter mimicked the sarcasm in his voice. "Nor does it do much to boost my ego."

She turned to look at him. "I think your ego is in excellent condition."

"You're right. If not, I'm sure that a few days in New Orleans gaming and...taking in some of the culture...will set it aright."

Lisette was too shocked by the jealousy that surged through her to reply. New Orleans meant women, lots of women. Women who would deem it quite something to have Nathan Rambler share their bed.

Her own ego smarting, she reminded herself that she had

a mission, and that was to put Henri Duschene behind bars and get back her birthright. She couldn't afford to let a dalliance with Nate or any man deter her from the course she'd set.

Nate settled his long frame onto the rocker and hooked his knee over the arm. "Now that we've established that you're filled with remorse over what happened last night and have no intentions of pursuing it further, perhaps you'd like to explain exactly what the hell is going on."

"What do you mean?"

He steepled his fingers together. His blue eyes were gemstone hard as he regarded her over their tips. "I mean, that you're a wanted woman, and I've been sheltering you in the bosom of my family for several months. I think it would serve both our best interests if you told me exactly what happened and why I shouldn't turn you over to Sheriff Purcell."

The quicksilver change in his attitude amazed Lisette. One moment he was anxious for her kisses; the next he was threatening, albeit subtly, to turn her over to the authorities.

"Come, Lisette. Tell me why you tried to kill your stepfather."

Where to start? she wondered. How could she explain all the things Henri had done to her family? "He's an evil person."

Nate laughed. "He's a pompous ass who holds himself in very high esteem—but evil?"

"He killed my mother."

"And how, pray tell, did he do this terrible deed?"

As Nate's sarcasm worsened, so did Lisette's control of her temper. Her voice held the chill of a winter night. "He poisoned her."

"Poisoned? And you can prove this, I imagine."

"No. All I have is Dodie's word."

"Dodie?"

"My mammy. That's who I went to see when I took Iron Warrior last night."

"And you think the sheriff will believe her?"

She shook her head. "She told me the sheriff would believe Henri. That's why I need your help."

Nate's eyes narrowed. "My help? Why me?"

"You...you're a man of the world. You know Henri's kind. You can help me figure out a way to bring him to justice."

For long moments, Nate just sat there, staring at her. Would he help her, or turn her away, as she had him?

"If you want my help, I have to know the whole story. Everything."

A sigh of relief soughed from her lips. She sat down on the tapestry-covered stool beside the bed. "It all started when I was a child. My father was hardly in the ground when *Maman* married Henri...."

Lisette told Nate about the changes loving Henri had wrought in her mother. She told him about Silvie's hero worship and how her feelings had grown into something more after Elizabeth's death. Lisette tried to present the facts as she saw them, stressing Henri's ability to charm the birds from the trees, but not forgetting to include Silvie's headstrong nature.

"And what makes you so certain that Henri poisoned your mother?"

"Dodie. She says she saw Henri getting some arsenic from the pantry.

"Maybe he used it to rid the stable of mice."

Lisette shook her head. "No. It was about that time that *Maman* started getting sick. The doctor called it gastric fever."

"Did her skin feel clammy? Did she have dizzy spells?

"Yes. Her throat burned and so did her extremities. She had the loveliest skin, but near the end, she was...yellow."

Lisette could picture her mother as she had been those last weeks.

"Did she have a rash?"

Surprised, Lisette nodded.

"She convulsed at the end, didn't she? Then she went into a coma. Then her heart just stopped beating."

There were tears in Lisette's eyes when he finished. "How did you know?"

"There's a club in London that has some strange members and some stranger practices. It's called the Hell Fire Club, and they have a dose of arsenic daily, gradually building up a tolerance to it. There've been a few who didn't make it."

"You believe me, then?"

"That she died of arsenic poisoning, yes. That Henri did it? Why would you think so?"

"To get the plantation, of course. In Louisiana, a woman has no control over her property. She has to relinquish her holdings to a man. The plantation my father left my mother would be run by a close male relative, in *Maman's* case, Henri."

"But if he had control of the plantation already, why would he find it necessary to kill your mother?"

"Because there was a chance Silvie or I would marry and he would lose full control. As time passed, he saw that Silvie was more likely to marry than I, so he seduced her."

"Why not marry her when he found out about the child, then?" Nate asked. "Wouldn't that have solved everything?"

"I believe that was his plan at first. Then something—someone—better came along."

"The widow Benoit?"

"How did you know?"

"Henri introduced us. She's quite a fetching piece. I see why he might be attracted to her."

Lisette wasn't prepared for the pang of jealousy that shot through her. "What attracted him," she corrected sharply, "was the fact that if he played his hand right, he could have not only Belle Maison, but Catalpa plantation as well."

Nate rested his elbows on his knees and leaned forward. "So tell me how you came to leave Belle Maison."

Lisette recounted Silvie's confession and how she had awakened when Henri came home. She told Nate about Henri trying to push Silvie down the stairs and his attempt to strangle her.

"He must have thought I was dead, or had lost consciousness, because he left me lying there and started after Silvie again. All I could think of was that she was *enceinte,* and that what was happening couldn't be good for the baby. I called his name, and he...ran at me. When he reached out to grab me, I...ducked, and he went flying over my head and down the stairs. Dodie didn't think he would live, and she didn't want Silvie or me to be around either way, so we left."

"She didn't want Silvie to be the cause of speculation if the truth came out?"

"No. She said Henri had done enough to our family without bringing Silvie shame. Whether he lived or died, she felt we should be far away, so we wouldn't have to explain what had happened—or why. If he died, she was going to tell the sheriff he'd come home drunk and fallen down the stairs."

"Clever of her. So you and Silvie left?"

"Yes." Lisette related their journey through the countryside and their parting at Thibodaux. She explained how she'd met Sister Dominique and told him about the explosion and her struggle to reach the bank.

By the time she finished, her hands were knotted in her lap. "The next morning, you came along and assumed I was Sister Dominique.'' She looked up, and there was earnest entreaty in her eyes. ''I didn't have any money. I had nowhere to go. At the time, the misunderstanding seemed like a godsend.''

He stood and, clasping his hands behind his back, went to the window. ''Is that all?''

''Yes.''

He turned and pinned her with a steady look. ''And it's the truth?''

''Yes.''

''So what is it that you want me to do?''

''Help me prove what Henri has done. Help me get Belle Maison back. It's mine,'' she said fervently. ''Mine and Silvie's. Our father built it, and it belongs to us.''

''Belle Maison means a great deal to you, then?''

''It means everything to me.''

Nate nodded slowly. ''And you would do anything to get it back.''

''Anything! I won't give up until I do.''

Without giving her an answer, he started for the door.

''Nate!''

He turned, the knob in his hand.

''Are you going to help me?''

''I don't know,'' he said solemnly. ''I'll think about it.''

Chapter Twenty-Eight

Nate closed the door to Lisette's room, misery and disillusionment settling over him like a pall. He hadn't expected their night together to mean so much to him, even though he had suspected for several weeks that he was growing to love her. Nevertheless, it had surprised him when their lovemaking totally destroyed the memory of all those who'd gone before.

Nate closed the door to his study and sank down behind the desk. He dropped his head into his hands and wondered how he could have been so wrong. Lisette had been an eager yet shy lover. Her touches were at once uncertain and curiously bold. She had offered no resistance and had given him her all. It had been an exhilarating, humbling experience that had filled him with a peace he'd never before experienced. He had carried her to her room, knowing that he was in love for the first time in his life and assuming his love was returned. Why else would she grant him such liberties?

Why else, indeed?

Love hadn't been her motive at all. She had taken him to bed, not because she cared for him, but because she wanted something from him. She wanted him to help put her stepfather away so that she could regain control of her ancestral home.

She didn't want him; she needed him.

What she wanted was a parcel of ground, a house, and to be lady of the manor. In that, she was like his father, the duke—or Karl—obsessed with owning things.

He had to admire her. As Krueger had, she had taken the cards she was dealt and played them with all her skill. She had used her beauty and intelligence and lured him into believing he had the winning hand. She had manipulated the situation to her advantage—not to mention that she had used the church most badly. But in the end she had gotten what she wanted, and to women like Lisette, just as to men like his father, the end always justified the means.

Nate couldn't believe that he, of all people, could be so easily duped. It wasn't as if he were an inexperienced youth who believed every word a woman said, but after living in the same house for so many months, he thought he knew what kind of woman she was. Dear God, when had he ever made so bad a judgment?

Furious at her and himself, and filled with a pain he didn't understand, Nate swept his arm across the top of the desk, scattering the ledger, the pen and inkwell to the floor. It wasn't until he heard the sound of shattering glass that he realized what he had done. His gaze moved to the polished floor where India ink pooled in a black puddle. It reminded him of his heart, shattered into a thousand pieces and bleeding…bleeding…

Nate reached for the decanter and poured himself a glass of Krueger's whiskey. He wondered if there might possibly be a way to prove once and for all just how important the plantation was to her.

The children had all been excused and had gone above stairs when Lisette faced Nate across the table, anxious to know what he'd decided. She had been on pins and needles, wondering whether or not Nate would help her, and racking her brain for some way to find Silvie and expose Henri, if he chose not to.

She had been plagued with worry all afternoon, trying to recall what she had said or done to make such a change in his treatment of her. Was it the fact that she had expressed her concern over the impropriety of her behavior?

"Still wearing the habit, I see."

His comment dragged her thoughts back to the present and her eyes to his. "Until my situation is...resolved, I feel that it's in the best interest of the children to keep up the charade."

"Best for yourself, you mean," he said, raising the wineglass to his lips.

The hurtful comment sent a rush of red to her cheeks. "Nate, I don't know why you're so short. If it's because I don't want to—" She paused, searching for the right word, and gave a helpless shrug.

"Sleep with me," he supplied, setting the stemmed glass to the table with a slight thud.

She nodded. "I hoped you'd understand that my emotions are in a muddle just now, and the children are—"

"It isn't important," he interrupted with a dismissive wave of his hand.

Lisette looked away. Though she had decided not to continue their intimate relationship, the fact that he could shut her out so easily hurt. She ignored the comment and addressed his initial statement. "For propriety's sake—as well as my safety—I feel that until I leave, it's best if I maintain my position here as Sister Dominique. Besides, I can hardly tell the children that I'm wanted for attempted murder."

"No," he agreed, "I suppose not."

Lisette grew uncomfortable beneath his penetrating stare.

"So you're just going to leave?"

"I have to find my sister. It's very important."

Nate shook his head. "What about the children? I can't believe you're sitting there so prim and proper, talking about leaving without so much as a thought as to how it will affect four children who have grown to love you."

"I have thought about it, Nate, but I have no choice," Lisette told him earnestly. "I'm just biding time here. There's no way I can stay forever. You know that. Whether or not you decide to help me, I must go, and soon. After two close calls with Henri, I'm afraid it's just a matter of time before he figures out where I am. The children have had a lot of adjustments to make. They'll make this one, too."

"They love you, damn it!" Nate said slowly. He leaned across the table, his control more menacing than outright fury might have been.

Lisette's heart ached at the thought of not seeing the children again, but she didn't know what to do to make staying possible. "It won't be easy for me, either," she told him. "Please believe me."

He twisted his mouth bitterly. "I don't believe in much of anything anymore, *Sister,* but I've decided to help you anyway."

Stung by his sarcasm and surprised by his decision, Lisette looked at him expectantly. "Do you have a plan?"

He held up his index finger. "First off, I don't think there's a chance in hell of pinning your mother's death on Henri. As you said, it would mean his word against a slave's. I do, however, believe we can get your plantation back."

Lisette sat up straighter. "You do?"

Nate offered her a half smile. "I do. And that's what's really important, isn't it, Lisette?"

She frowned and gave a small shrug, not knowing what he was getting at. "Of course, it's important."

He smiled thinly.

"What do you propose?"

"It's simple, really. Henri spends a lot of time in New Orleans. It will be easy to plan a trip that coincides with his. Once we arrive, I'll put out word that I'm looking for a high-stakes poker game. Your stepfather fancies himself a gambler, and he'll be invited to join us. That's when I'll win back your plantation, just the way I won this one."

Though Lisette would like nothing better than to see Henri brought to his knees, she wondered if Nate could actually pull off the same thing twice. "What makes you think you can lure him in that deep?"

"He has a colossal ego, as I'm sure you know. I'll pander to it a bit, and then I'll set him up. A good card player knows not only how to read his cards, but how to read the players. Trust me in this."

"I do trust you," she said, relieved that the end was in sight.

"There's only one minor condition."

"Condition? What kind of condition?"

There was a reckless gleam in his eyes that quickened her pulse, but instead of answering her question, he asked one of his own.

"I keep thinking about last night, Lisette. Do you?"

In truth, the memories had threatened to rob her of her sanity, but to admit as much would be admitting to weakness, and to show any kind of weakness was an invitation to heartache. "No," she said softly.

His laughter was soft and taunting, and his teeth were a white flash. "You're lying. I'm very good at reading people. The truth is in your eyes."

She dropped her lashes, unable, after all the changes she'd seen in him, to believe that he was capable of such deliberate cruelty.

"It's too late to hide it."

The mockery in his voice brought her gaze—steady now—back to his. "The condition, Mr. Rambler?"

"Oh, is it Mr. Rambler now? After all we've meant to each other?"

Lisette's face flamed. "It's quite obvious that it meant little to you."

"On the contrary. It meant a great deal. So much, in fact, that I'd like very much to do it again."

Shock robbed Lisette of her voice. "I...you..."

"We, love. We. We made love. You liked it. And I liked it. And if you want me to get you your plantation, that is the price."

"That's...blackmail."

"It isn't blackmail. It's barter. You trade one service for another. In this case, you get your plantation back, and I get another night with you in my bed...willingly."

Lisette stared into the cool blue of Nate's eyes and shook her head from side to side in denial. Perhaps she was right in thinking he was like Henri. It was obvious his feelings were not based on love. If he loved her, he would never have made sleeping with him a condition for helping. If he loved her, he would have pressed for marriage.

Stifling a disappointment she was only marginally aware of and understood even less, she nodded. If she wanted a home for herself and her sister, she had no choice but to comply with Nate's terms.

Chapter Twenty-Nine

The time for justice was at hand. Through the grapevine, Nate had learned that Henri was leaving for New Orleans in two days. Lisette could hardly believe that in less than a week her problems would be over.

While she was thrilled at the prospect of getting her birthright back, that anticipation was tinged with worry. What if Nate didn't win? Would he expect her to reimburse his losses or demand added nights in his bed? The possibility both frightened and excited her.

She tried to pretend that his cavalier treatment of her didn't matter, but that was another lie. It did matter—just as making Henri pay for his crimes against her family mattered, just as bringing Silvie back home mattered.

Bringing Silvie home. Ever since Nate had promised to help, Lisette had been consumed with the idea of accompanying him to New Orleans and bringing back her sister. There was only one way to see if he would agree to let her go, and that was to ask. Determined to make him say yes, she approached him in his study the night before he was to leave.

Stepping into the room, she saw that he was bent over the plantation journal, entering the day's happenings with bold strokes. His shirtsleeves were rolled to the elbow, revealing muscular forearms. Lamplight cast a blue sheen on his night-black hair, and Lisette curled her fingers into the heavy fabric of her habit, unsure which emotion was uppermost in her mind: the need to feel those strong fingers against her flesh or the desire to tangle her own fingers through the silky softness of his hair. It seemed like aeons instead of three weeks since she'd touched him, a lifetime since she'd felt his lips on hers....

"I'll be with you in a moment, Franz. Go ahead and set up the board."

The sound of his voice jolted her from her wayward thoughts. His abstracted tone told her that he was absorbed in his task; nevertheless, he hadn't forgotten the nightly game of checkers he played with Franz. Lisette was reminded again of the changes she'd observed in him.

When she made no move, Nate raised his head. Surprise flickered in his eyes, closely followed by the coolness to which she'd become so accustomed. He closed the journal and pushed it aside.

"What can I do for you?"

She swallowed and approached the desk. "I've come to ask you to let me go with you to New Orleans."

His heavy eyebrows snapped together. "Absolutely not. Your tagging along would serve no purpose."

The look on his face brooked no arguments, but she would not be swayed. Furious at his attitude, Lisette struggled to retain her calm. "I would not be tagging along. While you're setting the trap for Henri, I'll go to the convent and get my sister."

"What if she isn't there?"

Lisette blinked. "Not there? Why wouldn't she be?"

"What if she didn't make it to the convent? What if she didn't do what you asked? From what you've told me, your sister is a bit on the willful side."

The possibility had occurred to Lisette, but she had dismissed it. Silvie was stubborn, but surely she would not be so foolish as to put her life in danger the second time. Still, Lisette conceded that Nate's suggestion was within the realm of possibility. "I suppose it has been easier for me to deal with her absence if I think of her safe with the nuns."

"That's understandable," he said, striking a match and lighting a cigar. "What will you do if she isn't there?"

"I'll look for her."

"And how do you propose to find her in a city the size of New Orleans?"

That was an interesting question. Where would she look? Silvie had had little money. When it was gone, she would have been forced to find employment. But where? What kind of job could anyone as spoiled as Silvie secure, much less hold? Lisette tried not to let her concern show.

"I'll just...look at all the places she might have gone to find employment."

"You can't go traipsing around a city like New Orleans alone."

"Why not?"

Nate put down his cigar and rounded the desk. Fearing more of his anger, Lisette backed away, but he simply reached out and lifted her chin with a callused finger. His blue eyes roamed her face with the softness of a caress. "Because you're much too pretty," he murmured, brushing his thumb over her bottom lip. "Pretty young things can get swallowed up in a place like New Orleans."

She hardly registered the compliment or the way his touch caused her heart to race. Her mind was already making the connection between "pretty" and Silvie and "swallowed up..." Frightened by the possibility that her sister could be in trouble, she clamped her teeth over her bottom lip to try to hold the tears at bay.

"What is it?" he asked. For the first time in weeks, his voice held tenderness, not mockery.

She clutched his forearm and looked up at him through the tears gathering in her eyes. "What if the city has swallowed up Silvie?"

"Lisette—"

She dug her fingers into his arm. "I have to find her, Nate. She's my little sister, and I'm responsible for her. If she isn't at the convent, I have to try to find her."

Chapter Thirty

There was so much to see! Lisette thought, lifting the long gauze veil covering her face. She had not been to New Orleans since she was a child and, as she craned her head first one way and then the other, trying to take in as much of the passing scenery as possible, she felt as if she were a country bumpkin come to town for the first time. Bumpkin or not, frightened or not, she was here—after much arguing and pleading.

The only way Nate had even entertained the idea of letting her accompany him was if she agreed to maintain her nun's charade during their stay and if she would allow Levi to go with her when she went in search of Silvie. Nate felt that the nun's habit and Levi's six-and-a-half-foot, two-hundred-fifty-pound presence would afford her a certain amount of protection as she scoured the streets in search of her sister.

While she agreed with his reasoning, Lisette had pointed out that nuns took vows of poverty and would certainly not stay in a place like the St. Louis. She preferred staying with the Ursulines, but after considering the arrangement, realized that the convent rules forbade anyone's indiscriminate coming and going. Since she had no way of knowing when she might return at each day's end, she knew that staying at the hotel would afford her more freedom to conduct her search.

Since Nate felt, and she agreed, that it was best if no one knew they were traveling together, the problem became how to register her at the hotel without raising any eyebrows or any questions.

In the end, they had come up with the idea that Lisette would disguise herself as a widow—Mrs. Raoul Depardieu of Baton Rouge. As a widow she could travel alone, and the black veil of her widow's weeds would hide her face more effectively than the nun's wimple and veil. Lisette realized that she was exchanging one black costume for another, and vowed that when she and Silvie were safely at home, she would never don the color again. Still, as she rode through the streets of New Orleans, she had to admit that she felt a measure of safety with the sheer fabric covering her face.

Royal Street was a montage of Old World charm with its shops, banks, hotels and cafés, and the occasional exquisitely designed residence. Bourbon Street, once lined with shanties, now boasted the most elegant of homes. Looking at the changes and the signs of growth around her, it was easy for Lisette to believe the claim that New Orleans was one of the largest cities in America.

Because the spectacular St. Charles Hotel had not yet reopened after the fire that had gutted it two years before, Nate had elected to put them up at the St. Louis Hotel. That structure had suffered a similar fate in 1841 but had been rebuilt in exact duplication of de Pouilly's original design.

Lisette didn't know what she expected, but it certainly wasn't the massive edifice that took up an entire block. Located on the corner of Royal and St. Louis Streets and named after the patron saint of the city, the hotel, with its lofty dome and Tuscan columns was the most magnificent building she had ever seen.

"How many people can stay here?" she asked Nate as Levi pulled the carriage to a stop.

"Two hundred or so."

Her eyes widened. "I'll get lost."

"Of course you won't." He pressed some money into her hand. "Here. I want you to go in and register. I'll follow you in a few moments."

Lisette sighed and cast another awed look at the hotel's facade.

"Would you care to join me in my room for a late meal?" Nate asked, alighting from the buggy and extending a helping hand.

Lisette studied his steady blue gaze. In their current state of antagonism she wasn't certain she could bear to be alone with him. "No thank you," she demurred. "I have some bread and cheese that will do just fine."

Nate nodded his acceptance of her decision. Lisette took a fortifying breath and allowed him to help her from the carriage.

If the outside of the hotel was impressive, the inside was nothing short of magnificent. After registering as Mrs. Depardieu, Lisette declined the help of a porter and carried her carpetbag into the rotunda.

She stopped short at the panorama before her, struggling to absorb the magnificence of Dominique Canova's awe-inspiring design—from the circular staircase to the top of the dome, whose height, according to Nate, was a soaring eighty-five feet from the marble floors. Daily auctions were held in the vast interior, and everything from paintings to plantations to goods and slaves could be bought.

The rotunda doubled as a barroom, and it was obvious to Lisette that drinking hours were underway. Barkeeps were entrenched behind the half-moon shaped, marble-topped bar that extended half the length of the circular area. Crystal decanters flung bright shards of light from their glittering facets, and white-aproned waiters mingled among the elegantly attired men who were discussing their business in low voices, and arguing their politics loudly.

Feeling self-conscious—though there was no need since the gentlemen were interested solely in whatever it was that had brought them to the popular gathering place—Lisette made her way to the stairs. She located her room with little difficulty and closed the door behind her. With a sigh of relief, she turned the key in the lock and set her carpetbag on the bed.

The strain between her and Nate had made the trip seem overly long. Anxious to wash away the dust of travel and slide between the sheets, she let her gaze roam the spacious room, admiring the ecru lace curtains, the tapestry-covered chair and the elaborate carving adorning the French armoire.

It certainly was a fancy place, she thought as she removed her veil. Tomorrow, she would go to the convent and bring her sister back to the hotel. Silvie would love it.

Lisette awoke to the sound of birdsong outside her window. She rolled onto her side and, through the lace at the window, saw a fat robin clinging to the sill. The harbinger of spring ignited a flame of hope. Just as spring was a time of rebirth, the reclaiming of their home would signify a new beginning for her and Silvie.

Lisette was filled with excitement as they left the hotel and made their way down St. Louis Street. They were heading east on Chartres when she caught sight of the recently elevated spires of St. Louis Cathedral, whose new "French" look was less than a year old. Though the cathedral dominated the Place d'Armes, her interest was caught by another structure.

"What is that building?" she asked.

"The Upper Pontalba," Nate said. "Built by the Baroness De Pontalba. It has a twin at the other end of the square."

Lisette strained to see. "They're huge! What are they?"

"Living quarters—lots of living quarters for lots of families. They're called apartments."

Lisette looked doubtful.

"It's true. I've heard it said there's nothing like them in all America."

"Well, they may be the first, and they'll undoubtedly be the last. It's inconceivable that so many people can live together in one building." She gave a last lingering look at the Lower Pontalba. "They're lovely, though. The grill work is exquisite."

"It was made in France. Do you see the *A* and *P* in the design? The initials stand for the names of the baroness and her father."

"It must be nice to possess enough money and power so that you can leave your mark on an entire city this way."

Nate's lips tightened. "There are other ways to make your mark."

Lisette glanced at him, wondering what she had said to kindle the anger she heard in his voice. Whatever it was, he didn't speak the remaining two blocks to the convent.

Lisette exited the convent thirty minutes later, and as soon as the gate closed behind her, Nate knew the visit had been fruitless.

"Well?" he asked as he helped her into the buggy.

"She's gone. Mother Superior said that a Silvie Antilly had come to them in October but that she sneaked away on a trip to the French Market a short time later."

Nate didn't say anything. He just watched as Lisette tried

and failed to hide her disappointment and the sudden tears that welled in her eyes.

"You knew, didn't you?" she said.

"I suspected."

"How?"

He shrugged. How could he tell her that Silvie sounded like a stubborn chit who would do exactly as she pleased and the devil take the hind part? "Hearing you talk about her... She didn't sound like a person who would be happy with the regimented life of a convent."

"You're right," Lisette agreed. "When I think back on it, she said as much to me, but I didn't expect her to walk out the doors without a penny to her name."

She looked across the way, at the dozens of people going about their daily business. Nate could almost read her mind. The same thoughts were in his. Finding her sister would be an enormous undertaking...if not an impossibility.

"Where do you think she went?"

Nate placed his flat-crowned hat more firmly atop his gleaming head. "I have no idea," he confessed. "Did she have any skills she might use to make a living?"

Lisette grew thoughtful. "Planters' daughters are taught to manage a house, to care for a husband, children and their slaves. How to sew." She brightened. "Silvie did lovely needlework."

Not much to recommend a girl in a place like New Orleans. "You might try asking about her at some tailor shops," he suggested.

"That's a wonderful idea! I have a daguerreotype made just before *Maman* died. Perhaps if I show it around, someone will recognize her."

Despite his disillusionment with her, the hope that flickered in Lisette's eyes tugged at Nate's heart. "That's a good idea. Would you like me to go with you?"

"I...thought you had a game scheduled for this afternoon."

"I can cancel."

"No," she said, with a shake of her head. "My job is to find Silvie. Yours is to win back the plantation."

"Ah, yes," he said, "the plantation. We mustn't forget why we're really here. By all means, I'll get it back for you if I can."

"If you can? You have doubts, then?"

He shrugged.

"What...what if you lose? What if you lose a lot of money and I can't pay you back?"

His heated gaze caressed her face. "I'm sure I can think of something."

Wild roses bloomed in her cheeks. "And if you do win, when will you expect me to..." Her voice trailed away.

"Don't fret, love. I promise to give you fair warning."

Chapter Thirty-One

Lisette, dressed as a grieving widow, had been looking for Silvie for four days, and she was no closer to finding her now than she had been the day she arrived. Her sister's picture had been shown to dozens—no, hundreds—of people, but no one recalled seeing her. It was discouraging to realize that her search, which had started in the respectable part of New Orleans, was slowly leading her to the seedier section of town.

All day and to no avail, Lisette had been questioning people on Constance Street, the imaginary boundary that separated the Anglo *nouveau riches* of the Garden district from the Irish immigrants who lived in the area called the Irish Channel. She was ready to quit for the day when she spotted a woman strolling down the street, twirling a fringed parasol.

Lisette couldn't help noticing that the hennaed hue of the woman's red hair clashed violently with the ruby-red satin of her dress. The bodice was cut low over her ample bosom, and a beauty patch was pasted near the lace edging. Her lips and cheeks were rouged, and her eyes were outlined with kohl.

Judging from her attire, Lisette knew the woman was

what her mother would have termed a "woman of ill repute"—the sort a well-bred girl of her own background should not be seen conversing with this side of the grave. But Lisette was tired and discouraged and, if she were honest, she was approaching desperation. Had he miraculously appeared on the street, she would have confronted the devil himself.

When it became obvious that the woman intended to pass her by, Lisette reached out a detaining hand. "Excuse me," she said, "I was wondering if you would be so kind as to help me."

The redhead stopped, and glanced from Lisette to Levi. A dull flush crept into her sallow cheeks, and Lisette wondered if the woman was embarrassed.

"You shouldn't be here, lady," she said with a frown. "The only help I can give you is to tell you to get out of this part of town."

"Thank you for your concern, Miss—"

"Monique," the woman said, shifting her weight to one leg and placing a hand on her ample, satin-clad hip. "Monique Jones."

Lisette suppressed a smile, the first she'd been inclined to in days. Somehow she felt that the woman's name was a pseudonym, one she'd taken to help her conform to her present occupation.

She held out her hand. "I appreciate your concern, but it's necessary that I be here." She drew Silvie's likeness from her fringed reticule. "Have you seen this girl?"

The woman took the daguerreotype. She cocked her head to one side and tapped one long-nailed finger against her blood-red lips. "She does look familiar. What color is her hair?"

Lisette tried to squelch the tentative excitement building inside her. "Dark brown, like—" Remembering that her own hair was covered by her hat and veil, she caught herself. "It's very dark brown. So are her eyes. She's a very pretty girl."

"I can see that." The woman shook her head. "I don't know. She looks familiar, but I can't place her."

Lisette's burgeoning hopes were dashed once more. "Oh, please! I've been searching for her for days, and you're the only one who's even thought they might have seen her. Please, try to remember."

The fancy woman's eyes grew tender. She patted Lisette's shoulder. "The girl means a lot to you, doesn't she?"

Lisette nodded. "She's my younger sister. She's with child, and she's all alone in the city."

"With child?" The woman looked thoughtful; then her blue eyes brightened. "Well, why didn't you say so? I remember now! She came in when I was working over on Gallatin Street for Maggie O'Malley. That's been a couple of months ago. I'm working on my own now, but—"

"That's all right," Lisette interrupted. She was filled with relief that her search was almost at an end. "Can you tell me the house number on Gallatin Street?"

"Two-five-six," the woman said, handing the picture back to Lisette. "Maggie'll be able to help you."

Lisette smiled her appreciation.

"Look it's none of my business, but you really shouldn't go into that part of town alone."

"I have Levi."

"So you do," the floozy said with a resigned sigh. "But at least wait until morning."

"Thank you for your concern," Lisette said sincerely. "But I must go now." She pressed one of Nate's bills into her hands and smiled once more. "Thank you again," she said. "And God bless."

With a fresh coat of whitewash and bright-green shutters, Maggie O'Malley's place stood out among the mean houses of the neighborhood. Grass struggled to grow in the narrow yard, and spring flowers bobbed in the breeze. The sound of a tinny piano playing a rollicking song wafted through a partially open window and mingled with bursts of laughter and hoots of glee. It was a pretty enough place, Lisette thought, noting the well-swept walkway, but it was certainly noisy.

The thought had no more entered her mind, when a woman clad in bloomers and a corset ran squealing out the door, a rotund man with his shirt hanging open, close on her heels.

Lisette turned a wide-eyed look at Levi, wondering how the woman—the madam, she corrected herself—of this place could know Silvie. Perhaps Silvie had helped in the kitchen, or had been hired to stitch the outrageous dresses these women wore.

Levi shook his head. "Best you don't go in there, ma'am. That ain't no place for you."

"I couldn't agree more, but I must. If my sister is in there, I have to know."

"Yessim," he said with a nod.

He helped Lisette out of the buggy and, taking a deep breath, she climbed the steps and knocked on the door. A dark-haired woman in a bright-blue dress and a feather boa flung wide the portal. When she saw Lisette standing there in her widow's weeds, the smile on her face vanished.

"I'd like to speak to Maggie O'Malley, please."

"You're speakin' to her, dearie," the woman said in a thick Irish brogue.

"I am Lisette Antilly. I'm looking for a young girl, and I heard you might be able to help me."

She drew out the daguerreotype and offered it to the woman, who gave it a cursory look.

"I know her," she said, handing it back to Lisette.

"You do?"

"That's Silver Antilly."

"Silvie," Lisette corrected.

Maggie shrugged her plump shoulders. "Silvie—Silver. It's never their real name anyway."

"Does she work here?"

"She did." Maggie O'Malley's full lips curled into a wry smile. "She was one o' the best girls I've had in a long time."

Lisette felt her euphoria fade.

"It's too bad the baby ruined her figure," Maggie said, her coarse features set in a resigned expression. Oblivious to the agony in Lisette's eyes, she continued mercilessly. "I had to let her go." She winked. "You know how men are. They like those slim young things."

"Are you saying that Silvie was a..." Lisette couldn't go on. The thought was too terrible to voice.

"This ain't no charm school, dearie. Times is tough, and a body has to make a livin' somehow."

"I—"

"Look, is that all? I got a gentleman friend waitin' fer me."

Shocked, sickened, Lisette could only nod. The door had almost clicked shut when she cried, "Wait!"

Maggie poked her curled and beribboned head out the door. "What is it?"

"Do you know where she went?"

"I couldn't say for sure. One o' my girls heard Silver was down on Adele Street, living in some deserted building."

The door shut in Lisette's face. Sickness washed over her, and she placed her hand against the painted boards of the porch for support.

Silvie, selling herself to men. Making her home in a building not fit to live in.

"You all right?" Levi asked.

Lisette turned and saw that he stood a few feet away. She reached out blindly and felt him take her hand. "I—yes, I'm fine."

Trembling, she allowed him to help her down the steps and into the buggy.

"Do you want me to take you back to the hotel, now?"

"No," Lisette said, staring unseeingly across the street. "Take me to Adele Street."

"Beggin' your pardon ma'am, but it's gettin' close on to dark. Maybe we ought to wait till mornin'."

Lisette sighed. Levi was right. Waiting was the last thing she wanted to do, but she had heard too many tales to risk wandering around the roughest section of town at dusk. It certainly wouldn't help Silvie if she were killed trying to rescue her. There was nothing left to do but pray her information was correct and hope for an early sunrise.

"All right, Levi," she said. "Let's go back to the hotel."

"Hey, handsome!"

Agent Arnold Massey, better known in the area as Thomas Baird, watched from the shadows of a recessed doorway across the street from the fire-gutted building. He was glad she had finally decided to go out and hustle up some money. He was weary of sitting outside the hovel he and Donaldson shared while they kept an eye on her. Tipping back his cap to get a better look, he watched the young sailor look up at her throaty salutation.

The woman—she was hardly more than a girl, really—approached her victim, a smile on her face. Her clothes were dirty and ragged, and she was pitifully thin, except for her belly, which was distended in advanced pregnancy—a pregnancy Duschene had neglected to mention. Her curly dark hair hung in matted tangles down her back, and there were scratches on her cheek. Once a beauty, she reminded Massey of the place she lived—gutted. Empty.

She moved to within a foot of the sailor and put a pale hand on his chest. Massey couldn't hear what she was saying, but he could imagine.

He and Donaldson had been following her for months, keeping tabs on her in case the sister showed up. They had watched her swift decline from being one of the most popular prostitutes in the area to the pitiful creature she was now. When he'd first located her, Duschene's stepdaughter was one of Maggie O'Malley's best girls. But as her pregnancy progressed and her body had begun to thicken, fewer and fewer men wanted to share her bed. She'd had no choice but to leave Maggie's and go on the streets.

For the last several weeks, she had made her home in the burned-out dry goods store and had added thievery to her repertoire of tricks. If a man wouldn't bed her, she'd pick his pocket. And if she had no money, she stole from the street vendors.

Massey had watched her sink lower and lower into the quagmire of poverty and degradation. Seeing the changes in her bothered him, though he'd be damned if he'd admit it to anyone. Because he had a tender heart, he'd been known to leave a loaf of bread just inside her door on more than one occasion.

Now, he watched dispassionately as Silvia Antilly removed the man's pocketbook with a deft flick of her wrist, while murmuring into his ear. The man shook his head, and just as smoothly, she hid her bounty in the folds of her skirt. With a philosophic shrug and a smile, she moved on down the street, the man none the wiser...at least for the time being.

Duschene had charged him to keep an eye out for the sister. After so long a time, Massey had little hope of the older girl showing. But Duschene was willing to pay him to hang around, and if that's what he wanted, that's what he'd get. It was certainly an easy assignment; the hardest part was dealing with the boredom...and the sickening smell of the slaughter houses.

Ah, well, it would be over soon. If Arnold Massey had to guess, he would say the baby was due any time. And frankly, he didn't expect the girl to make it through the delivery.

Chapter Thirty-Two

Lisette finished the last bite of her breakfast and sighed with repletion. It would be a long day, and she needed all the nourishment she could get. She was wrapping a link of sausage and a slice of bread in her napkin when someone knocked at the door. Stuffing the leftovers into her pocket—just in case Silvie was hungry—she rose and turned the key in the lock.

Nate stood there, dressed for the day in gray trousers, a black-and-gray-striped vest and a black frock coat. As usual, when he looked at her with that intense blue gaze, Lisette had no control over her runaway heart.

He thrust the package at her and stepped through the door.

"What's this?"

He refused to meet her eyes. If she didn't know better, she might have thought he was embarrassed. "I thought you might be tired of the habit and widow black. I saw that in a shop down the street. Maybe you can wear it home."

Clothes? He was right; she was tired of the nun's uniform and beginning to hate the unrelenting black of her widow's attire. Lisette knew that clothing was too personal a gift for a lady to accept from a gentleman, but she wasn't sure she and Nate qualified for either of those labels, and besides, what was an item of clothing after she'd shared his bed?

"Thank you," she said. "May I open it?"

"Suit yourself."

Ignoring the disinterest in his voice, Lisette carried the package to the bed and untied the twine. Inside the brown paper was a pristine white blouse with tucking down the front, a round lace-trimmed collar, and a navy ribbon around the neck that overlapped in front with a pearl button. A navy faille skirt completed the ensemble. Its tailored simplicity was exactly the kind of thing she might have bought herself.

She turned, the blouse clutched to her breast. "Thank you. It's lovely."

"You're welcome," he replied. Then, as if he wanted the whole exchange finished and forgotten, he asked, "How did it go yesterday?"

Lisette shook out the skirt and laid it on the bed. She had no intention of telling him her sister had become a prostitute or that she intended to go into the worst part of the city to find her. If he even suspected that her destination was the Irish Channel, he would want to accompany her, or worse, forbid her to go.

"Not well," she lied, smoothing the collar of the blouse.

"I knew it would be a monumental task when you set out to do it." For once, there seemed to be genuine caring in his voice. "You know that we're leaving in two days, and I don't want you to be disappointed if you don't find her before then."

Lisette nodded.

"So where are you going today?"

"I thought we'd go into the Garden District," Lisette said, turning and looking him squarely in the eye. It was amazing how easily the lies came to her now. "Perhaps someone there had need of a housekeeper."

Nate's mouth tightened. "Just don't go beyond Constance Street toward the river. It's far too dangerous."

She turned away again. "So I've heard."

"Do you need any money?"

"No, thank you," she said over her shoulder. "I have plenty."

"Then I'll leave you to your search. I have an old friend stopping by early this afternoon and another game set up for tonight."

At mention of the game, she turned. "How are things going with Henri?"

"Well enough. I've lost some and won some, and he's winning enough from the others to make him stay. Tonight should do it, though."

"Why tonight?"

"Because," Nate said with a slow smile, "I'm tired of your stepfather's company, and I feel lucky."

If the look in his eyes was a measure of what else he was feeling, that something else had to do with her. She felt a flush sweep through her body. If he was right, she would have her home back by the next day. Would he exact his payment, then?

What the hell were the woman and her driver doing? Patrick Donahue wondered as he watched from his vantage point on the corner. As an officer of the law, it was his job to keep the peace in the hellhole he called home, but a few run-ins with the local toughs had taught him a thing or two: first, there was no stopping them, not with the paltry number of officers who were willing to work at this thankless job; and second, his life was worth more than most of those who broke the law. Officer Patrick Donahue had a strict policy to look the other way unless a body's life was in mortal danger.

The lady—and it was obvious she was a real lady, dressed as she was in that fine skirt and blouse—had stirred up considerable interest among the locals since she and her Negro had started poking around in the deserted buildings the better part of an hour ago. She was scared, and rightly so—that much was obvious, too. She was also determined to do whatever it was that had brought her here, or she wouldn't stay, not after that drunken sea scum had called out to her.

What the devil, or who the devil, was she looking for that she'd risk her virtue and her life in this place?

Donahue watched as they entered the third building. He yawned. At least their arrival made a welcome change from watching the tarts and thieves.

Hell's bells! The sailor was following the lady and her driver into the dilapidated house. It didn't appear that the seaman planned to let well enough alone after all. Donahue pushed himself away from the lamppost. He'd bet a week's pay that the sailor was up to no good. He crossed himself, clutched his stick tighter and took a resigned breath. Patrick Donahue was far from brave, but he couldn't let any harm come to a lady, now could he?

Across the street, in the shack he called home, Arnold Massey had been watching the woman's progress. Like Patrick Donahue, he was glad of the diversion, though he too wondered what was going on. But it was Paddie's job to keep the tenuous peace in the neighborhood, and his to keep an eye on the girl.

Massey saw the sailor ease toward the dark opening that had swallowed up the lady and her escort. Standing to get a better look, he rubbed a clean circle in the grime coating the window. Damnation! The seaman was going inside!

Glancing toward the corner, Massey saw the policeman start toward the building in a lumbering lope. Massey picked up his gun from the scarred tabletop and placed it in the pocket of his ragged coat…just in case he needed to give the officer a hand. Then he grabbed a bottle of gin and took a great swallow. Grimacing, he went to the door and lurched out into the sunshine.

If Lisette had entertained any idea that finding Silvie would be easy, she was wrong. It was a nightmare. Adele Street was near the river, and there were dozens of sailors and rowdies milling around the street, watching her every move. Though she was uneasy over facing the unseen perils inside the deserted buildings, she was more afraid to stay in the buggy.

The stench from the nearby slaughterhouses defiled the air with a sickening miasma that filled her nostrils. The only way she could keep from gagging was to hold her handkerchief over her nose. Fat blue blowflies swarmed in the dank air, buzzing around her head like a swarm of angry bees.

Abandoned buildings lined Adele Street, and her hands and face were soon streaked with soot and grime. So were the new things Nate had bought her.

As she had followed Levi into the second building, a drunk sailor had called out an obscenity that set her face to flaming. She'd cast an embarrassed glance at Levi, who pretended he hadn't heard. Obviously the drunk was not deterred by the size of the man accompanying her. Nevertheless, she stayed close to Levi and found herself wishing Nate was by her side. She was beginning to regret the woman's vanity that had urged her to leave the widow's garb behind.

Inside, the rancid smell of the slaughterhouse was partially, blessedly, overcome by the odors of mold and dust, charred wood and the peculiar scent of rodents. Shards of glass crunched beneath their feet and cobwebs ambushed them at every corner, eliciting shudders of dread and visions of the eight-legged creatures crawling down her collar. She could hear the rats scurrying through the piles of burned and rotting wood, could see their shadows darting about the dusky corners.

Lisette stopped short. What was that? She turned her head and looked behind her. Was that the shadow of a man? Her heart thudded painfully as she struggled to see through the semidarkness. A steamboat whistle blew. Someone yelled. Giving a shrill shriek, Lisette jumped and grabbed Levi's arm in a death grip.

"All right, now, sailor," came a rough command, thick with an Irish brogue and firm with authority. "Get those hands up over yer head and come on out in the daylight."

A crude curse scorched the air. The man who had followed them into the house raised his hands and retraced his steps to the exit. Lisette glanced at Levi, who motioned for her to follow him. They made their way carefully to the front door. Only when he saw the uniformed policeman standing near the exit and the sailor running down the street, did Levi motion for Lisette to come out.

She found herself looking into a round flushed face with merry blue eyes and a shock of orange hair that stuck out from beneath his cap. It was the kind of face one trusted on sight. Smiling, she held out her hand in greeting.

"Officer Patrick Donahue, at your service," he said, pumping her hand like the handle of a well.

"I'm Lisette Antilly, and this is Levi. We owe you our lives."

"Aw, get on with ye," Donahue blustered, his face going even redder. "He probably only wanted yer purse."

If the sailor's earlier comment was any indication, Lisette

felt certain that he had something entirely different in mind. She gave a slight shudder. "At any rate, I thank you."

"Ye're welcome." The policeman hiked up his trousers and pushed back his hat with his club. "I hate to be gettin' in yer business, ma'am, but what are ye and yer man doin' here, anyway?"

"We're looking for my sister." Lisette drew out the daguerreotype of Silvie. "I was told she might be in the neighborhood. Perhaps you've seen her."

Donahue had to examine the picture only a second or two. "Crimminy! I've seen her all right. She lives yonder." He pointed at a derelict building across the street. "She's yer sister, ye say?"

"Yes."

Donahue cleared his throat and pulled up his trousers again. He wouldn't meet her eyes. "I hate to be atellin' ye this, but it's best ye have no more surprises. The girl's pretty far gone with child."

Lisette found the policeman's concern for her sensibilities surprising and touching. "I know," she said with a wan smile. She looked toward the building. "Is she there?"

"I've not seen her leave this mornin'. Would ye like me to go inside with ye?" he offered.

"No, thank you," Lisette said. "But I would appreciate it if you would...keep an eye on things out here until we're ready to leave."

"My pleasure."

Thanking him again, Lisette and Levi crossed the dirt street and stepped through the doorway of the building.

Massey waited until the lady and her driver were well inside before he approached the policeman.

"Whas happened, Offisher Donahue?" he said, swaying toward the law officer and making certain the Irishman got a whiff of his reeking, gin-soaked breath.

Donahue closed his eyes and turned away, but not before Massey saw the worried frown on his face.

"Nothing fer the likes o' ye to concern yerself about, Baird," Donahue said with a hint of condescension. "Some seaman took more than a friendly interest in the lady and followed her inside that place yonder. I ran him off, that's all."

The man called Baird took another swig of gin, letting some drip down his chin. He swiped at his mouth with a ragged, grimy sleeve. "Whas she doin' down here, anyhow?"

Donahue stared at the building across the way. "She's lookin' fer that poor young thing that lives in the old dry goods store."

"Whas a lady like her want with that chit?" Massey asked around a loud belch.

"Not that it's any concern o' yers, but the lass is the lady's sister."

As Lisette entered the shadow-shrouded building that had once housed a store, she said a quick but fervent prayer that she would find Silvie well, yet somehow she knew it was a prayer that would go unanswered.

Half-burned counters still bore bolts of charred cloth and soot-ruined goods. The walls were blackened from fire and smoke, and the room was vacant except for the stray cat that streaked for the freedom of the doorway with a rat clutched in its jaws.

"Silvie!" Lisette called. The mocking emptiness echoed back the name. She brushed aside a spider's web and took a resolute step toward a door hanging on one hinge, praying her sister would answer. "Silvie, it's me, Lisette!"

Nothing. Lisette glanced behind her and saw that Levi was close on her heels. She stepped through the doorway to the back room, straining to see in the semidarkness. Tattered rags and broken boards had been hung at the windows to keep out the sun. Dust motes danced in the slivers of light that pierced the holes in the rags and lay in golden strips across the dirty floor.

Lisette made out a wood-burning stove, a table with one leg propped on a brick, a once-elegant cane-backed chair and what looked like a cot with a bundle of clothes piled on it. As she took another tentative step into the room, a racking cough came from the makeshift bed. It wasn't rags on the cot; it was a person.

"Silvie?"

Lisette bolted across the room and knelt by the side of the cot, her heart pounding in fear.

"Levi! Pull those rags from the windows!" she commanded.

"Yassim."

In a matter of seconds, a ray of sunshine lent a glimmer of light into the room. The girl lay on her side, her face to the wall. Her hair was dirty and matted, but Lisette knew she had found her sister. Reaching out, she eased Silvie to her back. Her beloved rag doll was clutched to her breast, like a talisman to ward off evil. But the good luck charm hadn't worked. The bones of her shoulders felt as fragile as a swallow's. There were hollows in her cheeks and around her eyes. Except for her belly, where Henri Duschene's child grew, she was terribly thin. And she was ill. Perilously ill.

Lisette smoothed back Silvie's hair and sank her teeth into her lower lip to hold back the tears. Silvie's breathing was shallow, and she felt feverish. Lisette swallowed back her misery. This was no time for weakness.

"Come, Levi," she said. "Let's get her to the carriage."

Without a word, Levi bent and scooped Silvie into his muscular arms. Lisette followed as he carried her out of the darkness of the rubble and into the warmth of the sun.

As she left the ruins, a drunk appeared from nowhere and staggered into her path. She fell back a step to take his weight, and his arms went around her as he struggled to regain his balance. Holding her upper arms, he straightened. For an instant, he looked her straight in the eye. Even as Lisette shrank from his touch, she received the impression of regular features, whiskers and brown eyes before he lurched away with a murmured "'Scuse me."

She watched him stumble down the street, and her heart ached for him and all the people like him who, unlike Silvie, had no chance of getting out. No chance at all.

Drawing in a deep, shuddering breath, she climbed into the buggy and drew her sister's head onto her lap. Levi clucked to the horse and they started off down the dusty street.

The jostling motion of the carriage must have disturbed Silvie's sleep. Her eyes fluttered open, and she looked up at Lisette, who smiled and brushed back her sister's tangled hair. "I'm here, *petite,*" she whispered.

Silvie's eyes widened and glistened with gathering moisture. Then she closed her eyes and turned her head away...but not before Lisette saw a single tear tremble on the tips of her lashes and slide down her cheek.

Chapter Thirty-Three

Lisette had never made a scene in her life, but when the people at the hotel refused to let her take Silvie to her room, she let go with a burst of righteous indignation that would have done the most hellfire-and-brimstone preacher proud. When she had finished telling the managers of the St. Louis that they were bereft of even the most basic of human kindnesses and offered to pray for their hardened hearts, they allowed her to put Silvie in her room if Lisette promised to clean her up and agreed to pay for the soiled bedclothes, which they would surely have to burn. Lisette assured them she would. She would have made promises to the devil, would have moved heaven and hell to see that her sister was properly cared for.

Once Silvie was settled in, Lisette ordered broth and bread brought up. Silvie was ravenous. Holding her sister's head against her breast, Lisette administered the hot stock spoonful by precious spoonful. When Silvie had eaten her fill, she wanted to sleep. Lisette sat by the bed and watched over her, praying it was a good sleep, a healing sleep, a peaceful sleep, one filled with happy dreams of a bright future.

Lisette could hardly wait to talk to her sister and tell her what Nate was doing for them, but that would have to be postponed until Silvie was stronger. Meanwhile, Lisette decided to wash away the reminders of her dismal morning and ordered a bath brought up.

After she had washed away the grime of the Irish Channel, she donned her widow's attire, intent on finding Nate and telling him of her good fortune...if he hadn't already heard, via the commotion she'd caused. She would also see to it that another bath was brought up when Silvie awoke.

Scrubbed clean, Lisette covered her hair with the hat and veil. She was weary of disguises. She hadn't realized just how weary until she had put on real clothes again. Reminding herself that she wouldn't need to hide her identity much longer, she reached for her reticule. In a few days, she could wear whatever she pleased, but in the meantime, Nate was right in insisting that she continue to pose as a widow—especially since Henri was on the premises. When she had made certain Silvie was still resting well, she went downstairs.

The rotunda was filled with people, all intent on partaking of the free lunch the hotel offered and looking over the slaves, which were auctioned every day from noon until three.

The sales area was set up across from the bar, and the sound of tinkling ice blended with the voice of the auctioneer, who extolled the particular virtues of the women on the auction block. The nicely dressed Negresses sat on chairs that had been placed on top of tables that extended to the rear of the room. They seemed unafraid, a little shy and a bit amused at the goings-on around them. While the whole ordeal was amazing to Lisette, it appeared to be of no interest to anyone other than the bidders.

Curious about the luncheon fare, she strolled by the table, which was laden with an array of sandwiches and olives. White-aproned waiters were busy ladling terrapin soup into china bowls. She was debating whether or not to get a sandwich for Silvie when she heard a familiar voice behind her.

She turned and saw Nate standing a few feet away, a buxom beauty clinging to his arm and his every word. He said something Lisette didn't hear, and the dark-haired woman pursed her full lips in a moue of pique. He laughed down at her, and she stamped her satin-shod foot in a burst of temper. Nate's grin broadened. Lisette wanted to throw something—perhaps a bowl of the hot soup—at Nate's companion.

Jealousy was a new and unwelcome emotion. She couldn't believe the rage that coursed through her at seeing Nate flirting with another woman. She told herself it didn't matter, that just because they had made love she had no hold on him. But it did matter. And in her heart, he was hers....

As if something compelled him, he looked up. Lisette turned away, fearful that even with the veil shielding her face, Nate might see her despair. Blinded by tears, she ducked her head and stepped away from the table, bumping into a hard, male body.

The apologies were offered simultaneously. Emotion lent thickness to Lisette's voice as she glanced up through the gauze veil. Fear snatched her breath. Henri! Even through the glaze of tears there was no mistaking him. Dear God, was she destined to see him at every corner? Skirting a trio of men discussing a recent purchase of a Mandingo woman, Lisette made her way to the stairs as fast as possible without drawing undue attention to herself.

At the top of the stairs she looked down to see whether or not her stepfather was in pursuit. The rotunda was so vast that it was impossible to make out the features of anyone below, but she found Nate by recognizing the teal blue of the dress Nate's lady friend wore. From where Lisette stood, she could have sworn he was looking up at her.

Henri nursed a tumbler of whiskey and paced his room, waiting for Arnold Massey's arrival. According to the note that had been delivered to him earlier, the agent had word of Lisette's whereabouts. A self-satisfied smile curved his lips. It had taken several months and a wagon load of money, but he had found both of Elizabeth's brats, and he would soon see them behind bars. But not until he was finished with them. Not until he was finished with the high and mighty Lisette...

A staccato rapping interrupted his thoughts, and he swung wide the door. Massey stood there, looking as plain and nondescript as ever. For the first time since their association began, Henri saw a hint of feeling in the other man's eyes. That emotion was exultation.

"Would you like a whiskey?" he asked.

"I don't mind if I do," Massey said, "since this is a bit of a celebration."

"You've found her?"

"Indeed, I did," Massey said smugly.

"She's here in New Orleans, then?" Henri asked, stepping aside so the Pinkerton agent could enter.

Massey smiled. "She's here in the hotel."

Henri almost strangled on the liquor. "What?"

"I followed her here myself."

"Followed her here? From where?"

"She showed up down on Adele Street, just as you said she would."

A self-satisfied smile toyed with the corners of Henri's mouth. "So she came looking for her sister?"

"Yes," the agent said with a nod.

"Did she find her?"

"Yes. She and her Negro driver brought the girl back

here to the hotel.'' Massey smiled and shook his head. ''I don't mind telling you I didn't expect her to show up...not after so long a time.''

Henri rolled the glass between his palms. ''Oh, I knew she'd come sooner or later. Lisette is very loyal to those she loves.''

''She has a lot of grit in her craw. I'll give her that. She's a looker, too.''

''She is rather pretty, isn't she?'' Henri concurred thoughtfully. ''You didn't do anything to make her suspect you were on to her, did you?''

''No, sir. As a matter of fact, I'm not certain where she's staying, exactly.''

Henri's dark eyebrows snapped together. ''What do you mean? I thought you said she was here.''

''She is. Right here in the hotel. That's a fact. I followed her here myself, but I couldn't follow her inside because I was dressed like a drunk from the Channel. I got cleaned up and came over as quickly as I could, but when I checked at the desk just now, there was no Lisette Antilly registered.''

''Damn!''

''Oh, that's no problem. It's obvious she's using an assumed name.''

An assumed name. Somehow, Henri couldn't imagine Lisette being devious enough to think of using a name other than her own.

''Donaldson and I will just watch the comings and goings at the front door. It won't be hard spotting her. She looked like an angel. Smelled like an angel, too,'' he said, closing his eyes as if doing so would sharpen the memory. ''After smelling the slaughterhouse for months on end, the scent of lilacs was a welcome treat. Most welcome.''

Lilacs. The word exploded in Henri's mind and reminded him of his earlier run-in with the widow in the rotunda.

She, too, had smelled of lilacs. Suddenly the intangible feeling that something he couldn't quite grasp was at his fingertips became as clear as the crystal decanters residing on the marble bar downstairs.

Anxious to be rid of the Pinkerton agent, Henri smiled and slapped the man on the back. "You've done well, Arnold. I'm sure it won't take but a day or so to get her."

"Shall we pick her up?"

"No. When you find out where she is, come to me. I'd like to confront her myself."

"That's a little unorthodox, sir," Massey said with a frown.

"Perhaps. But it isn't as if she's a hardened criminal," Henri said with a confident smile. "She'll come along nicely once she knows she has no choice. I'd like the satisfaction of turning her over to Sheriff Purcell myself."

As he spoke, Henri ushered the operative toward the door, indicating that the interview was over. "Tell Donaldson there will be a nice bonus for you both."

"Yes, sir, I will," Massey said, though he still didn't look convinced. "Thank you."

The door had no sooner clicked shut than Henri threw his head back and laughed. Damn, but the girl was clever!

The clue had been quite literally under his nose all along. He drew a monogrammed handkerchief from his pocket and wiped at his eyes. Lilacs. He'd smelled them the day at Magnolia Manor when he'd run into the nun. It was their sweet scent that had tantalized him in the kitchen of Belle Maison the night Dodie had supposedly been up with her rheumatism. He'd smelled them again just a few hours ago, when he'd collided with the widow downstairs.

Lilacs. Lisette's favorite scent. Henri chuckled again. Who would have dreamed when Lisette flew the coop that she would fool him—and the world for that matter—so easily, so completely? But then, who would have dreamed that she'd come to roost seven miles from home and hide herself behind the robes of a nun?

Chapter Thirty-Four

Nate's eagerness to pay back Henri for what he'd done to the Antilly sisters was diminished by the worry that had plagued him ever since Lisette's close brush with her stepfather in the rotunda earlier that afternoon.

After he'd given her the clothes that morning, Nate hadn't expected to see her until the moment he handed her the deed to Belle Maison. But when he'd looked toward the lunch table, there she'd stood, no more than fifteen feet away, her eyes filled with the same surprise at seeing him as he himself felt.

Seeing Maria with him, she'd turned away, as if she were…what? Nate swore. He was fooling himself if he imagined Lisette might have felt the slightest bit jealous. Still, he'd been cursing the Fates when he witnessed her collision with her stepfather.

Fear that Henri would recognize her despite her masquerade had made Nate's mouth go dry. He hadn't drawn an easy breath until he was certain Henri's only interest was in the terrapin soup. Nate watched Lisette's escape up the spiral stairs and saw her look his way. He hadn't been able to see her features, but his heart imagined that she was looking down at him and the woman on his arm with sadness.

Buoyed by several drinks and the knowledge that Lisette and her sister were within arm's reach, Henri dressed for the poker game with extra care. The news that she had been found only proved what he'd known all week: luck was with him. He'd been playing well, and he anticipated that tonight would bring more money into his depleted coffers. Paying the Pinkerton agency to find his stepdaughters hadn't been cheap, but it was money well spent. As soon as he finished with Lisette, the law would rid him of both the twits. Belle Maison would be his, and he would continue his pursuit of Patrice and her generous legacy.

Henri laughed. The smell of victory was sweet indeed. As a matter of fact, victory had the distinct odor of lilacs.

Properly chastened by her run-in with Henri, Lisette stayed close to her room. She'd hoped that when Silvie awoke she would be as anxious to catch up on Lisette's news as Lisette was to hear what had happened to Silvie during their winter of separation. But her sister had offered no tales and answered Lisette's questions lethargically, if at all.

While Silvie seemed eager to rid the scent of the Channel from her body and the snarls from her freshly washed hair, she was less anxious to submit to Lisette's ministrations. She had always been an independent sort, and no doubt part of her embarrassment had to do with her advanced pregnancy. Whatever her reasons, Lisette knew that had it not been for Silvie's poor physical condition, she would never have allowed Lisette's help.

As it was, Silvie sat with her eyes closed while Lisette scrubbed her skin to a healthy rose and dried it with gentle pats. Though she was far too thin, she looked more like her old self. Dirty skin had been washed clean. The scent of lilacs had replaced the cloying stench of the slaughterhouse. She wore freshly laundered nightclothes instead of the filthy garb Lisette had found her wearing.

Her outward appearance was much improved, but the vacant look in her eyes was the same, and it tugged at Lisette's heart. The spirited girl who had left Belle Maison in October with a bundle of clothes and a thirst for adventure was gone. Lisette could only pray that with care and love the Silvie she knew would someday return.

Ensconced before the fire, which had been lighted at dusk, Silvie submitted as Lisette brushed her damp hair and clipped away the worst of the tangles. She worked patiently, using her fingers and a comb to free a particularly stubborn snarl and quoting a teasing line their mother had used during their childhood.

"Here, kitty, kitty, kitty. Come get the rats out of Silvie's hair."

Hoping for a positive response, Lisette glanced at her sister's reflection in the cheval glass situated across from them. But instead of the smile she longed to see, twin tears slid down Silvie's pale cheeks. Laying the comb on the mantel, Lisette slipped her arms around her sister's shoulders and cradled her damp head against her breasts.

The tears started then...finally. Lisette's heart broke into a million pieces as harsh sobs racked Silvie's body, filling the room with her despair. Lisette rested her cheek against her sister's head and whispered words of comfort and love to her. Then, catching a glimpse of them in the oval glass, she closed her own eyes against the portrait of sorrow mirrored there.

The tap at the door came sometime after midnight, long after Lisette had helped Silvie between the clean sheets, long after Silvie's tears had dried and the occasional sob had ceased to shake her body. Ready for bed but certain she would never fall asleep, Lisette was dozing in a chair. The light knock intruded on a troubled dream of Henri chasing her and Silvie through the swamps, a pack of hounds close on their heels. She was thankful to open her eyes and find it was only a dream.

Giving a sigh of relief, she rose and went to the door. Nate stood there, dazzling in his dark dress clothes, a reckless look in his blue eyes. His gaze swept past her, found Silvie's form on the bed and came back to rest on Lisette. With the terrifying remnants of the dream still seeming to be real, she admitted to herself that she was inordinately glad to see him.

"You found her, I see."

"Yes."

"Why didn't you tell me?"

"I tried," she said, recalling her chance encounter with him and the woman in the rotunda. "You were... occupied."

Nate knew better than to try to explain. His gaze went to Silvie once more. "How is she?"

Lisette shrugged and, despite her efforts to halt them, tears filled her eyes. Monitoring the minor skirmish between her will and her feelings and gauging that her feelings were losing, Nate drew her into the hall and closed the door to her room.

"Come with me," he said, taking her hand and pulling her along with him. He half dragged her to his suite, where he indicated that she take a seat on the sofa. He poured them both a drink from the crystal decanter and pressed one into her cold hands. "Drink."

"You're always trying to make me drink."

A memory of the last time she'd made a similar statement tempered their present problems. Awareness sprang up between them as quickly as a grass fire in August. Hunger glittered in his eyes, but he masked his emotions by lifting his glass in a silent salute.

"You're always in need of it," he quipped, taking a generous swallow. He grimaced, clenching his strong white teeth against the bite of the liquor. "Have you called a doctor?"

The sudden shift in topic caught Lisette off guard. "Doctor? Oh, for Silvie. Yes. I had Levi bring one this afternoon."

Nate cocked a heavy eyebrow. "And?"

"He says that she has a fever, that she's malnourished, and that the baby will be here soon."

"I'm sorry she's had such a hard time," he said gently.

"She won't talk to me about it, but the place we found her was terrible. Terrible." Lisette pressed her lips together to hold back the threat of tears.

"Perhaps getting back home will make her better."

Home? Was Nate referring to Magnolia Manor or Belle Maison? Had he done what he said he would? Had he won back her home?

He set his glass to the tabletop and reached into the breast pocket of his frock coat. Lisette's heart leaped as he drew out some folded papers and handed them to her. Hardly daring to hope, she took them with hands that trembled. She skimmed the documents, and a wide smile banished the sadness from her eyes. It was the deed to Belle Maison! Silvie would be thrilled. They would go back and...

Lisette's euphoria vanished like a wisp of smoke in the wind. The deed had been signed over to Nathan Garrett Rambler, not Lisette Antilly. Had she misunderstood, then? Had she misunderstood that Nate was going to win back the plantation for her, just as she'd misunderstood the night they'd spent together?

A memory of his flirting with the woman earlier that

afternoon flashed through her mind. Had she truly believed the few short months with her and the Krueger children had changed a man like Nathan Rambler? Had she truly thought he would sign over the plantation to her for a night in his bed?

She raised her eyes to his. "Henri signed Belle Maison over to you." Her voice was low, strained.

"That's right."

"I...thought if you...won the plantation back, it was to be mine," she said.

A muscle jumped in Nate's jaw. His British accent, which she hardly noticed anymore, was back. "Are you implying that I'm not a man of my word?"

"I'm not...implying anything."

"Of course you are." His voice was as cold as the ice served in the drinks downstairs, as flat as the slick marble of the bar. "You want your damned plantation, and you'll have it, love, but not until I have what I want."

Her face drained of color, yet Lisette didn't know why she was so shocked. She'd known the terms. He had been more than clear about what he wanted in return for the plantation, and she had never expected him to act the gentleman and forfeit his demand.

Nor, she realized with a start, had she really wanted him to. "When?" Her voice was as soft as the caress of the wind against his skin.

"Now."

He took a step toward her. Reaching out, he slipped a callused hand beneath the heavy weight of her hair. His fingers were warm against her neck.

"Not after you've entertained another woman all afternoon," she said, trying to break free.

He held her with a look. "Now."

"What's the matter?" Lisette taunted as he drew her nearer. "Didn't she satisfy you?"

"That's really immaterial," he told her in a silky voice. "The question is, will you please me enough to make me sign those papers?"

"You never said anything about pleasing you. Only that I had to...give you one more night."

Nate's smile was crooked, mocking. "Surely you didn't think I'd be happy with a stick in my bed, now did you?"

Of course she hadn't. Nor had she expected that she could keep from responding to him.

"Why don't you kiss me and show me what's in store for the remainder of the night?" he suggested, drawing her into the V of his hard thighs.

Lisette shook her head in denial, but even as she did, excitement spread like warm honey throughout her body. His head moved toward hers. Their lips touched, and she felt herself being drawn into a montage of sensations: the scent of his skin; the taste of whiskey and cigars; the feel of bone and sinew beneath her clinging fingertips.

She melted against him and threw back her head to grant his marauding mouth access to her throat.

"Heaven help me, I want you," he groaned against her soft flesh.

The confession loosed the band of pain that had held her in its grip ever since she'd seen him with the strange woman. Responding involuntarily to the power that swept through her, she twined her hands in the thick silkiness of his hair and dragged his mouth to hers once more.

A slight shudder quaked through him. He kissed her long. Deeply. Sipping the sweet nectar from her lips, his stroking tongue dipped inside her mouth and stoked the fires of her need, branding her with the taste and the feel of him.

Silvie was forgotten. Henri did not exist. Belle Maison was a distant memory. Promises of not falling in love were replaced with the reality that she had. Dear God, she had.

Reality was the taste of Nate's lips, the magical touch of his hands and the need growing inside her.

He swung her up into his arms and carried her into his bedroom, where he placed her on the bed and pressed her into the soft down of the mattress with the weight of his body.

"You want me, too," he murmured against her ear. "Say you want me."

Denying the truth would be denying the next beat of her heart, her next breath.

"I do. I do." The words were groaned between feverish kisses that robbed her of breath and sanity. "I do."

Chapter Thirty-Five

Lisette awoke surrounded by warmth. She opened her eyes to find that she lay half sprawled across Nate's body. Her cheek rested against his chest, and one of her legs was wedged intimately between his. Even in sleep, his hand cupped her breast in a possessive way. Remembering how his mouth had laid claim to every part of her body and how she had explored every inch of his, she felt a rekindling of the desire he was so expert at igniting.

Despite her vow never to love, despite the unknown woman, despite the fact that she meant little to him beyond this, the night had been glorious. Needing to touch him, Lisette laid her hand against his cheek. He smiled in his sleep, and she felt a sharp pain shoot through her heart.

The night he demanded was over now, and he wanted nothing more from her. Careful not to wake him, Lisette disengaged herself from his arms, eased off the high four-poster and dragged her wrapper over her bare arms.

Morning crept into Nate's room as she crept out. Sneaking back into the room where Silvie slept, she donned her widow's garb as quietly as possible. She had to have some time away from Nate to think about what she had done and what she was going to do. Perhaps she could find some solace in the dawn of a new day. Thrusting some coins into her reticule, she let herself out of the room and started for the stairs.

As per his instructions, which were relayed late the following evening, Arnold Massey was stationed across the street, waiting for Duschene's stepdaughter to show herself. The planter had called him back to his room and told him he believed Lisette Antilly was masquerading as either a nun or a widow. Sure enough, the hotel registry had a Mrs. Raoul Depardieu listed, and she was indeed a widow.

Since it was hardly feasible to knock on every door in the hotel to see which room she occupied, the only alternative was keeping an eye out for her, and Massey was heartily sick of spying. He could have paid the night clerk to supply her room number, but he liked to keep from arousing suspicions whenever possible. The man might have felt guilty and warned her that some stranger was asking questions.

Massey smothered a yawn. At least he didn't have to associate with the kind who made their home in the Channel, and he could sleep in his own bed at night. As a matter of fact, he'd gotten really good rest the night before and had just come on duty to replace Donaldson.

The early-morning sun was creeping over the buildings in the east, and the early risers were starting to head for the French Market, eight or nine blocks away. He was debating whether or not to risk slipping down the street to the bakery for a cup of *café au lait* and some *beignets* when a flash of black in front of the St. Louis Hotel snagged his attention. Damnation! It was the widow! What if he'd been inside the bakery and missed her?

Vacillating between going after her himself or going to get Duschene, Massey watched as Lisette Antilly headed south toward Chartres Street. After a brief hesitation, he crossed the street and stepped inside the hotel. Duschene had made it clear that he wanted this done his way. Far be it from Arnold Massey to cross the man.

When Silvie was certain Lisette wasn't coming back, she climbed from the bed and availed herself of some of the bread and cheese wrapped in a napkin on the dresser. The knowledge that she had basic human comforts again brought tears to her eyes. Thank God Lisette had come for her.

She carried her breakfast to the window and looked out. Down below, a variety of birds scrambled for sustenance in the dirt street. As she watched, Lisette exited the hotel. Furtively, it seemed to Silvie, a man stepped out of the doorway of a building across the street and stood watching Lisette. The frisson of fear that trickled down Silvie's spine dissipated when the man ignored Lisette and crossed the street to the hotel.

Her stomach growled, and she tore off a bite of bread, the incident forgotten in the pleasure of having food again. Perhaps, she thought with a feeling of anticipation, Lisette would bring back some *beignets*. It would be nice to share a sweet with her sister.

The months since they had separated at Thibodaux had been a long, unending nightmare that Silvie had soon realized was of her own making. She'd been a fool to leave the convent. Boredom, however excruciating, was preferable to the indignities she had suffered on the mean streets of New Orleans.

She had learned many lessons, among them the fact that the pleasure of giving her body to a man of her choosing was a far different matter than having a man—any man—pay for the pleasure of using her body. As she'd lain sick and starving in the burned-out dry goods store, knowing that death awaited her, she realized that her own willful nature had, perhaps, cost her her life.

When she had roused enough to know that Lisette had come to her rescue, Silvie's first thought had been relief. The second had been shame, from which she could see no relief. She knew Lisette wanted to talk, to find out what had brought her to this end, but Silvie hadn't wanted to dredge up the memories. She'd wanted to forget. She hadn't wanted Lisette to look at her with pity and revulsion, or worse, disappointment. She'd disappointed her far too often as it was.

But Lisette hadn't berated her for the things she'd done. She had fed her and bathed her and held her in her arms while they cried for the loss of their innocence. Last night, for the first time in a long time, Silvie had fallen asleep knowing that tomorrow would be better.

Waking in the night, she had discovered that she was alone in the hotel room. She'd wondered where Lisette could be, but until she had returned a few moments ago wearing nothing but her wrapper, Silvie hadn't realized Lisette had been with a man.

Shocked, Silvie had lain there, feigning sleep, until her sister left. It hadn't seemed the time to admit she was awake. Lisette would be embarrassed, and Silvie did not want her sister's kindness repaid with embarrassment. She wondered whose bed her sister had slept in and what kind of man he was. Who was he? Where had they met? He would be someone very special, that much was certain. Lisette would settle for nothing less.

Her hunger satisfied at last, Silvie put another piece of wood on the fire to chase the early-morning chill from the room. Wandering back to the window, she pushed aside the billow of lace and looked out once more. Sunlight slanted through the narrow cracks separating the buildings. Across the narrow street two men stood, engrossed in conversation.

There was something familiar about them both, she thought, pressing her nose to the glass. Very familiar.

Then she realized that the man facing her was the same man she'd seen cross the street when Lisette had left the hotel. For no accountable reason, Silvie's heart began to pound heavily in her chest. She told herself there was no reason for concern. There was nothing menacing about him. He was just an average, nondescript sort of man. It was his companion, the man whose back was to her who was at the root of her discomfort. Something about him reminded her of Henri.

The child growing inside her kicked, as if to reject the thought. The other man made a wild gesture. That too reminded her of someone, but for the life of her, she couldn't think of who that someone was. As she strained to see, the dark-haired man turned and started in the direction the other man had pointed, his profile thrown into stark relief against the brick building.

Gasping in shock and fearful of being seen, Silvie took an automatic step away from the window. Her intuition had proved correct. The man who was headed in the same direction Lisette had gone was none other than her stepfather.

Silvie wrung her hands. Dear God, what was he doing here? How had he found her? Before she could consider those tormented thoughts, a new fear made her quake: Lisette. Had the man in the brown suit been watching? Was Henri going after Lisette?

Silvie moved cautiously back to the window. The man in the brown derby was still standing there, watching Henri's departure. After a moment, he started down the street in a jaunty strut. Silvie's eyes drifted shut in denial. Though the stranger looked far different than he had the last time she'd seen him, she would have recognized that strut anywhere. She'd seen it every day for the past two months. The man across the street, the man who had sent

Henri in the same direction Lisette had gone was Thomas Baird, the drunk who had lived near her on Adele Street.

Silvie backed away from the window and crawled back into bed with the sudden realization that she had been fooled. The man's name might be Thomas Baird, but she was one hundred percent certain he wasn't a drunk. He was someone in Henri's employ.

Chapter Thirty-Six

Nate awoke slowly, memories of the night tantalizing the sleep-fogged recesses of his mind. Lisette. He reached out to draw her nearer, but instead of touching warm woman, his hand encountered the smooth, cool cotton of the sheet. His eyes sprang open and confirmed the fact that Lisette was gone. Disappointment knifed through him. Regardless of the way he'd gotten her into his bed, he had hoped that once she was there she would see how much he loved her. He sank back onto the pillow and threw his forearm over his face. So much for hopes.

Sweet heaven, was there another like her? She roused more emotions in him than any woman ever had. She brought out the best in him, the gentle consideration he hadn't known he possessed before she came into his life. She infuriated him. She intrigued him. She made him smile. And her kisses inflamed him to a passion he'd only dreamed of.

He loved her. But loving her didn't erase the fact that she had used him to get possession of her precious plantation. Like his father, like Karl Krueger, the possession of things—whether they be lands or titles—was more important to her than it ought to be.

Could she change? Damn it, she had to. What he felt for her was too special not to hold on to. It was time to confront her with his feelings. He would find out once and for all if she was the woman his heart said she was.

As she'd prayed it would, the beauty of the spring morning brought a measure of peace to Lisette's heart. God was in his heaven and all was right with her world. She had found her sister. Belle Maison was once again in Antilly hands, and she was in love. Love. She hadn't wanted it to happen, but there it was, as Dodie would say.

She was in love with Nathan Rambler, a known gambler. A ladies' man. A man whose touch caused her blood to speed recklessly through her veins. Giving herself to him that first time had been foolish, yet even then, she'd known she could no more stop herself from making love with him than she could stop herself from falling in love with him.

The problem was what to do about the current state of affairs. Should she confront him about his intentions before they left New Orleans, or should she bide her time, wait until she and Silvie took up residence at Belle Maison and hope he came courting?

Calling herself a ninny and a fool, Lisette forced the quandary from her mind and tried to take pleasure in the world around her. People were gathered in droves, seeking the freshest fish and vegetables, haggling over prices and laughing because it was spring and they were glad to be alive.

She spied some ripening bananas and some exotic-looking fruits she didn't recognize. Silvie would love a banana, and it would be good for her. Lisette rounded the corner of a vegetable stand and started to select a half-dozen of the yellow-green fruits from the huge bunch when she felt something jab her in the ribs.

As she turned to see what was happening, a familiar

voice said, "Hello, Sister Dominique. Or should I call you the widow Depardieu?"

Henri. Lisette dropped the bananas and her heart sank to her toes. A thousand thoughts—none of them pleasant—raced through her mind. What was he doing out so early? How had he found out she was masquerading as a nun? How had he known she was at the French Market?"

"How did you find me?" she asked, turning to face him.

"I have my ways." His fingers bit into her upper arm. "Come along quietly, and I won't hurt you."

Glancing down, she saw that Henri had a small-caliber gun pointed at her middle. She looked askance at the vendor who was old and crippled with rheumatism. He would be no help. Henri gave her arm a hard jerk and started toward Decatur Street at a fast pace.

"I've given this situation a lot of thought," he said in a conversational tone. "The real nun was killed in the boat explosion, of course, and you took her place. It would have been easy enough to fool Rambler. He isn't accustomed to nuns." Henri chuckled. "Actually, that was a very clever move, Lisette. Very clever indeed. Pretending to be a nun, right under my nose."

"How did you find out?"

Henri guided them toward the Place d'Armes. "Always so curious! Don't you know that curiosity killed the cat?"

"Don't play games with me! Tell me how you figured out who I was and how you found out I was staying at the hotel."

He turned to look at her, and another smile slid across his face. "Vanity, my dear. Vanity."

"What do you mean?'

"I hired an operative to keep an eye on Silvie. I knew you'd try to find her sooner or later, and I was right. He was there when you brought Silvie out of the building on Adele Street."

"The drunk!" Lisette said in disbelief.

"The same," Henri acknowledged with a nod. "He followed you back to the hotel, but he couldn't find you registered as Lisette Antilly. He told me he'd traced you that far, and then he made a strange comment about your smelling like lilacs."

Henri stopped in front of the St. Louis Cathedral and looked down at her. "Suddenly it all fell into place. Each time you and I ran into each other, I knew there was something familiar, something I should know. It was the scent of lilacs, but I didn't realize it until the Pinkerton agent mentioned that you smelled of lilacs when you found Silvie. Perhaps if you weren't so vain, Lisette, you'd still be free."

Lisette didn't comment. She was too busy damning the vanity he was talking about and wondering how she could get word to Nate that she was in Henri's clutches.

"What I haven't figured out yet is how you talked Nate Rambler into bringing you here," Henri said.

"It was easy enough," she said, raising her chin. "We struck a deal."

"You and Rambler were in this together?" he asked, sweeping her with a shrewd gaze.

Lisette nodded. "He set you up to lose the plantation from the first day we arrived. Now that he's won it, he's signing it over to me."

She was surprised to see the frown creasing his forehead smooth and his smile return. "He's signing Belle Maison over to you, but what did you have to give him, hmm, Lisette? One night in his bed? Two? Or does he plan to keep you around a while?"

"That's none of your concern!"

"Oh, but it is." He brushed his knuckles across the sweep of one cheekbone. "You see, I'd planned on taking you myself."

"I'd die first!"

The look in Henri's eyes hardened, and he dropped the role of cajoling captor. "Never fear. I'll not take Nathan Rambler's leavings."

Rage prevented Lisette from answering.

"You think you're so smart," he said. "Well, you might not think so when I put you and your sister behind bars for trying to kill me."

"Your threats don't frighten me," Lisette said with a lift of her chin. "Besides, I told Nate the truth about what you did to Silvie and me."

For the first time since he'd confronted her, Lisette saw Henri's confidence slip.

"You told Rambler about Silvie?"

Lisette looked him straight in the eye. "About Silvie and *Maman.* You won't get away with this, any more than you got away with stealing our home from us, father dear."

Henri's breath escaped in a slow hiss. "You scheming bitch!" he snarled. "May you be damned to everlasting perdition."

"Perhaps I shall be," she said with a nonchalance she was far from feeling, "but I will take great consolation in knowing you're right beside me."

Silvie paced the room, waiting. During the hour that had passed since she saw the two men across the street, she had given the situation considerable thought. If the man she called Thomas Baird knew Lisette was in the hotel, he must know that she was, too.

Even though Silvie was worried about Lisette, she knew she was in no condition to follow Henri. Even if she chanced to find them, she could do nothing to prevent him from harming her sister. Considering all she had been through, Silvie reasoned that there was no sense leaving the safety of the hotel room and making herself a prime target for Henri's henchman.

As she did every few moments, she went to the window and looked out. Precious minutes were ticking by, but she had no choice but to wait. The task of rescuing Lisette would have to fall to someone more capable than she. It would have to fall to Lisette's lover, only Silvie had no idea who he was or how to contact him. But she knew the man, whoever he was, would come looking for Lisette sooner or later.

As if in answer to her thoughts, someone knocked at the door. Whirling toward the sound, Silvie placed a hand to her throat to still the pulse pounding there.

"Who's there?"

"Nate Rambler."

Silvie closed her eyes. Nate Rambler? That was no help.

"I'm looking for Lisette, Silvie."

Surprise brought her head up and headed her footsteps toward the door. He knew her name. "She isn't here."

"Where is she?" There was a sharpness in his voice that had been absent a second before.

"I don't know."

"Open the door. Please. I won't hurt you."

"How can I be sure?" she asked, tears of frustration forming in her eyes.

"Because I know what Henri did to you, and I came here with Lisette to take you home."

There was warmth in his voice. And calm. Even after all the lies Henri had told her and after all the indignities other men had put her through, she believed him. Turning the key in the lock, she opened the door.

The man standing before her was tall and broad shouldered. It was easy to see why Lisette had fallen for him.

"Where's Lisette?" he asked without preamble.

Silvie shook her head. "I don't know. She came in earlier to dress, but we didn't talk. I saw her head toward Chartres Street.''

Nate frowned. ''Do you think she was going to the French Market?''

''I don't know, but I do know that when I looked out the window later, I saw Henri heading that way, too.''

Chapter Thirty-Seven

Going on the assumption that Henri meant to do Lisette harm, Nate scoured the French Market, the Place d'Armes and every small shop between there and the hotel. Finding no sign of either, he returned to break the news to Silvie, who began to cry.

By midafternoon, he was wild with worry. By evening, he was ready to kill Duschene with his bare hands. He was pacing the floor of his suite and wondering what to do next, when a porter brought him a message. Ripping open the envelope, he drew out the note and devoured its contents. Then he swore, crumpled the letter and tossed it into the ashes of the dead fire.

"He's taken Lisette back to Belle Maison."

"Why?"

"Basically, he wants money. He's going to hold her until I tell him I'll give it to him."

Silvie's eyes filled with tears. "What are you going to do?"

"Give him what he wants, of course."

Nate drew on his coat and went downstairs, intent on making arrangements for him and Levi to go back to Magnolia Manor immediately. When he arrived at the station, he learned there were no more trains leaving New Orleans until early the following morning.

It didn't take much imagination to figure out that Henri had ordered the message delivered late in the day to guarantee him a day's head start. Nate had no choice but to wait until morning.

Then he remembered Silvie. What would he do with her? His heart told him to rush to Lisette's aid, but his head told him that Henri wouldn't harm her…at least not unless his scheme fell through. Nate also knew that after moving heaven and hell to find Silvie, Lisette would want him to care for her. He could not, in all good conscience, leave Silvie to her own devices in New Orleans, which meant he now had to go and shop for something she could wear on the journey.

Though Nate would not have gone back to his old way of living for anything, it seemed that the more responsibility he accepted, the more was heaped on him. Damning Henri Duschene, Nate bought three tickets for the following day and stormed back to the hotel. If Henri hurt Lisette, he would be sorry. Very sorry.

Worry was at its peak and patience was in short supply two days later, when Nate drove a flatbed wagon slowly into the lane that led to Magnolia Manor. The train ride had been no problem, but because she was still weak and sick, Silvie had been exhausted when they arrived, and he had been forced to stay in Thibodaux for the night. As soon as Silvie and Levi had been settled for the night, Nate had sent two messages: one to Henri at Belle Maison, which was just two short miles away, and one to Sheriff Purcell, who was, according to the deputy, out for the afternoon.

Rising as early as he felt would be acceptable for Silvie, Nate had driven them back to the depot, where he rented a flatbed wagon from Alvin Sturges. Together, he and Levi made a bed in the back so the weary Silvie could lie down. The nine-mile journey from Thibodaux to the plantation took the better part of the day. Alone, on horseback, Nate could have made the trip from Thibodaux in half the time. The road was bumpy, and he drove so slowly it seemed that they crawled. Even Silvie's bed must have been uncomfortable after the first couple of hours.

As he pulled into the lane and saw the familiar buildings and the fields of cane stubble, a poignant feeling of homecoming swept through him. It was good to be back. The children, who must have been watching for him, raced out the door. When he dismounted from the wagon, Monika and Heidi threw themselves at him, demanding hugs. Franz and Karl were more circumspect with their greetings, settling for brisk handshakes.

"Where's Sister Dominique?" Heidi asked.

"She'll be coming along later." Nate met Karl's gaze, and the younger man's eyes seemed to say that he knew something was wrong. Nate introduced Silvie to the Krueger clan and instructed Heidi to have Sadie ready a room downstairs. He didn't miss the curiosity on their faces or the questions reflected in their eyes, though they were polite.

Once Levi had carried in the luggage and Silvie was resting, with nothing to worry about but Sadie's hovering, Nate called the children into his study.

"I know you're wondering what's going on and who Silvie Antilly is." He poured an inch of *tafia* into a glass and took a swallow. "Silvie is Sister Dominique's sister, but Sister Dominique isn't really a nun at all. She is Lisette Antilly."

He could tell by the confused looks on their faces he was bungling the story. Closing his eyes, he pinched the bridge of his nose between his thumb and forefinger against a headache that was coming on.

"Where's Sister Dominique?" Monika wailed, tears in her eyes.

Nate gave the child a smile. "She's at Belle Maison."

"What's she doing there?" Karl asked.

Nate sighed. Perhaps he should tell the whole story, excluding, of course, all the salient details of Silvie's affair with her stepfather. It would be easy enough to paint Henri as a villain without making Silvie look bad.

"Lisette Antilly—whom we know as Sister Dominique—and Silvie, are sisters. When their father died, several years ago, their mother married Henri Duschene."

In as condensed a version as possible, Nate told them of Henri's "advances," of the argument where he'd fallen down the stairs, and the Antilly girls' flight from their home. He explained how Lisette happened to "become" Sister Dominique and told of Silvie's journey to the convent in New Orleans, omitting, for the younger Krueger's sensibilities, Silvie's descent into prostitution and thievery. He told of Silvie seeing her stepfather follow Lisette and how Henri had later sent the note, requiring one last game of cards to settle forever the issue between him and his stepdaughters.

At the end of the tale, Franz proclaimed the man insane and asked if he could have an apple before dinner. Heidi shuddered at the thought that Henri had stayed beneath their very roof. Monika was busy plucking leaves from a plant. Only Karl looked concerned and thoughtful.

"Whose child is Silvie carrying?" he asked when the door closed behind his siblings.

Nate considered the question and decided that Karl was old enough for the truth. After all, Karl had been playing a dangerous game himself.

"It's Henri's child."

"Did he...force her?"

"No," Nate said, opting for the truth. "But he seduced

her. He lied to her, flattered her and told her he loved her, when all he wanted was the pleasure she could give him."

"He should be shot!" Karl said angrily. "She's a beautiful girl, and her reputation, perhaps her very life, is ruined."

Nate realized suddenly that what Karl was saying could be applied to the situation with Lisette. Was he, Nathan Rambler, any different from Henri Duschene? Or Karl? Like Henri, he had seduced an innocent woman and made her no promises. What would he do if Lisette were with child? What would she do?

"That's what you were talking about, isn't it?" Karl asked.

The question intruded on Nate's self-castigation. "I beg your pardon."

"You were trying to make me see that the very thing that has happened to Silvie, could happen to Sara."

"Yes."

Karl offered a sheepish grin. "It's easy to see mistakes when they're someone else's, isn't it?"

"Very."

Karl went to the window and stared out. He turned suddenly. "Is Sister Dom—Lisette—in danger?"

"I hope not. But I'm inclined to agree with Franz that the man is less than stable."

"You care for her, don't you?"

Nate couldn't hide his surprise. He nodded.

"Then why aren't you riding hell for leather to save her?" Karl asked.

"Because Duschene is a little crazy, I think it's best to play it his way for the time being. He wants cards—we'll play cards. When Silvie and I got off the train in Thibodaux, I sent a message setting up the game for tonight, right here at Magnolia Manor."

"Do you think you can win?"

"I have to, wouldn't you say?"

Lisette heard the scraping of the key in the lock. She'd been back in her old home, her old room, for more than two days, a virtual prisoner to Henri and his whims. All she'd had to eat was johnnycake and water, and precious little of that. Hoping it was Dodie with something more substantial, she put the calico cat she was holding onto the bed and went to the door. But instead of the aging black woman, Henri stood in the aperture, tossing the key in his hand.

"Resting?"

"Trying to. I might be able to rest better if it weren't for the growling of my stomach."

"Hungry, are you?" he asked with a lift of his brows. "Well, perhaps I'll have Dodie bring you something later."

"That would be decent of you," Lisette said with extreme sarcasm. "What's going to happen to me—besides starvation, of course?"

"I doubt that missing a meal or two will cause you to starve." He smiled the smile that turned her stomach. "As to what I'm going to do with you, well, that depends on your lover."

"Nate?"

"Ah, you admit it, I see."

"Why shouldn't I?" she asked, too weary to argue with him.

"Why, indeed? At any rate, I have informed Mr. Rambler that you are with me, and I have invited him to play one last game of cards to settle this unfortunate situation once and for all."

"You want to play cards?"

"Now, Lisette, what better way for two gamblers to settle their differences? I had given him a time limit to let me know whether or not he agreed to my terms, and I'd begun to think that perhaps he didn't care for you after all. However, I just received word that we're to play this evening at his place. It seems I misjudged the depth of his feelings for you."

"What kind of terms?" she asked warily.

"If I win, Rambler will give me twenty-five thousand dollars." Henri drew a fountain pen and a piece of paper from his breast pocket.

To hide her agitation, Lisette went to the bed and picked up the cat. Holding the soft warmth of the animal against her cheek, she asked, "And what happens if you lose?"

"If I lose, I'll get out of your lives for good." He thrust the paper and pen at her. The tabby hissed and struck out at his hand, leaving a thin groove that quickly welled with blood.

Jerking back his hand, Henri swore and raised his knuckle to his lips. Bestowing a malignant look on the cat, he placed the papers on the edge of the bed. "Sign this. I must be on my way."

"What is it?"

"It's an agreement that says that if your lover wins, you won't prosecute me for your kidnapping or for any other...crimes you may have thought I committed."

Lisette shook her head, unable to believe the man's gall. Did he think he could erase the sins he had committed against her and her family so easily?

"Crimes like killing my mother?"

He gave a disbelieving cluck. "Such a suspicious child!"

In an act of defiance, Lisette swept the paper and pen to the floor. "Spare me the lies and half truths," she said in a voice that throbbed with pain. "I know you killed her."

Henri's smile faded, and his voice grew soft with menace. "Then you also know that if you don't do as I say, I can do the same to you. And don't forget Silvie, my dear.

With you gone, who will see after her and her bastard child?''

The look in his eyes told her that he would have no qualms about killing either of them. Freeing the cat, she stooped and picked up the paper and pen. Hating him and herself, she signed her name and handed back the agreement.

''Thank you,'' Henri said cordially, refolding the paper and returning it to his pocket. He swaggered to the door and swung it wide. ''Don't wait up, Lisette,'' he said, as if it mattered. ''I'll probably stop by Patrice's place to celebrate.''

Chapter Thirty-Eight

From her vantage point in her old room, Lisette stroked the cat and watched Henri take his leave, the agreement he'd forced her to sign secure in his pocket. She hated giving in to him, but it would be so wonderful to have him out of her life that the compromise was almost worth it. But if things went according to the tentative plan forming in her mind, it wouldn't matter anyway.

She had toyed with the idea of escaping, but Henri saw to it that the doors were securely locked—with the key in his pocket—and the windows nailed shut. If it were summertime, she'd be smothering. As it was, the room was uncomfortably warm.

With Henri gone for the night, she might have a chance. Lisette figured that if Dodie could get the door unlocked, it would be simple enough to take a horse from the barn and ride into Thibodaux for Sheriff Purcell. Surely he would believe her. Even if he didn't, perhaps she could convince him to take her to Magnolia Manor where Nate and Silvie could corroborate her allegations against Henri.

"Lisette? It's me, honey. I come to let you out."

The sound of Dodie's voice gave hope to Lisette's plan and brought a smile to her face. There was a scratching in the lock, the knob turned, and Dodie tottered in, carrying a tray with two biscuits, a glass of milk and a bowl of grits with milk and butter floating on top. More precious than the food was the wide smile wreathing the black woman's face and the love in her eyes.

Dodie set the tray on the dresser, and Lisette was folded into a warm embrace. For the moment, food and hunger were forgotten.

"How did you unlock the door?"

Dodie held up a long hairpin. "It's easy if you know how. Are you all right, child?"

Lisette smiled. "I'm fine," she said, shooing the cat away from the tray and picking up a biscuit and the milk. "I'm hungry, though."

"Humph! This ain't much. I fixed some hot grits and bacon drippings and took 'em out to that sick houn'dog of Hank's. When I come back in, the master had dished you up a bowl and tol' me to bring 'em up to you. I wish it was fried chicken."

"It's fine," Lisette assured her. She took a sip of her milk. "I found Silvie."

"No!"

Lisette nodded, and her smile broadened. "When Henri and I left, she was at the hotel with Nate Rambler. I'm sure he'll bring her back with him."

"Is she all right, then?"

"Not really," she said, her smile fading.

"What's the matter?"

Lisette set the milk and biscuit back on the tray, not even noticing that the cat was busy lapping up the warm grits.

"She was living on the street when Levi and I found her. She's sick, and the baby could come anytime." She took a deep breath and forced a brightness she didn't feel to her voice. "But she'll be better soon. All she needs is love and care."

"And we'll sure 'nough give it to her and that youngun' of hers."

Hearing the love in Dodie's voice, a soft glow filled Lisette's eyes. She laughed softly, recognizing for the first time the goodness associated with Henri's sin. "We're going to have a baby to love!"

"So it seems. But first we got to get rid of Henri."

"Don't worry," Lisette said, breaking off a piece of the biscuit. "Henri is headed to Magnolia Manor to play cards with Nate. While he's gone, I'll ride into Thibodaux and tell Sheriff Purcell what's happened."

"Lord amercy!" Dodie cried, but the comment had nothing to do with Lisette's plan. "Would you look! That cat done ate all your grits. Git on, now!"

She waved her apron at the tabby that jumped down from the dresser and rubbed against Lisette's skirt.

Stooping, Lisette scooped him into her arms. "Bad kitty," she scolded, rubbing her nose against his silky fur.

"I'll bad kitty him," Dodie threatened. Then she smiled. "Bring that varmint on down to the kitchen while I fix you something else to eat. If you're gonna go traipsin' all over the country, you'd best do it on a full stomach."

"That would be wonderful," Lisette said. Doing as Dodie bid, she followed the black woman down the stairs and out to the kitchen.

"You want these grits or should I fix you something else?"

"Oh, grits are fine." The cat in Lisette's arms gave a howl and dug his claws into her arm. "Ouch! What's wrong, kitty?" she crooned. "Do you want down?"

She put the cat on the floor, rubbed her arm and looked over Dodie's shoulder at the congealing pan of grits.

"Are you sure?" Dodie asked.

"They're fine."

Dodie shrugged. She was dishing the hominy grits into

a clean bowl when the calico cat gave another horrible howling noise and began to convulse in the middle of the kitchen floor.

"Dear God!" Lisette said, dropping to her knees beside the writhing feline. "What's the matter, baby?" she said, reaching for the cat.

"Leave him alone," Dodie said sharply, placing her hand on Lisette's shoulder.

Lisette looked up, a question in her eyes.

"He'll just claw you all up. Ain't nothin' you can do for him anyway."

"Why? What's the matter with him?"

"Poison," Dodie said with a shake of her head. "Arsenic, if I had to guess. You'd best be countin' your lucky stars that that cat got into your grits, or it'd be you layin' there 'stead of him."

"What do you mean, Sheriff Purcell isn't here?" Lisette said, holding back the urge to cry. After the cat had died of poison meant for her, she'd changed her clothes and had Hank hitch up the buckboard. Then she'd headed straight for Thibodaux and Purcell's office.

"I'm sorry, ma'am, but he got a message about some murder, and he thought he ought to follow up on it."

At the word "murder," Lisette felt the blood drain from her face. Had Henri told Purcell he had her locked away at Belle Maison? No. That didn't make sense. Henri wouldn't have tried to kill her if he wanted the sheriff to lock her up. There were bound to be other killings he had to investigate. Nonetheless, she felt a little foolish and had a great desire to get out of the vicinity of the jail.

"I really need to speak to him," she said. "Do you have any idea where he's gone?"

"I'm not at liberty to discuss official business with you, ma'am," the deputy said.

"I understand. Thank you."

Stifling her disappointment, Lisette stepped back outside onto the wooden sidewalk and unhitched the horse. She would have to go to Magnolia Manor alone.

Chapter Thirty-Nine

Henri swayed in the saddle as his horse plodded along the dusty lane that led from Patrice's house to the main road. Wearing a satisfied smile, he took a cigar from his pocket. There was nothing like an afternoon in a woman's arms to make a man feel lucky, he thought, guiding the horse onto the road that led to Magnolia Manor. He bit off the end of the cigar and rolled the other end in his mouth. Striking a match, he held it to the tobacco and drew the smoke deep into his lungs.

Hmm, he thought, shaking out the tiny blaze and glancing at the road ahead, it looked like another rider. Henri kicked the horse into a faster gait. A little company for the journey might be nice. Besides, he didn't want to be late. Not when things were going his way.

Nate paced the study, awaiting his guests and assuring himself the plan should work. Once the ordeal with Duschene was over, Nate planned to concentrate on resolving his feelings for Lisette and getting his life in order. But he had to get Henri out of everyones' lives first.

Nate hoped the deputy in Thibodaux had passed on his message to Sheriff Purcell. Without mentioning any names, the note had said that if the sheriff would take a ride out to Magnolia Manor he could hear some startling news and pick up a new resident for his jail—the plan being that Nate would worm a confession out of Henri in Purcell's presence. So far, the sheriff hadn't made an appearance, and Nate was growing concerned.

Henri, however, arrived at dusk.

Though it galled Nate to sit at the dinner table with a murderer and a kidnapper, he could ill afford to arouse the man's suspicions. After partaking of a light supper and idle chitchat, he invited Henri into the parlor for a brandy and a cigar, stalling the game in the hope that Purcell would make an appearance. A table had been set up near the fireplace, specifically for their game.

"You have the money, I assume," Henri said, taking his place opposite Nate.

"Is my personal check sufficient?"

"I should think so."

Nate picked up the deck of cards. "Then I suppose we're ready to play."

"Not quite. I have a paper here I'd like you to sign."

Henri's attitude grated, but at the moment, nothing could be done about it. Purcell would take care of it when he arrived. Where the hell was Purcell, anyway? Nate wondered. He couldn't keep Duschene here all night.

"What kind of paper?"

"An agreement that says neither you nor Lisette will try to have me arrested for her abduction or for the murder of her mother."

With the cigar clenched tight in his teeth, Nate perused the paper bearing Lisette's signature. He peered at Henri through the cloud of smoke.

"I might sign it if you admit you did it," Nate said, throwing caution to the wind. Something had obviously held up Purcell. But even if the law officer didn't hear Duschene's confession, Nate wanted to.

Henri shrugged. "I had no choice. I grew up dirt-poor, Rambler. As the son of a duke, as you are rumored to be, you wouldn't understand that. All I had were the looks I was born with and a way with the ladies." He smoothed a hand over his sleek head. "I was fortunate enough to talk Elizabeth into marrying me when her husband died, but she had two daughters. One of them was bound to marry sooner or later."

"You could have married Silvie and had her half of her mother's estate."

Henri tapped the ash from his cigar. "Half isn't enough. I want my own land. My own place. Besides, Silvie was good for little besides bedding. If I'd married her, I'd have gone crazy inside six months."

There it was again! Nate thought. That need to own land. But Henri was worse than either the duke or Lisette. Henri wanted land so much he was willing to kill for it...had killed for it.

Nate gritted his teeth and hoped he could keep from leaping over the table and strangling the debonair Acadian. "I trust you've been treating Lisette well since the kidnapping."

"Kidnapping? Isn't that a bit strong? I'm just holding her as a bit of security until you and I complete our business." He smiled around his cigar. "But to answer your question, she was playing with her cat when I left. Now, can we dispense with the dillydallying? Just sign the paper and let's get on with the game. I have a lady waiting for me."

Patrice, no doubt.

Though it went against the grain, Nate signed his name below Lisette's. It didn't really matter. Win or lose, he had no intention of letting Duschene leave the house with his money or his freedom.

Nate returned the fountain pen and broke the seal on a fresh deck of cards. "Choose the game."

"Monte. Best three out of five," Henri said, leaning back in his chair and regarding Nate through a cloud of blue smoke.

"I thought you only wanted to play one game?"

"I changed my mind."

The statement was made with the attitude that whatever he decided was the way it would be. Nate shrugged and slapped the cards onto the table for his guest to cut the deck. What the hell? Perhaps Purcell would show up yet.

Henri's arrival awakened Silvie from a sound sleep. Even after all this time, his voice sent shivers of apprehension dancing down her spine. How could she have believed his lies? How could she have thought there was any decency in him? How could she have loved him—or worse, believed he loved her?

Aware of a dull ache in her back and in her heart, she pulled the covers up over her head and curled into a tight ball of misery. Like his mother, the child in her womb drew into a painful knot that took her breath.

After a few moments, both the pain and the voices faded away. Did Henri know she was here? He must at least suspect it. And what had he done with Lisette? Had he left her at Belle Maison unguarded?

Silvie poked her head out from under the blankets, her mind working feverishly. If Henri was here, and staying for dinner and cards, it would be a good time to sneak back to Belle Maison and set her sister free. She owed it to Lisette after the way she'd just stood there the night Henri had tried to kill her.

That may be true, Silvie, but how are you going to help

her? You certainly can't ride horseback, and you don't know how to hitch up a buggy.

She gave a groan of frustration. Besides, she wasn't that strong, yet. She was feeling better after several days of good food, but she wasn't up to any more travel so soon after the trip from the train station.

So you're going to let her down again?

"I can't help it," Silvie said in a harsh whisper. "I can't!"

You can get a gun and kill him.

"No..."

You can. You can do it for Lisette. You can do it for your baby.

Silvie grew thoughtful. Could she? Killing was a sin, but then, what was one more added to her list of transgressions? Would God count Henri's death a sin if it set aright so many things he had done wrong?

Silvie rose from the bed and slipped her arms into the wrapper Sadie had left for her. Trembling, she slid her feet into the mules left at the bedside, opened the door a crack and stuck out her head. She saw no one, but she could hear Nate's and Henri's voices in the dining room.

Her slipper-shod feet whispered across the polished cypress floors as she made her way to the study. The door had been open when she arrived and, as she passed, she'd seen a rifle hanging above the mantel. Silvie would stake her life that the gun was loaded, and though she'd never fired one, she'd watched Henri enough to have a general idea of what to do.

She stretched her arms high and lifted the rifle from the rack. Another pain elicited a guttural moan and almost caused her to drop the rifle. The agony passed in a few seconds and, carrying the gun, she eased down the hallway and out the back door.

The grass was wet with dew, and her feet and the hem

of her gown were soon soaked and chilling. She hardly noticed. Passing the dovecotes, she skirted the slave quarters, staying close to the edge of the cane fields, thankful there was no moon to expose her.

Despite her bulk, she moved swiftly, purposefully. She had a mission, and she intended to carry it out.

Chapter Forty

Nate dealt three cards each to himself and Henri. It was the fifth and final game of monte. Nate had won the first two games; Duschene had won the next two.

"I'll take two," Henri said, discarding two of his three cards. Nate dealt two new cards for Henri and looked at his own hand again. His cards were high: a pair of sixes—any pair was death in lowball—and a jack. Nate discarded all his cards and took three new ones. This time he got a four, ten, ace.

"One more draw," Duschene said. "Make it good."

He discarded one card. Nate threw away his ten.

"What do you have?"

Henri spread out his hand. He had a two, three, four.

"Good," Nate said, clenching his cigar between his teeth. "but not good enough." He spread his cards on the table for Henri to see. "Ace, two, four wins. That's three games for me."

Henri stared at the cards as if he couldn't believe the turn in his luck. Nate held out his hand; Henri looked at him blankly.

"The paper. The one Lisette and I signed. I believe I'll

have it back now. Then I'll ask you to go. I have some things that need my immediate attention."

Henri's face turned red, and he swore. Pulling the paper from his pocket, he laid it on the table. "You're lucky," he said. "Very lucky."

"We're all lucky sometimes," Nate said with a shrug. "I lose as often as the next man."

Instead of answering, Henri prepared to take his leave.

"I expect you out of Belle Maison by the eighth, and as far away from here as you can get," Nate told him as they strolled toward the door. "Otherwise, I'll have to pay a visit to the sheriff."

Instead of more bad humor, Henri smiled. "I'll be out long before then. I'd hate to have Purcell after me."

"Good. I'll see you outside."

Henri plucked his flat-crowned hat from a brass spike of the hall tree. "That won't be necessary."

Nate plunged his hands into the pockets of his trousers and watched with a thoughtful expression as Henri let himself out. In a matter of seconds, he heard the sound of hoofbeats as the horse galloped off into the night.

Strange. Duschene had taken his loss far better than Nate had expected.

Damn the Englishman to hell! Henri couldn't believe he had been so lucky as to catch up with Purcell—who had inadvertently told his destination and wound up trussed like a Christmas turkey in the bushes alongside the road near Patrice's—and then so unlucky as to lose the game, twenty-five thousand dollars and his freedom, if he didn't leave the state.

Cursing the Fates, Henri rode through the quarters. It was pitch-dark, and he had to rely on the animal's instinct to stay to the road. His mind was on other matters. Like how he was going to get the money to set himself up in a new location. Even though he hadn't dealt with Silvie to his satisfaction, Henri knew that since he'd seen to it that Lisette suffered the same end as her mother, it was imperative that he move on. Silvie's fate would just have to remain in God's hands. The problem was, he needed the money Nate Rambler had cheated him of.

Patrice would give him money. At least enough to start over someplace—especially if he promised to send for her. Who knew? Perhaps someday it would be safe to come back. He smiled, the matter settled to his satisfaction. He would stop by Patrice's, get the money, pick up a few things from Belle Maison and be on his way.

He was perhaps a quarter of a mile down the road when his horse whickered and sidestepped, distracting him from his plans for the future.

''Whoa, now,'' he said, pulling the gelding to a stop and patting his neck. ''What is it? Coyote?'' Henri scanned the wooded area to his left, but could see nothing beyond the black silhouettes of trees. The horse whinnied again, and Henri's gaze moved toward the right, stopping at the figure standing in the middle of the road.

Fear thundered through him. Someone stood several yards away. A woman. A woman holding a gun. Lisette? he thought wildly. Sil—

A shot rang out, and Henri felt the impact of the bullet. Pain and shock and rage swept through him as he tumbled off the horse's back onto the ground.

Nate was pulling on his boots when he heard the sound. He cocked his head and listened, but there was only that single, faint cracking sound. A gunshot? Grabbing his coat, he started for the door, but it burst open before he reached it.

Karl stood there, his blue eyes wide with worry. ''Silvie's gone! I went down to see if she needed anything, but she wasn't there."

"What?" Visions, none of them pretty, paraded through his mind. Had she run away, or had Henri…

"She left a note."

Nate snatched the paper from Karl's hand. The rounded letters looked like the writing of a schoolchild, and the hand that formed them had obviously been shaking. The contents were disjointed, and the sentences half-formed. But the message was clear: she had to do it. She'd let Lisette down. She hoped God would forgive her.

Could Silvie have gotten her hands on a gun? Dear God, had she gone somewhere and tried to take her own life?

"Come on, Karl. Let's go get our rifles and wake up Levi and Old Jim. We have to find her. She's in no condition to be outside at night."

Heidi awaited them outside the room. "What's wrong?" she asked.

"Silvie is missing. We have to go look for her," Karl said in a take charge voice that hinted at his imminent manhood.

"What can I do?"

Nate squeezed Heidi's shoulder and started for the stairs. "Pray we find her."

In their haste to get to the study, he and Karl took the stairs two at a time. The first thing Nate saw when he entered the study was the absence of the gun over the mantel.

"Do you think she plans to…kill herself?" Karl asked.

"I don't know. It certainly looks likely. Alive or dead, we have to find her."

He wasn't dead. Henri raised himself to one elbow and looked toward the sound of the harsh weeping. It was Silvie. He'd heard her cry enough to recognize the sound. Fury overrode the pain in his arm. The little tart had tried to kill him! He looked around and saw that his horse hadn't bolted. It was munching new shoots of grass a few yards away. Henri's searching fingers encountered a wet stickiness. Pulling the monogrammed handkerchief from his pocket and using his teeth, he managed to tie a rough bandage around the wound.

Gritting his teeth against the pain, he struggled to his feet and started toward Silvie. The bitch thought she'd killed him, and she was crying so hard she didn't hear his approach.

Reaching down, Henri grabbed a handful of her hair and jerked her head back. She gave a sharp sob of fear.

"Scream, and I'll kill you right here. Right now," he said in a menacing voice.

"Wh...what are you...going to...do with...me?" she asked around hiccuping sobs.

Still holding her hair, Henri hauled her to her feet and pushed her toward the horse. "I'm going to take you back to your home. After that, we'll just have to wait and see."

Lisette was getting sleepy, and she was tired to the bone. Because she was trying to save the poor horse, it seemed she had been traveling forever. Since she had to pass by Belle Maison to get to Magnolia Manor from Thibodaux, she had stopped to feed the horse, grab a sandwich and change into some of Dodie's grandson's clothes. It promised to be a long night, and she'd learned that trousers made traveling much more comfortable than skirts.

Not only was she worn out, Lisette was scared. The difference was the security she'd felt with the strength and stamina of Iron Warrior compared to the tired animal and the relative clumsiness of the buckboard—all that stood between her and the unknowns out there in the dark.

She had no idea of the time, but it seemed she had been in the dark and alone forever. She had just passed Patrice

Benoit's place and figured it was approximately five more miles to Nate's when she saw a figure lurch out onto the road. Her heart leaped into her throat.

"Whoa," she said, pulling the horse to a stop a safe distance from the stranger. Should she turn around or whip the horse into a faster gait and race right by the man? What if he had a gun? What—

An owl *who-who-whoed,* and she jumped in surprise.

"Help!" the man cried. "Whoever you are, please help me."

"Who is it?" Lisette yelled back.

"Purcell. Sheriff Purcell."

Purcell? What in heaven's name was he doing out here in the middle of the night? She clucked to the horse and drew the buckboard to the man's side.

"Thank God," he said, dragging himself into the buggy. He settled into the seat with a sigh. "Thank you...whoever you are."

"I'm Lisette Antilly," she said, clucking to the horse. "And I've been all the way to Thibodaux looking for you."

Purcell sat up straighter. "Antilly? One of Duschene's stepdaughters who tried to kill him?"

"I'm one of his stepdaughters, but your story is a bit confused. Henri tried to kill me and my sister."

Purcell rubbed the lump behind his ear. "Why don't you tell me what's going on?"

Thankful that he was willing to listen, Lisette launched into her account of what happened the night Henri had fallen down the stairs. She told him everything, including Silvie's pregnancy and Henri's rejection. She explained where they had both been these past few months and how she'd found Silvie in New Orleans. Lisette finished with the tale of her abduction and the death of the cat earlier in the day.

"I'll be damned," Purcell said with a disbelieving shake of his head. "I'll just be damned."

Obviously he believed her. "What happened to you?"

Purcell rested his elbows on his knees and looked out at the black shadows of the trees lining either side of the road. "Nate Rambler sent me a message that said to come out to his place. Said he could get me a confession on a murder."

"Murder!"

"Yeah. He didn't say who it was, but I figured I'd better check it out."

Lisette gave the sheriff's story thoughtful consideration. Had Nate figured out a way to make Henri confess? While she was trying to figure out what Nate was up to, the sheriff put his hand on her arm.

"Don't panic, and keep your eyes straight ahead. I think I saw some movement in the trees over there. Just keep on going, nice and easy unless someone jumps us. Then ask this nag for his very life."

Every muscle in Lisette's body tightened, and it was all she could do to keep from whipping the horse to a faster gait.

It seemed like an eternity but was only a minute or two before Purcell said, "Let's go a little faster now. Just a bit."

Lisette did as he commanded, and after a few more tense minutes, the sheriff sighed in relief. "Must have been a bear or something."

"Do you mind getting back to your story?" Lisette asked. "You were telling me about being called to Magnolia Manor."

"Right. That's where I was headed when your stepfather came riding up behind me. Not too far from where you picked me up. He asked what I was doing out here, and like a fool I told him. Next thing I know, I'm waking up in a pile of sawbriars, a lump the size of a goose egg on the back of my head and my hands tied behind my back." He fingered his scalp gingerly. "I didn't think I'd ever get loose. I 'preciate you picking me up."

"My pleasure." She felt much safer with a man along.

Purcell gave a bitter laugh. "I was wondering how come Henri coldcocked me like that, but since I heard your story, it makes a lot of sense."

"The man is insane," she said.

Nevertheless, Lisette felt a certain amount of relief. She had survived Henri's attempt at murder, and the sheriff believed her story. Silvie was safe with Nate, and Belle Maison was back in her possession. Even if Henri won the game tonight, the worst that could happen was that he would get off scot-free and use Nate's money to set himself up somewhere else.

She gave a sigh of relief and contentment. Henri Duschene had done his worst, and the Antillys had survived.

Chapter Forty-One

Nate, Karl and the two Negro men had split up. They had been searching for hours. The fire of their torches glowed orange against the black of the night as they searched the area surrounding the house. Nate's search led him farther and farther from the house. Holding his torch aloft, he had accidentally found the trail of footprints in the dew, which led him past the quarters and beyond the lane and onto the road. From there, the footprints left by Henri's horse were easy to follow.

About a quarter of a mile from the lane, Nate stopped. There was a large indentation, as if someone had lain in the dust. A dark splotch stained the dirt. Stooping, he reached out and scooped up a handful. It was damp, and when he carried it to his nose, he could smell the cloying scent of blood.

He tossed the dirt to the ground and wiped his hand on his pants. Whose blood was it? If Silvie had done this to herself, where was she? He lifted the torch and called her name. The glow of the light glinted off something in the center of the road. Drawing nearer, Nate was surprised to see his rifle lying in the dirt.

Picking up the firearm, he stood and looked back at the

place where he'd found the blood. A picture began to form in his mind. Silvie had taken the gun. She hadn't intended to harm herself; she'd come out here to ambush Henri, and had. Unfortunately for her, the wound hadn't been fatal. Henri must have recovered, overcome her and taken her with him. That had to be what happened. In her condition, Silvie certainly couldn't dispose of Henri's body. And if she had, she would have come back to the house and shouted it to the world.

Nate started back toward the house at a fast lope. He had to get Iron Warrior saddled and be on his way. There was no doubt in his mind that Duschene would take Silvie with him to Belle Maison where he would have both sisters in his clutches. God only knew what he would do to them.

Nate was almost to the lane when he heard the sound of an approaching horse and buggy. Who would be out at this time of the night? he wondered, wishing the rifle was loaded. In a matter of minutes, the buckboard was bearing down on him, and he could see that two people shared the seat. As the rig drew nearer, Nate was able to make out the features of Sheriff Purcell and what looked like a young boy. The buckboard came to a stop in a flurry of dust.

"Nate!" a familiar voice cried.

The single word held relief and joy and something else he couldn't define. The other person wasn't a boy at all. It was Lisette, who threw herself into his arms and held on to him as if she would never let him go.

Nate took the sheriff and Lisette inside and plied them with food and drink while each related his encounter with Henri's brand of maliciousness. In turn, Nate told of his evening with Henri, Silvie's disappearance and the evidence he'd found on the road.

"I was getting ready to head for Belle Maison when I

heard the buckboard coming,'' Nate explained. ''Now that I know you're all right, I'm going after Silvie.''

''I'm going, too,'' Lisette said.

''No,'' he said, pushing her back down onto the chair. ''Stay here. I can make better time by myself, and you're exhausted.''

There was pleading in Lisette's eyes. ''She's my sister. She might need me.''

She didn't need to say more. Nate capitulated with a sigh.

''I'm coming, too,'' Purcell said. ''It's my job.''

''What about your head?''

''It doesn't hurt as much as a bad hangover,'' he said with a wry smile.

Nate shrugged in defeat. ''I have a couple of fresh horses in the barn. Let's saddle up.''

Silvie was almost unconscious by the time Henri's horse deposited them at the door of Belle Maison. It had been a long night, and the trip from Magnolia Manor had been made without any encounters on the road. There had been one tense moment—not far from the place he'd left the sheriff—when he'd heard a buggy approach, but he'd guided the horse deep into the shadows of the trees and waited until it passed.

The night was drawing to a close, but it was still dark enough that he tripped on the step as he half carried Silvie through the door. He should have left the bitch alongside the road somewhere, but he wanted to see Dodie's face when she realized that all her scheming and lying to keep the girls safe had been for nothing.

Henri deposited Silvie on the parlor sofa and lit a lamp. She groaned and opened her eyes to look at him. Pain and condemnation dwelt there. Neither was an emotion Henri wanted to deal with. Nor would he. Striking another match, he lit a second lamp and started through the house, bellowing for Dodie.

The first thing he saw when he reached the top of the stairs was that the door to Lisette's room stood open. He ran to the aperture and found his suspicions correct. Rage filled him. Neither Lisette nor her body was anywhere to be seen. She was gone, and it was Dodie's fault.

When he turned, the black woman stood there in a faded wrapper, a steady look in her dark eyes.

"Did you unlock Lisette's door?" he asked quietly.

"Yassir."

"Why?"

"You told me to bring her somethin' to eat, master. Did you forget?"

Henri squeezed his eyes shut. He had forgotten. Dear God, so much had happened, so many hours had passed, that it seemed aeons ago that he'd given his instructions to the black woman.

"Why didn't you lock the door behind you?" he snapped.

"We ain't never locked no doors at Belle Maison. I guess I forgot. Besides, master, you had the key."

The wild look in Henri's eyes mirrored his exasperation. "Then how did you get in?"

"A hairpin," she said with a lift of one shoulder. "They can unlock a door, but they can't lock one back."

Henri stifled a curse of fury. The woman was a simpleton, but she was twisting the whole thing so that Lisette's escape was his fault. "So you just let her go?"

"What could I do? I'm an old woman. She hitched up the buckboard and took out of here like a flash of lightnin'."

Buckboard? Henri's stomach churned sickeningly as he recalled the buggy that passed him on the road. It had been Lisette. He knew it as sure as he knew the sun would rise in the east in less than an hour. He ran a hand down his whisker-stubbled face. What to do?

"You want me to see to your arm, master?" Dodie asked, her head bent.

Though her voice held the proper mix of subservience and humility, Henri would stake his life on the fact that her eyes did not. Ah, hell, what did it matter? She was old and unimportant. What was important was finding Lisette and getting rid of her and her sister once and for all.

"Bring the bandages to my room," he commanded. "And when you finish, fix me something to eat. I'm famished."

"What about Silvie?"

"Leave the bitch alone."

"Yassir," Dodie said. "I'll go fetch the ointment and bandages now."

Silvie awoke from a light sleep and opened her eyes. Someone had covered her with a quilt. Dodie, she thought. The gray of dawn had entered the room while she slept. She wondered where Henri was and if Nate had missed her yet and if Lisette had managed to escape while their stepfather was at Magnolia Manor.

Without warning, her stomach knotted in another cramp that took her breath. This time she recognized the pain for what it was. Henri's baby was about to demand entrance into the world, and its birth would usher in her own death. She had known it for a long time.

Fear wrapped its arms around her. She felt tears gathering in her eyes. Tears for the happiness she should be feeling. Tears for the love she would never know and for the sorrow her actions had brought to Lisette. If she could do one last thing, it would be to free Lisette from the possibility of Henri ever hurting her again.

As if on cue, she heard him call for Dodie.

"Get yourself up here, woman! Now!"

The sound of his voice grated on Silvie's nerves. Why, oh why, hadn't God let the shot she fired find the blackness of his heart? Why should someone as evil as he be allowed to live when she and her baby were condemned to die? For the first time in a long time, Silvie began to pray.

Holy Mary, Mother of God...

So much had happened. So many things gone awry. Perhaps if she tried to talk to him, she could make him see that his best course was to repent of the things he had done and seek forgiveness.

...pray for us...

As she finished her prayer, a curious peace stole through her. Facing death wasn't as frightening as before. Filled with a new determination, she pushed herself to her feet and made her way through the parlor to the hallway. Another pain struck, and she clutched her belly, moving slowly toward the stairway. Clinging to the railing, she dragged one foot and then the other up the steps.

Henri's door was open, but his room was empty. Then she saw that the double doors that led to the upper *galerie* were open and he was sitting at a small table, eating breakfast. The sun was climbing over the stand of pines in the east, and a chorus of different birds sang sweetly. The scent of jessamine and magnolias filled the air. Though a touch cool, it was going to be a glorious spring morning.

"Henri."

He looked up, and surprise flickered in his eyes. His shirt was off, and his right arm was swathed in white. As she approached him, her eyes moved over his body, the body she knew as well as her own. It was hard to believe that she had once found pleasure in those strong arms or that his mouth could be tender.

"What do you want?"

"To talk," she said, crossing the room and standing in the doorway.

"Talk!" he snarled. "What could the two of us possibly have to talk about? The advent of our child's birth?"

She laced her trembling fingers together and rested her hands on her abdomen. "I thought perhaps we could talk about forgiveness. Your soul."

Henri laughed and reached for a wineglass filled with ruby-red liquor. "Whose forgiveness, Silvie?" he asked, lifting the glass to his full lips. "Yours for acting the slut, or mine for taking advantage of you?"

"Both."

"I'm not interested." The crystal thudded to the tabletop. The crimson liquid spilled over the edge and spread over the white cloth. Henri wiped the back of his hand across his wine-stained lips.

Before Silvie could think of anything else to say, she heard the sound of hoofbeats. Looking over the top of Henri's head, she saw three riders coming down the lane. Swearing, Henri scraped back his chair and reached toward the *galerie* railing.

He was reaching for a rifle.

"You'll never get away with it."

"Won't I?" He raised the gun to his shoulder and took careful aim, waiting, waiting for them to get close enough to get a good shot.

Do something, Silvie.

What? What could she do? Wrest the gun away from him? Impossible. Cry out to whomever was coming to her aid? They would never hear her. Tears of frustration tumbled down her cheeks. She was going to do just what she had done the day Henri had fallen down the stairs. She was going to stand by and let someone get hurt because she didn't know what to do.

Four steps carried her to his side. "Henri, please," she said, grabbing his arm.

"Get away from me!" he yelled, shaking free and shoving her aside.

The force of her fall sent the table's contents crashing to the floor. Silvie was on her knees trying to rise, when another pain knifed through her abdomen. She couldn't stop the cry that escaped her lips.

The sound of hoofbeats grew louder and louder, or was it the sound of her heartbeats? The pain, unending, consuming, clawed at her. Like the pain, she reached up and grabbed at Henri's belt in an effort to gain her footing.

Another contraction struck and exquisite agony coursed through her. A scream ripped from her throat in tandem with the firing of the rifle. She was vaguely aware of something warm and wet against her legs and of a great groaning and cracking sound that mingled with Henri's hoarse cry of surprise.

Then she was falling....

For an instant she was a child again, and her father was tossing her up, up into the air. She could see his handsome face and the love in his eyes. She could feel the tickle in her stomach as she squealed and giggled her pleasure. She could almost hear his deep chuckle as it melded with the light, happy sound of her own laughter. Then, as always, he caught her safely in his arms....

Dear God! Henri had actually pushed Silvie, Lisette thought, as her horse raced toward the house. She saw Silvie cling to Henri as she tried to rise, heard the shot ring out. By the time she realized that neither she, Nate nor the sheriff were hit, she saw the *galerie* railing—the same railing her mother had begged Henri to repair—give way.

No! Not now! Not when help was so near...

Even over her own scream, Lisette heard Henri cry out,

saw him and Silvie fall, and strangely, eerily, she heard Silvie laugh, a light, tinkling sound that reminded Lisette of happier days when they were young.

By the time the riders reached the bodies, tears were racing down Lisette's cheeks. She slipped from her horse's back and started for Silvie's side, but Nate grabbed her arm, stopping her.

She looked up at him, and he shook his head. Didn't he understand that she had to go? Jerking her arm free, she knelt at Silvie's side. Reaching out a trembling hand, Lisette stroked the dark hair away from her sister's pale face. She was warm, and her skin was as soft as it had been as a child's.

"Race you to the barn, Lisette."

"Silvie, you'd better get out of Maman's *toilet water."*

"I hope I'm as pretty as you when I grow up, Lisette."

"You're prettier, Silvie," she said aloud. "Much prettier."

A harsh sob fought its way up Lisette's throat. She felt Nate's hands on her shoulders and allowed him to pull her to her feet and into his arms. Her heart beat out a painful cadence. So young. So young…

Chapter Forty-Two

Nate sat behind his desk, waiting for Karl to answer his summons and thinking about the changes the past few months—and especially the last week—had wrought in his life. He was a far different person than the cocky, shallow man who had ridden into Magnolia Manor with the idea of selling it out from under the children who belonged there. He hoped he was a far better man. One worthy of Lisette's love.

It had been over a week since Silvie was buried in the small cemetery next to her parents, over a week since Lisette had moved back home where she belonged. A week since he'd seen her, a week of trying to come to terms with who he was and where he was going. Where was he going? Did he belong anywhere?

He didn't know, but he knew that he had to talk to Karl, and after that, he would see.

Lisette crossed herself and rose from her kneeling position beside her sister's grave. She wondered if she would ever laugh again and if she would ever forget the things that had happened to her and Silvie. She blinked back her tears and cast a wistful look in the direction of her mother's grave.

"She was a good girl, *Maman,*" she said. "She was just headstrong."

Sighing, Lisette brushed the moisture from her cheeks and started back toward the house. The April day was filled with signs of rebirth and renewal, but her heart was empty.

She had spent the ten days since Silvie's death ridding the house of every trace of Henri Duschene. She had even sold his horses and the buckboard. She was going to start over. From now on, Belle Maison would be filled with love and hope, not heartbreak and despair. Hank had already started the repairs, and she would begin refurbishing Belle Maison tomorrow. It would take time, but she intended for the house to live up to its name.

Lisette was almost to the barn when she saw the gray horse tethered to the hitching post near the door. Her footsteps faltered. Nate. Why had he come? Seeing him would only stir up the longing for something that was not destined to be. The past few months had provided hints that he was nothing like Henri. The past few weeks had proved it.

She loved him, but he showed no signs of reciprocating. Though he had been helpful and considerate in the days just after Silvie's death, he had never once indicated that his actions were motivated by anything more than common decency. He had given no sign that he cared for her and had made no mention of his feelings. Lisette could only assume that the nights spent in each other's arms meant nothing to him.

Taking a deep breath, she stepped inside.

"Master Nate's waitin' for you in the parlor."

"Thank you, Dodie." Lisette smoothed back the loose tendrils of hair that had come free of her chignon and shook the wrinkles from her skirt. There were grass stains where she'd been on her knees praying, but she supposed it didn't matter.

He was standing at the window and turned when she entered the room. "Hello, Lisette."

"Hello." She clasped her hands behind her back. He looked wonderful—fit and strong and handsome beyond belief. "Did Dodie get you something to drink?"

"Some lemonade, thank you."

"What brings you this way?" she asked. "Have you come to say goodbye, or have you sold Magnolia Manor yet?"

"I'm not selling."

"Why?" she asked, hoping her surprise didn't show.

"Because it belongs to the Krueger children. I went into Thibodaux last week and had some papers drawn up. I'm their legal guardian until they reach an accountable age, and as soon as Karl is old enough to bear the responsibility of running the plantation, it reverts back to them."

"B...but I thought you were going to sell it and buy yourself a gambling den."

Nate shrugged. "Somehow that doesn't appeal to me anymore. Perhaps it was a passing fancy." He offered her a wry smile. "When I first came here, I thought I'd landed in a hell of my own making. I'd never worked a day in my life, never had any responsibility. But the last few months have opened my eyes. You and those four children showed me what love was and that there was far more to life than what I had."

"You...make it sound as if your family didn't love you."

"There's no doubt my mother loved me, and I suppose my father did, after a fashion. But he was an important man who had a lot of standing with the Queen. He took his pleasure in possessions and power, and my brothers and I were expected to behave a certain way. I refused. Even though I knew I was a disappointment to him and, even though I knew my actions were driving a wedge between us, I couldn't seem to stop.

"Do you remember the night we spent together?" he asked.

Scarlet stained her cheeks. She would never forget. "Yes."

"Well, I found out the next morning that Karl was sneaking around seeing the Whittaker girl. When I look back, I remember that night as a sort of déjà vu with role reversal. Karl was I, and I was my father. We had a hell of a row, and he asked me if I could imagine how he felt. His father was dead and his home was as good as gone. Actually, I understood very well."

"I don't understand."

He gave a sigh of frustration and scraped his hand through his hair. "I'm bungling this. That night, I was raking Karl over the coals for sneaking out to see Sara. I knew it was a dangerous game he was playing, because it was one I'd played many times myself." He forced his gaze to hers. "Does that surprise you?"

"No," she told him truthfully.

He paced to the fireplace and back. "That night, as I talked with Karl, I could see myself. He was rebellious, angry, doing the same things I'd done. Somehow, it helped me to see why I'd behaved the way I had. It also helped me to see my father's side...though I still don't care about owning anything."

He looked away. "Before I came to America, I had an affair with a married woman. When her husband confronted me, I wounded him in a duel. The Queen told my father to straighten me out, or he wouldn't get his title. Since he knew he couldn't make me toe the line, he asked me to leave."

"He disowned you?" Lisette asked in horror.

"He didn't go that far, but he did request that I change my name."

"You're not...Nathan Rambler?"

He clicked his heels together. "Jonathan Garrett Ramble at your service."

Lisette was having a hard time taking in the consequences of Nate's upbringing. "Have you made your peace with them?"

"No."

"But you should!" she cried earnestly. "Family is the most important thing there is—not your stubborn pride!"

Nate frowned. "But...you said this plantation meant more to you than anything."

"Next to my family it does. But not in a material way. It means so much to me because of the part it has played in my life. It means a lot to my heart. That's why I had to get it back. I grew up here, and so did Silvie. It's home."

He believed her. His head had known for weeks that she wasn't like his father, but his heart had known from the first.

"I love you," he said, and as soon as the words were out of his mouth, he wished he could call them back.

Lisette wasn't sure she'd heard correctly, but the heaviness in her heart lifted, nevertheless. "Did you say you loved me?"

He nodded. "I know my reputation leaves much to be desired, and that I'm not nearly good enough for a girl like you—"

Not good enough? For the first time in weeks, she felt a smile tugging at her lips, a welcome smile. "Not good enough for a girl who lies about who she is, you mean?'

The reminder stopped his tirade, and the look in her eyes gave him courage to continue. "I'm a gambler."

"You gave away an entire plantation to some orphan

children who you have also agreed to be responsible for until they're grown."

"I'm a womanizer," he said, wanting to lay all his faults out for her close inspection.

Lisette shook her head, and there was a definite smile in her eyes. "Not anymore. Your wife will never stand for it."

"Wife?"

"Yes." She shrugged. "Now that word is out that I spent months under your roof—unchaperoned—my reputation is ruined. You'll have to marry me."

"I would be proud to marry you," he said in all seriousness.

"No," she said, cradling his cheek in her palm, "it is I who will be proud to marry you."

Nate drew her into his arms and lowered his head until their lips met, sealing their promise, sealing their love. When they paused for breath, he said, "I want to ask a favor."

"What?"

"Would you mind terribly if we renamed Belle Maison?"

Lisette thought for a moment. "I suppose not," she said. "What did you have in mind?"

"Rambler's Rest. Because it was in your arms that I found the peace I'd been searching for all my life."

The tenderness in his voice brought tears to her eyes.

"You've bewitched me," he said, kissing away a teardrop that clung to her lashes.

Smiling, she turned her head to give him freer access to her neck. "It must be Tante Mabel's *Poudre de Perlainpainpain.*"

"Powder de what?" he asked, drawing back to look at her.

Lisette laughed. "It's a magic potion. Guaranteed to snare a man's affections."

The corners of Nate's lips lifted in a smile. "And how does this magic potion work?"

"It's complicated," she said, breaking free and backing away from the glint in his eyes. "First you bury three white beans in a pile of table salt for three days."

"Hmm." He reached out and pulled one pin and then another from her chignon.

Lisette shook her head and her dark hair cascaded over her shoulders. "Then you wait for a windy day and collect seventeen floating seeds from a thistle pl—"

Nate hushed her with a kiss. When he raised his head, there was a bemused look on each of their faces. Lisette continued, though her words sounded as scattered as her thoughts.

He kissed her eyelids.

"Take the down off the...seeds, and watch for a honeybee...Nate, stop that...be sure it's...Nate, please..."

He looked at her questioningly. "Be sure it's what?"

"Be sure the bee is gathering pollen from a clover... um...drooping to the north."

His hands moved to her hips and pulled her close. Their lips were a mere kiss apart, her voice but a whisper.

"You catch the bee with your bare hands—"

Nate drew back, his eyes dancing with mirth. He grinned. And started to laugh. "A bee? With your bare hands?"

Lisette gave him a playful punch on the arm. "Don't make fun of me. It worked, didn't it?"

He stilled his laughter, but his smile was wide and warm. "Indeed it did."

"There's more," she said as his hands worked the buttons of her blouse free.

"Tell me later," he growled into her ear. "I'm busy right now."

Epilogue

The buckboard rumbled down the dusty lane, and the breeze whipped the hot summer air through the trees.

"Who was that?" Nate asked, chucking his ten-month-old son beneath the chin.

"The old drunk who works for Alvin Sturges at the livery stable," Lisette said.

"What did he want?"

"He brought this package. It's come all the way from England."

"I'll be damned. The duke has certainly been generous since he considers me properly wedded and bedded."

"Nate!" A pink blush spread over Lisette's neck and face.

He laughed. "Well, open the bloody thing and let's see what it is."

"It" turned out to be an original painting by Landseer and, according to the accompanying letter, it was a small gift in honor of the birth of their son.

When Nate had written his family to tell of his marriage some twenty-two months before, the duke had responded with abject apologies and the assurance that he would have contacted Nate sooner, had he known where he could be reached. Since that time, the letters back and forth from Thibodaux to England had been frequent, and Lisette felt that the chasm between her husband and his family had been breached.

"Look, Jon," Nate said, pointing at the painting. "What do you think?"

Jon, who was chewing on his fingers, made some unintelligible noise.

"My opinion exactly," Nate said with a smile. "Tell Mama to take the picture inside. We want to play. Do you want to go high?" he asked.

Jon waved his arms up and down with glee. Lisette could swear the child knew what Nate was talking about.

Nate tossed the boy high in the air, and Jon chortled with glee. "Not so high, Nate," she cautioned, but he only tossed the child again. The baby's laughter filled the air, and, along with the sound of his laughter, came the sudden and unmistakable sound of another child's laughter, a light, silvery sound...the way Silvie had laughed as a child.

Lisette almost dropped the painting. "Nate! Did you hear that?"

Frowning, Nate caught Jon and held him close. "It sounded like Silvie," he said. "The way Silvie laughed the day she died."

Lisette's eyes filled with incipient tears. "That was the way she laughed when Papa threw her up into the air the way you threw Jon."

Nate put his arm around Lisette's shoulder and drew her close. He pressed a kiss to her forehead, and Jon threw his chubby arms around her neck.

"If she's laughing, I guess she approves. Or maybe," Nate added as an afterthought, "she's happy again, at last."

It took a while for the locals to get used to the change from Belle Maison to Rambler's Rest, and there were those who persisted in calling it Gambler's Rest. Nate decided that he had grown used to the name Rambler and decided to take legal steps to keep it. He and Lisette lived long and happy lives, and the gambling blood ran strongly through the coming generations.

Though Nate found his peace, there are those who are certain that, despite Nate's wish, Silvie did not. They say she still roams restlessly through the old plantation home, but it is the young, saucy Silvie who haunts the mansion, playing tricks on unsuspecting visitors and causing hearts to beat more rapidly.

Not to worry, the Ramblers always tell their guests. Someday, as the legend goes, when she redeems herself for not coming to Lisette's aid the night of Henri's accident, Silvie will find her own rest. Until then, they should remember that the unexpected bell-like sound they hear is only Silvie's laughter, carried on the wind through the moss-draped sentinels guarding the secrets of the Bayou Lafourche.

* * * * *

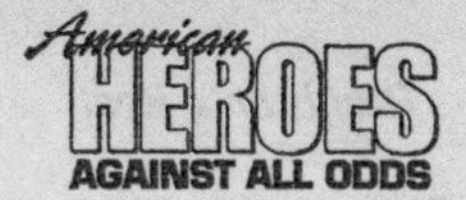

1. ALABAMA
After Hours—Gina Wilkins
2. ALASKA
The Bride Came C.O.D.—Barbara Bretton
3. ARIZONA
Stolen Memories—Kelsey Roberts
4. ARKANSAS
Hillbilly Heart—Stella Bagwell
5. CALIFORNIA
Stevie's Chase—Justine Davis
6. COLORADO
Walk Away, Joe—Pamela Toth
7. CONNECTICUT
Honeymoon for Hire—Cathy Gillen Thacker
8. DELAWARE
Death Spiral—Patricia Rosemoor
9. FLORIDA
Cry Uncle—Judith Arnold
10. GEORGIA
Safe Haven—Marilyn Pappano
11. HAWAII
Marriage Incorporated—Debbi Rawlins
12. IDAHO
Plain Jane's Man—Kristine Rolofson
13. ILLINOIS
Safety of His Arms—Vivian Leiber
14. INDIANA
A Fine Spring Rain—Celeste Hamilton
15. IOWA
Exclusively Yours—Leigh Michaels
16. KANSAS
The Doubletree—Victoria Pade
17. KENTUCKY
Run for the Roses—Peggy Moreland
18. LOUISIANA
Rambler's Rest—Bay Matthews
19. MAINE
Whispers in the Wood—Helen R. Myers
20. MARYLAND
Chance at a Lifetime—Anne Marie Winston
21. MASSACHUSETTS
Body Heat—Elise Title
22. MICHIGAN
Devil's Night—Jennifer Greene
23. MINNESOTA
Man from the North Country—Laurie Paige
24. MISSISSIPPI
Miss Charlotte Surrenders—Cathy Gillen Thacker
25. MISSOURI
One of the Good Guys—Carla Cassidy
26. MONTANA
Angel—Ruth Langan
27. NEBRASKA
Return to Raindance—Phyllis Halldorson
28. NEVADA
Baby by Chance—Elda Minger
29. NEW HAMPSHIRE
Sara's Father—Jennifer Mikels
30. NEW JERSEY
Tara's Child—Susan Kearney
31. NEW MEXICO
Black Mesa—Aimée Thurlo
32. NEW YORK
Winter Beach—Terese Ramin
33. NORTH CAROLINA
Pride and Promises—BJ James
34. NORTH DAKOTA
To Each His Own—Kathleen Eagle
35. OHIO
Courting Valerie—Linda Markowiak
36. OKLAHOMA
Nanny Angel—Karen Toller Whittenburg
37. OREGON
Firebrand—Paula Detmer Riggs
38. PENNSYLVANIA
McLain's Law—Kylie Brant
39. RHODE ISLAND
Does Anybody Know Who Allison Is?—Tracy Sinclair
40. SOUTH CAROLINA
Just Deserts—Dixie Browning
41. SOUTH DAKOTA
Brave Heart—Lindsay McKenna
42. TENNESSEE
Out of Danger—Beverly Barton
43. TEXAS
Major Attraction—Roz Denny Fox
44. UTAH
Feathers in the Wind—Pamela Browning
45. VERMONT
Twilight Magic—Saranne Dawson
46. VIRGINIA
No More Secrets—Linda Randall Wisdom
47. WASHINGTON
The Return of Caine O'Halloran—JoAnn Ross
48. WEST VIRGINIA
Cara's Beloved—Laurie Paige
49. WISCONSIN
Hoops—Patricia McLinn
50. WYOMING
Black Creek Ranch—Jackie Merritt

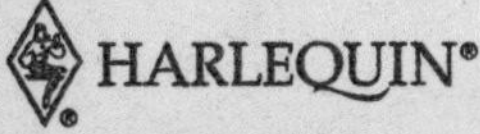

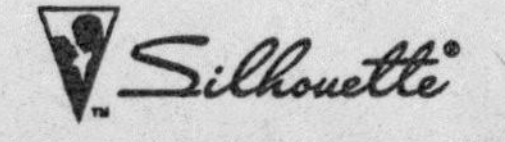

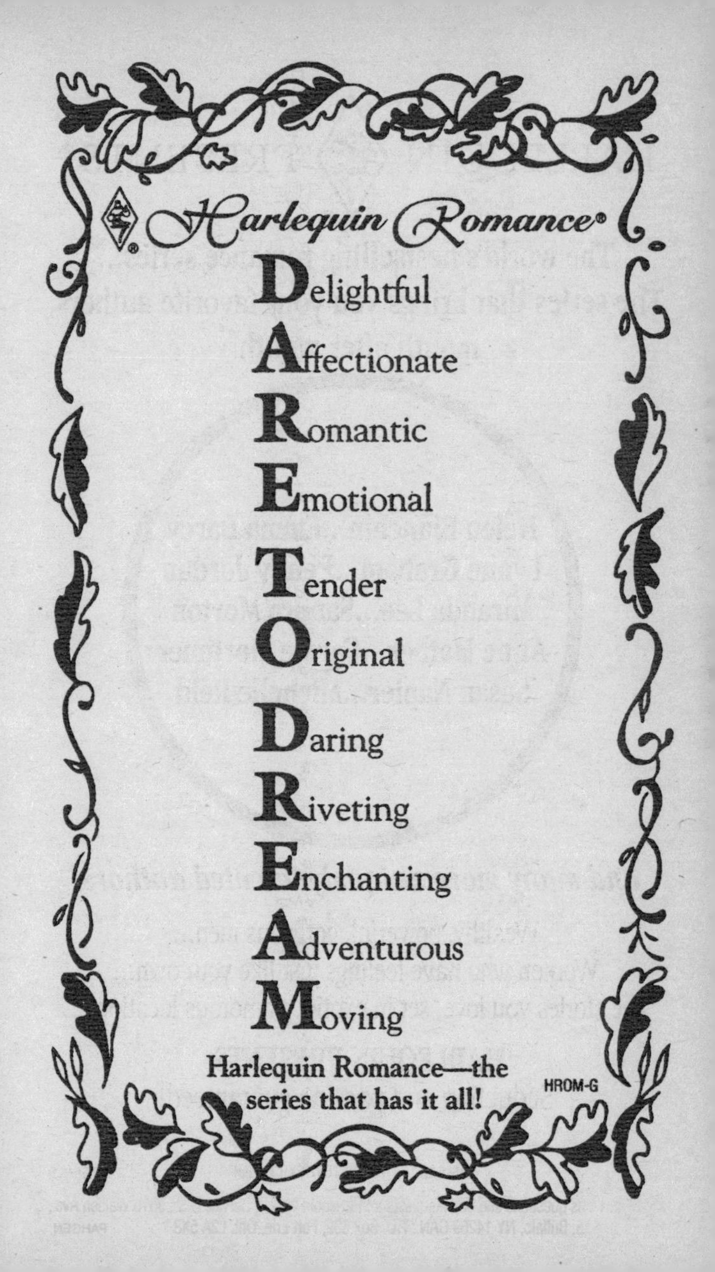
Harlequin Romance®
Delightful
Affectionate
Romantic
Emotional
Tender
Original
Daring
Riveting
Enchanting
Adventurous
Moving
Harlequin Romance—the
series that has it all!
HROM-G